cop.2

Herlin, Hans
Which way the wind.

Which Way
the Wind

Which Way the Wind

Hans Herlin

Translated by
Richard & Clara Winston

cop. 2

St. Martin's Press
New York

Library of Congress Cataloging in Publication Data

Herlin, Hans, 1925-
  Which way the wind.

  Translation of Feuer im Gras.
  I. Title.
PZ4.H553Wh   [PT2668.E748]   823'.9'14   78-4013
ISBN 0-312-86709-3

Other books by Hans Herlin
COMMEMORATIONS

Which Way
the Wind

FROM: PM, 1ST ARMORED DIVISION/APRUT-PM//

TO: CDR, 1ST M.P. BN./ARDZP-ST//

SUBJECT: NOTICE OF UNAUTHORIZED ABSENCE FROM US ARMY

1. THE FOLLOWING INDIVIDUAL IS WANTED BY MILITARY POLICE FOR BEING A DESERTER FROM US ARMY:

> NAME: DAVID HERRON
> GRADE: PVT
> SSN: 119-38-5230
> ORG: COB, 2/52 INF
> AGE: 24
> COLOR HAIR: LIGHT BROWN
> COLOR EYES: GRAY BLUE
> COMPLEXION FAIR
> HEIGHT: 72 IN
> WEIGHT: 170 LBS
> RACE: CAU
> SEX: MALE

2. IDENTIFYING MARKS: TATTOO, LEFT FOREARM, CRUCIFIXION

3. HERRON WAS TO RETURN TO DUTY IN VIETNAM. AWOL FROM HIS UNIT SINCE 8 JUL 71. SEE PHOTOGRAPH ID TYPE, AND REPORT, MANNHEIM PCF.

4. HERRON'S WHEREABOUTS UNKNOWN AT THIS TIME.

5. ANY INFORMATION OBTAINED AS TO WHEREABOUTS OF HERRON CAN BE REPORTED TO PM, 1ST ARMORED DIVISION.

DISTR: 1-PCF, MANNHEIM 1-PD, MANNHEIM 1-CG, 1ST ARMORED DIVISION

SEC CLAS: UNCLAS E F T O FOUO

SOURCE: PM, APRUT-PM 3202//14 OCT 71

Part One

1

The church was gray, neglected, abysmally ugly, a hodge-podge of styles. A graffito scrawled in large letters on the western side read; *We need Jesus, not Zuckermann!*

With the beginning of summer and the arrival of tourists in Vienna, the church was illuminated after dark. But the only effect was to prompt people to wonder why, or presume that the lighting had something to do with the jail that adjoined it. During the day people scarcely noticed the church, because it was so encased within the district's fabric and because of the heavy traffic that flowed past it.

The pickup truck circled the church for the fourth or fifth time, the driver obviously looking for a parking space. As soon as someone approached a parked car, the driver made a kind of dash, exhaust smoking, then dropped back to a slower speed.

The truck was an old, rusty pickup, and, like the church, it was a composite of many models and parts. Two hubcaps were missing, a fender was crushed; bulb and wires dangled from one of the two headlights. It had been patched and painted over so often in all shades of red, orange, pink, violet, and carmine that it looked altogether out of place in these gray surroundings, like a brightly colored ferryboat that had left the river and lumbered onto dry land. The driver seemed to have adjusted to this image by the way he drove, cruising smoothly around vehicles, pedestrian islands, and pedestrians themselves as though they were buoys set out to mark the shallow waters.

The three persons on the front seat of the truck sat close together. Two were old and looked very much alike in their gray clothes and with their gray hair. The driver was young; with his left arm thrust far out of the window he gave hand signals: stop, pass, turn. He had a colored kerchief tied around his neck and wore a khaki shirt. In spite of the intense heat, he had not rolled up the sleeves. Only the cuffs were turned back. From time to time, as he signaled with his left arm, the cloth slid up somewhat, revealing a tattoo on his forearm. Just enough of his skin was exposed to show that the tattooing was there, not what it represented.

"This is another one of your crazy ideas!" The woman sat between the two men, stiff and erect, her face stony. She wore her gray hair cut short. She pointed out the graffito. "Of course if anyone would strip his church, it would be Zuckermann. But what makes you think you can get past his old lady?"

"Getting past old ladies is my job." The man at her side was wearing old, gray clothes too, secondhand and worn out.

The woman turned to the young man on her left. She stopped speaking dialect; instead she used those short, excessively clear phrases people adopt when speaking to children or foreigners. "This your idea?"

"Don't bother him," the man said. "Watch him. Ever seen a better driver? I was born and raised in this district, but he knows every stick and stone—isn't that so, Sailor?"

The young man, concentrating on the traffic, did not reply. He had at last discovered the empty parking space he had been looking for. His outstretched arm signaled another vehicle to stop: the pickup darted forward, back, forward again, a ferry docking at a crowded pier. In the attempt to maneuver the truck into the short gap in the line of cars, the wheels momentarily mounted the sidewalk. Then, after a last lurching movement of the truck and a loud gasp from the muffler, the young man switched off the motor and pulled up the hand brake.

The old man and woman left their seats. The door slammed behind them with a tinny noise. Pigeons, gray, like everything else here, flew up from the narrow meridian strip that encircled the church like a life preserver. White spots on the pigeons' heads showed they were ringdoves. Someone in the city government had had the notion of exterminating all ordinary city pigeons and replacing them with ringdoves, which nested only in trees. That way all the monuments and churches in the city—and there were plenty of them—would be safe from pigeon droppings. For a while it had worked; but by now the ringdoves behaved like ordinary town pigeons.

The woman watched them as they flew up. They tried to light on the sills of the high, narrow windows on the western side of the church, but could not because of the plastic strips that had been installed there, offering no purchase for the pigeons' claws. They flew on in a sharp rise to the roof of the church, fluttered about, and finally settled down in the embrasures of the bell tower. Compared to the size of the church, the tower was scarcely impressive; and in fact a tall antenna reached up far above it. The antenna was held by three metal cables; with its struts it looked like a modern cross.

The woman kept her eyes on the ringdoves.

"That Zuckermann doesn't like pigeons!"

"How can you say that?" In spite of the heat—a leaden sultriness that had hung over the city for two weeks now, hot days followed by nights that brought no relief—the man had an embroidered woolen scarf crisscrossed under his jacket.

"He must hate them. Why else would he have put up those plastic strips? They say he sets out poison for them."

"No one's ever going to make that work, poisoning pigeons. If you were a pigeon"—he gave a short laugh—"a pigeon in this city, you'd have gotten used to all kinds of poisons long ago. They can't get rid of the junk dealers either, can they? This town'll always have pigeons and junk dealers like us."

"A priest who hates pigeons!" She shook her head. "No wonder the church is going to the dogs."

"And what luck for us." The man noticed that the main door of the church stood open, presumably to let the heat in, but he took it as a good omen. "Where else would we get all these fine pews! You have to admit this new vogue for stripping churches is the best thing that's happened to us for years. We haven't had a boom like this since they threw out the Jews. So what are we waiting for?"

"Will that priest be there, that Zuckermann?"

"No, only the sexton. Go on ahead. I'll just get the tools."

He let down the tailgate. They had started out early, and the truck already held a mixed bag of a morning's work: chairs, tables, a dish rack, boxes of broken toys. But they had plenty of room for the two confessionals they had come for.

Again he gave that short laugh, which somehow sounded old and secondhand like the things he bought and sold. For a junk dealer a church had more desirable articles than just confessionals. A pew, for instance, could be turned over to good profit in an hour; restaurants in the process of being refurbished could use them, and they made a nice piece of decor in fashionable shops. Church paintings also had a good market. Old embroidered vestments sold easily. Not to speak of candlesticks and artificial altar flowers. But he'd always wanted to have a confessional.

Imagine all the sins that had been spoken of in one of those! Generations upon generations of sins. Had they grown worse? Had they increased? The priests knew. All his life he'd envied Catholic priests that privilege of hearing confessions. All the lovely sins they heard about! But that, too, would soon be over and done with. A good many priests had already stopped hearing auricular confessions. Who knows, next they'd be getting married...

He took his work smock down from the truck and put it on, carefully buttoning the many buttons. It was a long smock, rumpled, dirty, with a few blotches of red paint, reaching down almost to his ankles. It made the dealer look even skinnier. Toolbox in hand, he went over to the young man, who had not stirred from his seat at the wheel.

"I hope you won't pay any attention to what she says," the dealer said, jerking his head toward his wife, who was waiting at the open church door. "She talks a lot of junk." He laughed as though he were proud of the joke he had made or was about to make. "Dealing in junk doesn't mean you have to talk junk.

I always tell her, 'A man needs ideas to live by!' But that's just what she has against me. To her ideas are wicked and dangerous. I tell you, Sailor, one of these days we're going to carry out our great idea. Right?"

He looked up at the young man, who did not speak or stir from his seat. His arm rested on the lowered window; his shirtsleeve concealed the tattoo. The dealer had never actually seen it, although he had tried; he merely knew it was there, which was why he called the young man "Sailor"—because of the tattoo and because of the language the young man often used. He had never asked his name. That was the junk dealer's rule: Don't ask where things come from, and so he had stuck to the name "Sailor."

"We'll make it go, won't we," he tried again, "our idea. Right?"

"Sure we will someday." The young man might have smiled but his voice indicated the smile more than his face did. It was curious how little his face changed when he smiled. It was an ordinary face, the face of an average Joe, the sort of face that looked so intrinsically familiar that it would be hard to remember it.

"Not someday, Sailor. Soon. The two of us will do it together. I'll order the differential for the Land Rover before this day's out, then when it's installed we'll..."

"Then off we'll go, sure." He spoke an odd German. Sometimes it seemed almost perfect, fluent, tinged with Viennese dialect; but then it became apparent that it was more a kind of mimicry, that he had the knack of imitating something he might not always understand.

"I mean it, Sailor."

"I know. Nothing can stop us."

It was very hot in the pickup's cab, but there was no sweat on the young man's face. He had light-brown hair, cut a bit short for his age. His face was tanned, and it was obvious that he had done his shaving last night rather than this morning. The junk dealer had noticed that long ago; the young man shaved in the evening rather than in the morning; it was always the last thing he did, as though he expected important things to happen during the night, not during the day.

"Are you coming along?" the dealer asked.

"I'll stick it out here. It's a no-parking zone."

"If a cop comes along, open the hood. They're easy on junk dealers whose trucks have broken down." He laughed. "The ones that aren't all new and clean."

"It's certainly not new and clean."

"Not like our Land Rover. Sure you don't want to come along?"

"I'll be here when you need me to carry the stuff out."

"You know, I've had my eye on that rectory for years! It's stuffed with treasures; the attic must be full of old things. I was on good terms with the old priest and I'd almost got him to the point where he would have let me into the attic. Then this Zuckermann came in... I've never got past his mother, the old lady. Are you really sure they'll let me have the confessionals?"

"Pretty sure, yes." The young man leaned back and closed his eyes, as though he were on the point of falling asleep.

The dealer knew he had the knack of falling asleep at once, any time and any place, even amid the loudest noise, with people around him; he could fall asleep whenever they had a long wait somewhere, and a secondhand dealer waited a great deal. Still, whenever you woke him, he was instantly alert. This was another of the sailor's traits he admired; for one thing, it was a splendid talent to have for the great trip they'd be taking together one day.

"I'll order the differential today," he promised again, and then walked over to the woman, who stood waiting for him in the shadow of the portal. The wide smock flapped around his legs.

The young man remained calmly seated. At one point he reached out for the box of cigarettes that lay on the dashboard, but then he did not take a cigarette after all. His hands played with the wheel; he released the brake, then pulled it up again, shifted gears, drew out the key and replaced it in the ignition. The restlessness of his hands contrasted with his body, which lolled motionless in the seat, and with his face, which looked sleepy. No matter what he did with his hands, nothing seemed to quiet them.

Finally his hands untied the kerchief from his neck. They

began twisting and turning the cloth, winding it into a knot, and suddenly the cloth seemed to take on life. It became a kind of puppet that he held in his right hand, the head formed by his index finger; his thumb and middle finger were the two outstretched arms. He did all this without even looking, sitting as if asleep at the wheel, eyes half closed.

2

It was the early-afternoon flight from Rome, and naturally there were often priests among the passengers, but as far as the stewardess could recall, no priest had ever flown first class. At least, not a priest in a cassock.

There were only two other persons in first, and so the stewardess had lavished much attention on the priest, her best smile and that stooping very low that few of the passengers rated. But he remained unapproachable. He had refused everything offered him, food and drinks, even the daily newspapers. And he did not smoke.

For a moment the thought occured to her that it might have something to do with a fasting period, some special time in the church calendar that she was unfamiliar with or had forgotten about. She had even gone to the pilot and asked about it, but he had only turned in his seat, laughed, and commented, "Fasts? Do priests still bother with that?"

She could no longer remember the last time she had gone to church, but his answer had shocked her all the same, even more his mocking smile. After that she had been still more attentive to the priest, but to little effect. Of course, it could be that he was simply afraid of flying. He never did unbuckle his safety belt, although it was a quiet flight in a cloudless sky. Only now, as they made their landing approach to Vienna, did they pass through the first clouds. Fear it must be, for right after they began taxiing at Rome airport he had taken out a black book with many colored ribbons dangling from it, but had left it lying on the seat and had not even glanced into it.

The three stewardesses whispering in the galley up front agreed on many points: that his clothes were plain but expensive, even custom-made; that his shoes were top quality, likewise his black leather attaché case with the initials "C. Z." in gold. Nor was there any disagreement among the three concerning his age: about fifty, a somewhat lean man with balding forehead. But there was a discrepancy between these signs of means and the man himself, with his careworn face. The stewardess who from the start had awarded him her best smile remarked that he actually looked the way a priest ought to— pale and spiritual—and that she would have recognized him as a priest even if he had not worn a cassock. But the others were not quite prepared to agree with that.

The plane had lost altitude, and as it began swinging in another wide turn, the river came into view for the first time. Then it vanished again.

Czepe Zuckermann looked out the window. He was glad that the flight would soon be over. He had been well aware of the attention bestowed on him. He was used to that, and to a certain extent he liked it. The cassock produced an effect, especially nowadays when priests rarely wore it. It yielded benefits when they were particularly welcome—in hotels, at information booths, in planes, of course. It was as though you were visibly wearing the sign of a highly prestigious Diners Club. In Rome, overcrowded as always at this season, he had been given one of the best and quietest rooms in the hotel, had been served first in the restaurants. And it made no difference what city you happened to be in: Rome of the true faith, or Calvinistic Geneva, where he had recently participated in an ecumenical congress.

And he had to admit he liked flying first class, where he had the entire row of seats to himself and room enough for his long legs. When he flew tourist, he always hurried ahead of the other passengers so that at least he would have the row by the emergency exits, which were farther apart than other rows.

He looked at his long legs with pleasure. He had never

been particularly concerned about being tall, although that was of help to a priest when he stood there at the front of the church. But he liked his long legs, or rather, he took pleasure in them, because they did not tire easily. Someone had once told him that he walked like an African, with the long strides of a person accustomed to great distances. Few things more gratifying could have been said to him.

The Danube reappeared. Its waters were gray; even the banks, overgrown with reeds, were gray. There were deeper shadows within this gray, either from clouds or from the plane's wings. It was now flying in a tight turn, losing still more altitude. He could not recall that this had ever happened before. He glanced to the side, endeavoring to conceal his sudden anxiety from the stewardess, who had settled down in the seat beside him for the landing.

He had never been able to overcome this fear of flying, and the landings were always the worst moments. He felt nauseated, could scarcely breathe; saliva collected in his mouth. He swallowed it and opened his lips to relieve the pressure in his ears. The pressure diminished, but the fear remained.

Never, he recalled, had he had this fear at sea, and the sea was also deep, a veritable abyss. Was there any difference between a body that fell through the air and one that sank toward the bottom of the sea? Flying always evoked such images in him; the thin aluminum skin of the plane opening beneath his seat and he himself falling through; or, worse yet, the window at his side breaking and the strong suction seizing him and pulling him out.

Flying was a a true ordeal for him, a martyrdom every time. Nevertheless he exposed himself to it again and again as if it were an indispensable spiritual exercise. And how could his great dream ever be realized without flying? In the vast expanses of Africa, or on the continent of South America, flying priests were needed because the widely scattered parishes could be reached only by small planes. For a time he had hoped that he would feel better in small planes, but found that he was even more afraid.

But now, he thought, that no longer mattered. The trip

had been a failure, a wretched defeat. Taking his request to Rome directly, over the heads of his superiors—he had done it only in order to make a last try. The result? He could still see them; no more than five hours had passed since he had confronted them for the last time. Those faces looked benevolent, but behind the mask they were icy, letting him feel their full displeasure at his attempt to bypass the authority of his archdiocese.

Through the window on his right he saw the private planes parked on the ground. They were already very close, and he closed his eyes and opened his mouth, freezing in his seat as the plane's wheels touched the runway. They struck unusually hard, three, four times—he could already see them bursting, going up in flames. Did the pilot know of his fear, did he take pleasure in making him suffer even more? He heard the noise as the jets reversed. It sounded loud and frightening, but it also meant that he had survived it.

"So that's over."

The stewardess included herself. After she had unfastened her belt and once more stooped low over him in her low-cut service dirndl, she pointed to the small black book with the colored place ribbons. "Don't forget your breviary." All through the flight she had been frantically trying to recall the word; now—surprised when it fell from her lips—she was both proud and strangely stirred.

3

The man from the flower stand at the corner of the church had been watching the pickup as it circled the church repeatedly, and as it finally squeezed into the tight parking space. Business was slow this morning, so he had time to observe what was happening around him. Saturday actually should have been the best day in the week; on Saturdays people generally bought more flowers than usual. Besides, the weather was good, perhaps a little too hot, but better than rain.

With a flower stand you were dependent on the weather and on people's moods. He had been counting on a good day. He had stocked up heavily this morning at the wholesale market: snapdragons, peonies, the last anemones, violets, and, of course, carnations. It was a good mixture of what was available at this season, except for the Canterbury bells, perhaps, and the first larkspur—he'd let himself be carried away when he bought them—and if he didn't sell them today or at the latest tomorrow morning, they'd be spoiled. Finally he'd taken lilies and gladioli—on top of everything else!—in the hope that Zuckermann's sister would turn up.

The secondhand dealer's garish red truck was a kind of institution, as much a part of this neighborhood as his own flower stand, which he'd owned for almost thirty years and which had been sixty years in his family. Secondhand dealers stuck to their neighborhood. If they were genuine dealers, they never lost touch with their home turf; sooner or later they returned. It was like the whores who had their beats around here; they started out here when young, then disappeared for years—and one day there they were again, right back where they'd started.

He had been eyeing this dealer's truck casually, out of boredom; it was only when the driver carried out his parking maneuver that the flower vendor's real interest awoke. He knew only one man who could maneuver a clumsy old vehicle like that; he'd seen him do it often enough in the streets around the wholesale flower market. The chaos there was unbelievable between five and six in the morning, when all the suppliers arrived and retailers like himself came along with their flower carts. And so, with a last look at the pedestrians who were hurrying past, he walked over to the parked red pickup.

"Sure enough, it's the orchid man." He stared at the young man behind the wheel. "I guessed it from the way you maneuvered—but then I thought, That's not possible! Orchid Man in the junk business!"

The young man did not move in his seat, and the man on the sidewalk could not see what he was doing with his hands.

"Rags and bones." The flower vendor shook his head. "I kept wondering where you'd gone to. You disappeared from the market. Why?" He adjusted his hearing aid, an old-fashioned model with a rather thick cord that dangled down from his ear and disappeared behind his shirt collar.

'Time for a change."

"You call it a change? Rags and bones, Orchid Man? Okay, they're going to tear down the flower market, they're going to kill us street vendors with that new flower supermarket, but junk dealing? Is that the future?" He pointed to the objects in the back of the truck. "Why? What's so good about that?"

"Gets me around the city."

"A guy who knows flowers like you do!"

The young man leaned out the window of the truck and looked over at the stand. "How's business?"

"Rotten."

"On a day like this?"

" I don't understand it either, but it's terrible!" When the young man hesitated, he went on, "Come on, Orchid Man, tell me what's wrong. It's a good day and people ought to be buying, but they aren't."

The young man jumped down from the truck. He seemed taller now that he was standing, but he was not strikingly tall; his height was average, like his face. He still held the knotted scarf in his right hand, but it was no longer a puppet, merely a lifeless piece of cloth.

"I've missed the market." This time he clearly smiled.

He had worked there a few weeks, driving a delivery truck to the airport at night, when the planes from Hong Kong and South America came in with the orchids. Hence his name among the flower dealers, though he had handled more than just orchids. The flowers came from many countries, which was one of the reasons he liked the job; savoring the names of remote places and picturing the routes the flowers had traveled: gladioli from South America; roses, iris, and gerberas from Israel; narcissi and tulips from Sicily; and carnations—these had come from the U.S.A., of all places. At first he found it hard to believe, but there they were, long, narrow cartons, whole truckloads of them. He had looked at the invoices and seen that most of them came from Florida.

He laughed aloud at the thought that he'd had when he first saw them: all Vienna swamped with carnations from Florida! That, at any rate, was something he would never have learned if he hadn't come to this city.

"What's so funny, Orchid Man?"

The young man rearranged the kerchief on his hand, and when he held it up, it was again a puppet.

"It's the carnations, all the carnations; that's what's so funny." It was the puppet that answered, in a puppet's voice; the young man's lips scarcely moved as he lent his voice to the puppet.

The flower vendor did not seem surprised. In the café across from the flower market, after the market closed and everyone lingered for a time, not yet disposed to start the day's work, this young fellow had sometimes produced his puppet.

And so the flower vendor entered into the game: "What's your name, Beautiful?"

"Oh?" the puppet responded coyly. "I never give my name to stangers."

"Then, do you know anything about flowers?"

"Of course I do." The puppet stretched its neck, as though challenged.

They moved over to the flower stand with its racks and an awning. It could be folded up at night and wheeled away. The young man studied the arrangement. He shook his head.

"Too many big flowers. Okay when it rains but not on a day like this. And larkspur! How can you hope to sell that?"

"I knew it was risky."

The puppet had vanished; the colorful kerchief was tied round the young man's neck again. He began rearranging the flowers on the racks. The gladioli and lilies at the bottom, the peonies in front of them, the Canterbury bells at the top, snapdragons on the sides, violets in the middle. He seemed to be arranging not so much by varieties as by colors. And he worked swiftly, without hesitating, only stepping back briefly now and then. Finally, he turned around.

"What do you think of that?"

"I guess I get the idea."

"Well, let's see whether it works."

The young man looked at the passersby, waited, and finally concentrated on a woman who had paused. He took a bunch of violets and with the flowers in one hand, went up to her.

"May I give you a few violets, ma'am?"

"Give me?" Her face was tired, harassed, and she was carrying two heavy shopping bags.

"Look at the color of them," the young man said, "almost as lovely as your eyes."

"My eyes?"

"Violets blue, the flower for you. Violets to wear, dancing on air."

The woman laughed, her expression changed. "Imagine!" She was looking at the young man. "My eyes are that blue?"

"Like violets. Or rather, like this larkspur. It's the first this year. The first is always the loveliest."

"Well, then... I'll take the larkspur... Let me have five sprigs. It's always best to take an odd number. Do you know that?" She suddenly seemed to have plenty of time. Finally she said, "So my eyes are the color of larkspur? Nobody's said anything so nice to me in a long time." Her eyes were on the young man...

The peddler watched her walk away. "You have a way with the women! That's the first time she ever bought larkspur from me."

People began buying flowers as though a spell had been lifted. The two men had only time to exchange a few words in between customers.

"I'll take you on any time, Orchid Man. Rags and bones—what kind of merchandise is that? Now, flowers, that's something more than just selling. There's soul in that."

"Someday, maybe."

"I have a second old cart; all it needs is painting. And the location isn't bad. A big hospital, lots of births."

"We'll talk about it."

"Only had to give it up because my brother...Hey!" He broke off as he caught sight of the white-clad figure of a young woman approaching the flower stand from the side of the church.

"There's the girl!" he said. "Now I'll get rid of my lilies and gladioli too."

It was strange that the flower man also called her "girl"—a woman of thirty-eight. The young man knew, because she had told him that she was fourteen years older than he was. Still, she had been just that, a girl, ever since their first meeting.

It has something to do with the way she walks, he thought as she came closer, hesitantly, as though she could not quite trust her feet, or the ground. The very first impression made one ask, What's odd about her? Eventually one would hit upon it: she had the body of a modern young woman and a face that did not fit at all; the face of a beauty from another age, as though she were a painting that had been done in two distinct historical periods, the head centuries earlier than the body.

She had reached the flower stand, and turned to him. "Hello, David."

The flower vendor looked around first at her, then at the young man. "David? That's your name, Orchid Man? A real name?"

"The gladioli—are they fresh?" the girl said.

"Oh yes," he replied. "Cut this morning, the gladioli. I was beginning to think you wouldn't be coming today."

"Give me the lilies too."

He took the flowers from the containers, let the water drip from their stems, and was about to wrap them up when the young man said, "I'll carry them."

The flower vendor looked at him. "Think it over. You can come on board any time—David."

"I will."

The young man needed both arms to carry the flowers; it was astonishing how heavy they were. Only now did he become aware of how strong the perfume of the lilies was.

"I'm sorry about the name." She had followed him, after paying for her purchase, and was now walking alongside him. "I know I shouldn't have used it."

"It's all right."

"No, it isn't all right. It just slipped out because it was such a surprise to see you."

"It doesn't matter. You can call me David." He could not recall why he had revealed his name to her. It had been a mistake, and he knew he could afford few such mistakes. But he believed her regret was genuine. Secrets seemed safe with her.

"It was really only because I was so glad to see you."

Her voice was low, gentle, darker than her appearance suggested. She wore a white linen dress, a shiny black belt its only ornament, white shoes, no stockings, and a long scarf. He had never seen her without a scarf. They were all much alike, very long and narrow, twined twice around her neck, ends reaching below her waist, made of thin, translucent stuff: silk or chiffon. The colors differed, but were always very light pastels: a mild lime green, a light pink, or, as today, a delicate violet. The pastels suited her pale skin and her hair, which was very blond and never properly combed. The only sharply contrasting feature was her eyes, dark and large, almost too large for her face.

"I thought you had left!" he said. It had not occurred to him that he might meet her today.

"Oh yes, they usually send me away during the summer."

"Weren't you looking forward to it? I mean, you told me about the park, and all the greenery and trees you could find there in the summertime."

"I told you all about that? Well, Mother and Czepe, they think it's better for me; they send me away when it gets too hot in the city."

"Didn't you go?"

"I did. But as you see—I'm back. I have my little tricks too." She laughed.

As far as he could make out, she used no makeup, only lipstick, and she did not seem able to handle that properly. When she laughed, he could see smudges of lipstick on her teeth.

"I went straight to the flower market and asked for you—not by name—I was very careful, I swear. You left suddenly, didn't you?"

He had met her at the wholesale flower market. He had noticed her there several times. The market was only for retailers, but she seemed well known there. And later, when they talked, it had been about flowers. Once or twice she had watched as he put on performances with his puppet at the café, and that was when he had first noticed the lipstick on her teeth. He found out that she was the sister of the priest whose parish this was. That was all he knew about her. And her name, of course: Milli. It was a name that suited her, he thought.

They had arrived at the main portal of the church and were standing in front of it, already in the shade.

"Are you going to work for him?" She gestured toward the flower stand. "Did I understand that right? I'll find you in the market again?"

He found it hard to lie to her. So he said nothing. From the open church door came the sound of hammering, drowning out the street noises. She listened, and her face took on a trace of tension.

"Are they taking away the confessionals?"

"Yes."

"Czepe will be pleased when he comes back. Mother's against giving them away, and Czepe has a hard time putting anything through against her will. What a fuss there'll be tomorrow, when Mother sees they're gone!" She laughed again, but it was a different kind of laugh this time, spitefully pleased, almost with a touch of malevolence.

He had previously had occasion to observe this in her, too, this sudden shift: one moment a shy, youthful girl, the next a shrewd, rather guileful woman.

"Give me the flowers," she said.

"I'll carry them in for you."

"Do you want us to be seen together?"

"Maybe better not."

"So."

He wondered how much she knew, or surmised. He had never intentionally told her anything about himself, and had also never, so far as he knew, given himself away. Yet it sometimes seemed to him that she knew, if only because in her life she had had experiences similar to his.

She had taken the flowers; her arms were so full that she could scarcely see over them.

"How heavy they are! And what a strong perfume the lilies have. I don't really like that smell."

"It will be better in the church."

"Yes." She smiled at him. "So—I'll see you again." She vanished in the darkness of the church.

He waited for some time before he entered the nave. When you came from the sunlight outside, the interior seemed dark, the high, narrow windows being caked on the outside with dust. You had to become accustomed to the dimness, and to the coolness, which increased the farther you went into the building.

The old altar had vanished; the new one, a simple, heavy

slab of stone, had been set up close to the whitewashed wall of the apse. The pulpit was still there, but it was not used. In its place there was an ambo, a lectern made of the same stone as the altar, with a microphone on an adjustable metal arm. The cables ran along to the nave, and the loudspeakers affixed to the pillars were so large and so numerous it appeared as though a hi-fi fanatic had been given his head. The pews were of old oak with fine carving that would fetch a good price. It occurred to the young man that he was already looking at things with the eyes of a secondhand dealer.

He had come along just at the right time. The confessionals had been moved away from the wall and dismantled. The dealer was standing beside the sexton, paying him from a thick roll of bills girdled with a rubber band. Milli was at the altar, arranging the flowers in tall vases, absorbed in her work. When she knelt down to the vases, her long scarf touched the floor. The young man had now started the removal of the confessionals, but all the while he worked he was aware of her presence. The scent of the lilies spread slowly, adding to the atmosphere of the church something that had been missing.

4

As soon as the priest left the plane, the heat assaulted him. It was much hotter than in the plane, and very much hotter than in Rome; the coolest June in years, they were saying there. But he could bear heat a good deal better than flying. As a matter of fact, he felt particularly good when it was hot, and every morning he got up not just *una hora ante missam* as was customary for priests, but *two* hours before Mass, and would run his regular ten kilometers. At least ten—and at a good fast pace, until he was bathed in sweat.

He was well aware that some people found the sight of a not-quite-so-young priest running through the streets in a blue jogging suit with luminescent orange stripes altogether ridiculous. But he would not be deterred from his morning run; it made him feel good, especially afterwards, when he showered and put on fresh clothing. Then he was ready for lauds and the first Mass.

Now, too, he was not bothered by the heat. With his big strides, he led the line of passengers. His long legs made his black skirt flutter like two beating wings giving him additional propulsion. He reached the airport building first, went through the passport check.

He had not counted on being met, but while waiting for his baggage he caught sight of the chauffeur. He was wearing his brown uniform, double-breasted, five buttons on each side, visored cap in hand. The priest smiled involuntarily at the livery and the gloves; even on the hottest days the chauffeur would not take them off.

The priest followed him out to the car. It was a big gray limousine, polished to a high sheen like the chauffeur himself. Kropik deposited the suitcase and attaché case in the trunk, and was reaching out for the black umbrella the priest was carrying.

Czepe Zuckermann looked up at the sky; there was no wind, but the streaked clouds looked like rain.

"I'd rather keep it."

The chauffeur opened the door to the back seat, but the priest shook his head. He got into the front beside the driver. He would really have felt ridiculous sitting alone in the back of the limousine.

"I am not the vicar-general, Kropik." He noticed the silver plaque his mother had had installed on the mahogany dashboard, a St. Christopher, and the thought of his mother prompted him to add, "Even though my mother thinks I should have been one long ago."

He knew he ought to have asked how she was, but he would be faced with all that again soon enough. Involuntarily, he thought again of Rome. Five hours—that was too short a time even for a man like himself who had come to terms with so many defeats in the last several years. He would need a little more time. He would come to terms with *this* as well—and that was truly a mournful thought.

The car stopped in a long line of traffic; a railroad line crossed the principal artery into the city.

"How is everyone?" he asked at last, as though he had been away a long time rather than three days. Kropik replied at once, as though he had barely been able to contain himself.

"Lilo was run over."

That was one of his mother's two Pekineses. He was unable to summon up any sympathy; he detested the dogs. The way they spread themselves in the apartment, moving around like vain little mannequins.

"How could that happen?"

"Milli took them out in the afternoon..."

"Milli?"

"She must have released the dog from the leash. I can't see any other explanation."

"Milli's back? Since when?"

"I drove out for her yesterday and brought her back."

"Why? What happened?"

The chauffeur did not reply at once. Czepe Zuckermann was familiar with that: Kropik was struggling with himself, wondering what he was supposed to say, what not. Kropik, after all, was his *mother's* chauffeur—he ran her errands, drove the *gnädige Frau* into town, to the seamstress, the beauty parlor, to her morning café and her evening bridge parties—and whenever possible Kropik made him aware of it.

"Your sister couldn't stay there."

"Why not?"

"There was trouble. She couldn't find her room at night. I mean, she mixed up the rooms, just went into another one and thought it was hers. The day before yesterday she was found in another guest's room, asleep on his bed... So they didn't want to keep her any longer."

The barrier in front of the tracks had been raised. They drove into town by the direct route, not by way of the port, along the river, a longer route but one the priest preferred. He looked at his wristwatch, a rectangular gold one with Roman numerals, expensive, a gift from his mother for his fiftieth birthday, which was already a year ago.

He could see the sky behind the poplars along the edge of the road. It would probably rain in the evening and then it would come down in sheets, possibly even hail. Any protracted heat wave in this city always ended in a cloudburst that flooded the streets.

"Stop here. I'll walk the rest of the way." He had recalled that it was Saturday and that he had scheduled a choir rehearsal.

When Kropik let him off, the heat was more oppressive than ever. He walked along streets lined with gray houses—some of them still bearing dried birch branches from the Corpus Christi celebration—and felt his disappointment easing, just as he had hoped it would. The traffic was already lighter; in the evening there would be only a few cars in the streets, driving slowly past the small, shabby hotels: men looking over the prostitutes who frequented this quarter—mere curiosity seekers, voyeurs. The real clients came on foot.

He knew this—and was proud of knowing it, for this was his community. For many years he had served in this parish, first as assistant priest and then, for the past nine years, as parish priest. He could have asked for a transfer, and his mother perpetually urged him to do so, but on this point he had never yielded. At first the reason had not even been that he was particularly attached to the parish, but simply that one of these days he'd leave Vienna for good, or so he told himself.

At the beginning, he'd wrestled with this neighborhood, just as if it were a remote mountain parish somewhere in the Andes, and his flock consisted of Indios who had to be converted. He loved this comparison—but after all these years little remained of such adventurous notions. The work had become routine: baptisms and funerals, sick calls and house calls, Sunday school and counseling engaged couples. And the masses, of course. He had an excellent percentage of church attendance, far above the average of other parishes in the city.

A great deal had been said and written about him, but it was not all praise. He provoked graffiti on the walls of the church, anonymous letters with threats, occasional obscene telephone calls that his mother took with the greatest composure. The fact that he wrote texts and music for oratorios— some people called them religious musicals—and put these on himself in his own church, was surely the least of it. From his superiors he earned severer criticism for the interest he showed in strippers, taxi girls, musicians, and bouncers attached to certain disreputable night spots that were part of his parish. Were such concerns truly among a priest's duties? And his chess-playing convicts. What a fuss he had made to get permission for a team of convicts, some with long sentences, to participate in the official Viennese team chess championship tournament. Zuckermann was one priest who seemed to court notoriety in every way possible.

He saw the church ahead of him. The flower vendor was packing up. Members of the choir had gathered in front of the main portal. He crossed the street to the jail.

The interior always gave him a sense of uneasiness, especially the cramped cells. There were three tiers of cells one above the other, and accessible only by an iron structure that extended through all three stories. This huge, open stairwell always frightened him: the reverberation of his footsteps on the iron steps, the voices, the keys. Every time he visited the prison he felt the same oppression until he reached the reception room where he studied chess problems with the convicts.

He waited at the high, close-meshed wire grating through which the prison yard could be seen, paved, clean—this being Saturday, it would have just been scrubbed. At the far end of it lay the laundry, where most of the prisoners worked. A door in the gate was opened, and closed immediately behind the guard.

"How did it come out?"

The guard knew exactly what he was referring to. "What do you think, Father? An important match, wasn't it? Well, I won't keep you hanging: they won five, drew two, and lost one."

Czepe Zuckermann had the standings in his head and so could tell that no matter how the other matches had turned out, the prison team had retained second place.

"That's good news. How about Oplatka?" He was the youngest of the eight players on the team, and the most gifted.

"Oplatka—well, you know him better than I do!"

"I'm sorry—I have so little time!"

"He could easily have had a draw, but he pushed too hard and in the end lost the game. If..."

"I really am in a hurry. I only wanted to know the results. Thanks very much."

The guard took off his cap and wiped his forehead. "What do you say? Will it rain?"

It was odd how all kinds of people were always asking him about the weather, with utmost faith that what he said would happen. Maybe it was simply because they knew he once had been to sea.

"Yes, it will," he said.

He felt better when he was out on the street again. He

hurried, making his big strides even longer. He noticed that the graffito, which his mother had ordered painted over, was showing through again. With a smile he switched the names, as if to read: *We need Zuckermann—not Jesus.* I'll have to confess that, he thought. That was the way it always was with him: it was not his flesh that bothered him but his mind.

The members of the choir were waiting for him. Most of them were young—the long-haired boys in jeans and colored shirts, the girls even younger, most of them wearing their long hair hanging loose with ribbons bound across their foreheads, and their hands spangled with strange rings. Their bracelets made a tinkling sound as they shook hands with him.

It was cooler inside the church. He saw at once that the confessionals had been removed, and for the moment that cheered him. He had always found confession an unpleasant chore. He noted the wealth of fresh flowers, but he had expected that on hearing that Milli was back.

The rehearsal room was alongside the sacristy. As he went there, the sexton tried to hold him back, remind him of other matters: tomorrow's Mass, a funeral that he would have on Monday. But Czepe Zuckermann listened impatiently, distractedly, because he could hear the voices of the girls and boys. At last, with something approaching irritability, he cut the conversation short. He did not calm down until he had taken his seat at the piano, the singers gathered in a semicircle around him.

They rehearsed three times a week, and he always looked forward to these hours.

"Ready? We'll begin with the second movement. The passage that goes 'Faith is easy for the fisherman, if the catch is large'..."

He sang the passage to them, without piano accompaniment, in a surprisingly low bass.

"Not too slowly. Very legato."

He had unbuttoned his white collar and laid it on top of the dark piano. The wide skirt of the cassock was spread carefully over his legs. His right hand lay on the keys; he held his left hand raised. The boys and girls, music sheets in their hands, looked at him.

"All together. And start right out in full voice!"

He gave the sign with his left hand, and his other hand vigorously struck the first chords.

5

It belonged to the city, was fed, nourished, and filled by the city, and yet it was an island unto itself. Some people even called the neighborhood that: Broken-Glass Island, because among the many things abandoned there were broken window glass and empty bottles. Shortly after the war a whole hill had arisen here, composed of windowpanes shattered in the Allied air raids; some claimed to recall that this mountain of glass had even misled commercial pilots, who mistook its glitter in the morning and evening hours for the beacon lights of the nearby airport.

It was not only glass that found its way here. More or less everything that was torn down or left behind ended up at Broken-Glass Island. It came from the city all day long in handcarts or pickup trucks, flowing through the narrow lanes that separated the different sites of the secondhand dealers: huts framed in sheet metal, wooden sheds on stone blocks, abandoned factories, or simply fenced-in areas where junk piled up. Rags bulging out of old burlap bags, newspapers, clothes, metal, broken furniture.

The roads that led into Broken-Glass Island turned to deep mud even in a light rain. But on a day like this they were dry and dusty. The red pickup truck sent up a cloud of dust as it drove alongside a fence made of old railroad ties. The dust settled gradually after the truck passed through a high gate and into the inner courtyard of a former laundry. The truck slowed, glided under the overhanging roof of a brick building, and stopped at an elevated ramp.

Men appeared at once and helped to unload the things. The dealer, who stood by, marked each of the pieces with a chalk mark that only someone in the trade would understand. The unloading and identifying went swiftly. The people were practiced, and soon the truck was empty and the helpers had vanished inside the big building. Now and then a shadow passed in front of the dirty windows. The young man took no part in the unloading, but went off by himself.

One of the two confessionals had been left standing in the glass-roofed forecourt; it was already temporarily reassembled. The dealer took off his smock, crumpled rather than folded it, and tossed it in through the open window to the front seat of the truck. Out here too it was sultry and oppressive, without a breath of wind. The dealer seemed not to mind the heat. He walked around the confessional, studying it from all sides. Finally he drew aside the purple curtain, opened the door, and seated himself inside. From the priest's cubicle he smiled at his wife.

"Anything to confess?"

But she was watching the young man, who strolled about at the far end of the yard. Then she looked up at the sky, where narrow strips of cloud had appeared.

"Do you really think we'll have rain?" Faint, distant thunder could be heard, but that happened every evening without any rain.

The dealer in his confessional recalled what the young man had said on the drive here. Pointing to the streaks in the sky, he had called it "mackerel sky." Looking up now, the dealer agreed that mackerel was indeed what he saw.

"Since he said it would rain, it will."

"Knows everything, eh, that sailor of yours?"

"What do you have against him? Sit down there and confess!"

"Don't make a joke about everything. And come out of that box."

He felt comfortable there. It was hot inside, had a curious smell, and gave him the strangest thoughts. He leaned back to close his eyes and absorb even more of the odor.

"I wish he would go away," he heard his wife say.

"He'll go away all right—one of these days," he said, as though it had occurred to him only this moment.

"I know what the two of you are cooking up. Don't think I don't know it."

"It's your confession, not mine."

She turned to him and looked at him, with a face that was so much like his, except for the blue of her eyes.

"Maybe you'll have yourself tattooed like him, eh?"

He wondered whether she could have seen any more of the tattoo than he had.

"What's so bad about a tattoo?"

"No decent person has anything of the sort. They wouldn't even bury you with that. Any priest would refuse. A decent person goes out of this world the way he came into it. The way God created him—without marks."

"Poor woman!" He adjusted his voice to his whereabouts, spoke unctuously. "No one goes out of this world the way he came into it. And besides, it's only the Jews who believe in that. They don't bury anybody with a tattoo. It's in the Old Testament somewhere. Look it up on Sunday."

"Don't try to change the subject. You've made up your mind to leave and you mean to have yourself tattooed, some kind of indecent marks on an indecent part of your body."

"You'll say three Hail Marys for that." He leaned forward. "I didn't know you had so much imagination. Woman, don't you know imagination comes from the devil? I think I'd better assign you two rosaries extra."

All around them were the usual noises of a late Saturday afternoon: gates being closed, trucks driving away, dogs barking because they had been left behind, a single plane in the air, possibly circling because it had not yet received permission to land, and everything muted by the heat. Few people lived out here, and on weekends the island subsided into silence, as though its distance from the heart of the city were increased.

The dealer hated weekends: the house in a fine neighborhood—_her_ house, where the drapes had gold fringe, the glass cabinets were filled with too many knickknacks, the rugs piled too thick, where the furniture was too heavy and dark, where nobody knew that they dealt in secondhand goods.

"Who is that kid?"

He leaned forward. Way at the back, in the unfenced area he had rented, stood a tan Land Rover. A set of steps attached to the rear of the vehicle led into the interior. There, at the foot of the steps, stood the young man with a girl.

She was a dark-skinned child with black braids on both sides of her head that hung far down. She was clutching something firmly. The young man was stooping down to her.

"Must be one of those gypsy kids," the woman said.

In the summertime gypsies sometimes camped along the edges of the island. The dealer had seen several of their caravans.

"They hang around everywhere. What business does he have with her?"

With a gesture, the dealer silenced his wife. He stood up, stepped out of the confessional box, and watched the two carefully as they talked to each other. Several times the child pointed in the direction of the city. Then the young man nodded, placed his hand briefly on her shoulder, and mounted the steps. The door of the van closed behind him. The child sat down on the steps.

Just then the employees emerged from the building. The dealer produced his roll of bills and paid them, and the men left, one after the other.

"Do you mean to leave the confessional standing out here? What if it should rain?"

He merely shrugged; he was watching the Land Rover as though he could manage to see what was going on inside it.

"All right," she said, "I'll do the books and then change. If it's going to rain, I'd like to be home before it comes so I can stake the delphinium. Otherwise they'll blow over in the rain. Aren't you coming?"

"In a minute." She walked away, and he pictured to himself the way she would emerge in half an hour, a totally changed person in her black crepe dress with that ridiculous bonnet trimmed with cherries, and the way she would drive the Mercedes out of the garage. He did not know which he hated more: the house, *her* house, or this respectable elderly lady at the wheel of the Mercedes.

He went over to the Land Rover. He walked slowly, as though to gain time, to absorb the picture: the van with its roof rack, to which all those canisters were strapped, green ones for gasoline and blue ones for drinking water...

6

The laughter came from the living room. It was the laughter of a woman who was no longer young but was evidently enjoying her age. On the stairs—coming from the rehearsal—Czepe Zuckermann imagined he had heard something else behind that laughter, a very old phonograph record, played often, scratched, with a tone that waxed and waned as in shortwave transmissions...But now, as he entered the hall, the only sound he could still hear was his mother's laughter.

One noticed her presence immediately on entering the apartment; or maybe only he, her son, would notice the scratched doorknobs. When they moved in she had insisted on new brass knobs for all the doors, and now the surface of the metal showed the scratches of her many rings.

The rooms were distributed over two stories, and connected by a wide stairwell. They could be reached directly from the church, since this had been part of a convent run by Ursuline nuns, and one section of the apartment consisted of rooms formerly occupied by the mother superior of the convent.

It was the dog, the one remaining, that betrayed his arrival; otherwise he might have managed to go upstairs unnoticed. He was not in the mood to meet anybody. The door to the living room stood open; that was one of his mother's ways, which she justified on the ground that she needed space and air. The Pekinese had come out through that door and barked at him.

For a moment there was silence. The laughter stopped. In the quiet that followed, it seemed almost as if something were changing, as if the rooms were reverting to the stillness that must once have prevailed when silent nuns in long robes moved through these rooms.

Only a single sound was audible; it came from his mother's long dress, which swept the floor.

"Is that you, Czepe?"

His given name was Stephan, but she insisted on calling him Czepe. She loved everything Hungarian; she herself spoke the language fluently, and she counted Vienna's Hungarian clergy among her favorite guests.

"Czepe?" She stood there, waiting for him to approach and kiss her.

It could not be said that she looked like a priest's mother. It was easy to imagine the beauty she must once have been. She was still a fine figure of a woman, with her aristocratic nose, her dark eyes that sparkled with alertness, and the sleek jet-black hair.

She was sixty-eight. In recent years she had put on some weight, but her waist was still slender. She liked long dresses. She always wore them in certain hues: violet, red, sometimes black, as though she were observing the colors prescribed in the liturgy. The one liturgical exception was white; her son had never seen her in that.

She extended her hand with all the heavy rings on her fingers—an unequivocal indication of what she expected. But when he still did not come forward to kiss her, she said, "I have a guest. You ought to say hello to him."

"I want to change."

"It's the vicar-general!"

Formerly such an occasion would have resulted in a test of strength between them, but now he had other methods.

"I've been in these clothes since this morning." In a way he really was not surprised. Though secretly he had hoped they would give him time. "I won't be long." The dog sat on the floor in front of her, pressing against her dress; its tail curled carefully beside it, it watched him closely with those ugly eyes in its crushed little face.

"I heard about the dog," he said, making an effort to show some of the feelings she expected and which he did not feel—pleasure at being back and sympathy for the loss of the dog. "I'm sorry."

She looked down at the dog.

"I really am sorry," he repeated.

"At any rate, it was lucky I didn't happen to look out of the window when it happened. It was all over when I heard about it. I hope Kropik had the blood cleaned off the pavement. I'll get another Pekinese."

He might have known it. She spoiled the dogs, sent for the vet when they had the slightest indisposition—and then said such things, resigned herself to the facts, went on with the day's agenda.

"It never would have happened if they would just get around to making the street one way."

"It is a one-way street."

"Is it? Since when?"

"For more than a year."

"A minor miracle! It's as I always say: you have to put pressure on them, then something is done. Without pressure nothing ever happens here. And imagine—they didn't want to send an ambulance, said they have no ambulances for dogs!"

"You called an ambulance?"

"Should I not have, just because it's an injured dog? They were quite insulting on the telephone. Well, I suppose you had better change first. These planes are always rather dirty. You didn't use the toilet, I hope? I don't know, do they have special toilets in first class?"

"I can't tell. I didn't use it."

He hated himself for this conversation, but this was what they ordinarily talked about. She had not so much as mentioned Milli, and he had not asked about her. He mounted the wide staircase. With its many doors heavily framed in carved oak, the second story was even more reminiscent of the convent that had been. He went to one of the doors toward the rear and listened. He heard nothing. When Milli was in her room, the radio was always going. He knocked, but there was no answer.

He turned. The walls of the hallway were hung with pictures. The original ones had been removed and were now stored in the attic; they had been replaced by oils his mother had bought—landscapes and, above all, paintings of animals. Not because she had any particular fondness for them, but because she regarded paintings of this type as the soundest of investments. The only remaining religious art was on the ceiling; it was a rather hackneyed fresco representing St. Ursula and her virgins being slaughtered by the Huns at Cologne.

As he looked up, he recalled out of habit the first two lines of the hymn he had sung as a boy:

> *Sankt Ursula ein Schiff regiert*
> *Mit engelreinem Blut geziert*

He knew no more of the text, only the melody. Humming it under his breath as he entered another room, he went directly to the desk, took out some music paper, and noted down the melody. If he changed it a little, he could surely make something of it. He had never fooled himself; he had only a mediocre talent and was dependent on others for his musical ideas.

The room he had entered seemed bare. He ignored what his mother did with the rest of the rooms, how she filled them to overflowing; but in his suite, two rooms and a bath, nothing accumulated. He seized every possible opportunity to reduce the objects to a minimum. A single picture hung on the wall, a crudely framed photograph of a medium-sized freighter, with snapshot portraits of the crew inserted into the foreground. Otherwise the study contained only the desk—heaped with papers and books—a utilitarian lamp, and two end tables on which books and pamphlets were similarly piled.

He entered the next room, which was even barer: an old-fashioned high bed, a nightstand and lamp, a footstool, on the wall a simple, small wooden cross without a figure of Christ; there were Venetian blinds instead of curtains; no rugs. One entire wall of the room was taken up by a built-in closet; the inconsistency of this appeared only when the doors were opened to reveal the wealth of clothing in Zuckermann's wardrobe. He had, as he too well knew, an inclination toward vanity, and he was particularly proud of his turtlenecks. There were whole drawers full of them, in all shades from blue to deep black, from simple cottons to sinfully expensive pure silks.

He took his time, washed, shaved—he had fairly heavy dark whiskers—and changed his clothes. He rarely wore the cassock, since the priestly uniform was no longer stringently prescribed; but for this flight to Rome it had seemed to him the proper garb. He definitely did not want to wear it in the presence of the vicar-general. He put on black slacks, a black corduroy jacket, and a matching turtleneck.

He left his cassock hanging outside the wardrobe so that it could be cleaned. For a moment it occurred to him that he was missing his other cassock, which had been sent off for cleaning at some time or other.

He was ready now, but he hesitated to leave. For a moment he thought back to the flight and the surprise he felt when the captain's voice announced that the outside temperature was 58 degrees below zero, at an altitude of 31,000 feet. This remarkable fact had astonished him—such icy cold up there in the radiant, sunlit sky. Now he thought, Maybe that's how it is with God—the closer you come to him, the colder he feels to you.

This was truly a day full of sinful thoughts.

Finally he left the room. He returned once more to listen at Milli's door, but again heard nothing.

"Czepe, aren't you coming!"

The vicar-general... It was obvious why he had come. He had appealed to Rome over the vicar-general's head. He had done this because up to now the vicar-general and the archbishop, whom the vicar-general preferred to hide behind, had turned down all his requests to be transferred to missionary work. Not just one request. He had turned down all of them over the years, again and again. Was his mother behind this, he had often asked himself. He had been told he was "overqualified" for such employment, and when that argument no longer availed, there came that final "much too old."

"Czepe!"

"I'm coming." He glanced at the narrow staircase that led up to the attic. The room specially built for him there held his shortwave radio station. That was his real *sanctissimum*. He regretted he could not withdraw to it at once.

7

Many evenings they had sat together inside the van, completely furnished with everything that two would need for a long trip: two benches along the sides that could be converted into cots, a folding table, a small refrigerator, a two-burner gas stove. But he had never entered the van without being asked.

The secondhand dealer saw the young man's silhouette through the back window of the Land Rover. From his movements he could tell he was packing. For a moment the dealer stood there without budging. He looked at the child. As soon as he approached, she had got up and run off a few steps, but she had stayed nearby. There was no doubt she was a gypsy, with her dark hair and dark eyes. At last he turned and knocked.

He remained outside after the door opened, waiting to be asked in. And perhaps he hoped that he had merely interpreted all the signs wrongly. But there was the young man and there was the duffel bag, a long, green duffel bag of canvas, with a carrying strap and lettering that was no longer legible. He had been carrying the bag when he first turned up here.

"Come in."

The dealer looked at the young man and thought, He's changed, though he could not have said why he thought it. He always wore nearly the same clothes: a khaki or checked shirt, the khaki slacks with the two patch pockets, the Clarks. Sometimes he also wore a tan windbreaker, and he always had one of those kerchiefs around his neck. He was dressed the same now, had only changed his shirt, and yet he was different, as though he were adjusting to a new role. Even a good observer could not have pinpointed exactly how he'd achieved this transformation. The young man was like one of those entertainers who change their whole appearance right on the stage, using a trifle, a cigarette, a hat, a cane, but he made the change without such props, from inside, like a chameleon changing its color.

"You're leaving?"

"Just changing places."

"Today?"

"Yes, have to. Old superstition. They say sailing on Sunday brings bad luck. But if you have to do it all the same, change your anchorage on Saturday. Move your vessel a few ship's lengths, then when you do sail on Sunday you can always say you started your trip Saturday. Pure superstition, of course."

"But why?" He watched as the young man pulled his shirt out of his trousers, buckled a wide canvas belt with several compartments around his waist, then covered it with his shirt again. He did this without the slightest embarrassment. "Why so suddenly?"

"I may be gone only for a short while. A week, two weeks. I don't know yet."

"Leaving the city?"

"Not necessarily."

"Don't like the city?"

The young man smiled. "I haven't found out yet."

"But..." The dealer waved his hand at the interior of the van. "I had the feeling you liked it here..." He broke off as if he felt that what he meant to say would only worsen matters. "I've never asked any questions, have I? I didn't question you when you came here."

"No, you didn't."

"You see a secondhand man knows how to keep secrets." His voice took on a pleading note. "No dealer wants to say where his things come from or where they go. Sometimes in town I look at windows of antique shops, and spot pieces that passed through my hands. All I have to do is look at the shop, the street, and I know how much they'll make on that piece. But I'd never tell anybody. No real secondhand man would. Ethics. Understand?"

"Sure, I understand. Let me put it this way: I've received a message..."

That actually came fairly close to the truth. A message that was the way it always happened. Almost like the way junk dealers got their information, by word of mouth. Someone told someone else, and the message traveled swiftly. It might take no more than an hour from the city out to here, yet if you investigated for days you would still not trace the exact route it had taken. That was why he was calm; he knew he had plenty of time.

"I'm just moving my anchorage to deeper water," he said. "Maybe I'll come back soon."

He was holding a knife in his hand. Resting his arms on the tabletop, he used the sharp point of the blade to split matches. He divided them with care and concentration, first the wood and then the head, so that afterwards he had three matches instead of one. He always busied himself doing something of this nature when they sat here and talked; he did it now with all the quiet and patience such tasks required, and the dealer's hopes revived.

"If you stay...wait, hear me out. This city is a real paradise for secondhand men. In all other big cities they've been tearing everything down for years. Slum clearance, you know. Soon there won't be anything left. But it's different here. This was an emperor's city, an empress's city—the city's still chock-full of things hardly anyone knows about. It's still full of gold, secondhand man's gold, and will be for a long time to come. There's more money in it than you may think."

The young man smiled, but it was a grave smile and vanished quickly.

"It's not for me. I would have thought you'd know that."

"Yes, I do know." The dealer felt exhausted from talking, from the heat inside the van. Sweat gathered in his thick eyebrows. He gave a sigh. The young man replaced the divided matches in the box. The green duffel bag lay on the bench beside him, packed; the young man's arm rested on it. His manner did not convey any impression of haste.

"And besides"—it was apparent that this was the last thing the dealer had to say, the argument he'd saved up—"I thought we were going to take that trip…"

He did not have to say more; there was no need to explain. They had talked about it often, here in the evenings; that is, he had talked and the young man had listened: the trip, the ever-present promise that someday he would really take it. Anatolia. Or rather, many names: Kumluca, Hacibektas, the Gediz River—in ancient times Hermos—and many other mellifluous names. A landscape dotted with archaeological sites ranging from scattered secret graves to huge, magnificent cities, full of gold and silver ornaments, bracelets, diadems, necklaces, scepters, statues, painted pottery, weapons, the treasures of millennia…all there to dig up!

As he conjured it up in his mind once more, he realized that he had never found anyone else who could listen so well to his dreams. Nor would he find anyone ever again.

"I know," the young man said, as though there were no more to be said.

"I was counting on you getting the stuff out of the country. As tough as smuggling opium, and just as valuable. I always told myself, If anybody can handle it, he's the one."

The young man stood up. He glanced around. "Guess I have to go."

The secondhand dealer looked around. "You haven't forgotten anything?"

"A sailor never leaves anything behind."

"So you're really a sailor?"

The young man just smiled. He stooped and brought a package tied with string out from under the bench.

"Next time you burn something, toss it in, just as is. Will you do that?"

"Sure. Anything you say. And no questions asked." He took the package, which was tightly wrapped in plastic and tied several times.

They went outside. The young man unhooked the steps and stowed them under the van. Moving very deliberately, he locked the door and held out the key to the dealer.

"Okay. Till later, then."

"We could give you a ride…"

"Thanks. I enjoy walking after a long day behind the wheel."

The dealer made a movement of reaching into his trousers pocket, but the young man shook his head.

"I don't need it, really not."

"I haven't paid you this week."

The young man's hand touched the Land Rover, gave the metal side a pat. "Keep it in shape!" He picked up the green duffel bag with one hand, his windbreaker with the other; then slung the bag over his shoulder by its cord. "See you!"

The gypsy girl came running up to join him. As they walked side by side down the narrow lane between all the heaped-up objects, the child laughed at something he said, her long black braids swinging. The mackerel pattern in the sky thickened. Across the river the sky was black, but it was still not raining.

The junk dealer walked back to the building as slowly as he had come. The child was standing outside the gate waving something colorful, but the young man was no longer in sight. The junk dealer knew it was a kind of betrayal, but he could not resist; perhaps he wanted to make up for the loss he had suffered by finding something else. Hastily he untied the cord and unwrapped the plastic.

The first thing he saw was black cloth, solid cloth of the best quality—he could tell that by the feel of it. But only when he found the white collar did he realize that the package contained a priest's clothing; collar, cassock, and cincture.

He stood looking at it, not knowing what to make of it. Then he remembered what he had promised and tied the package up again. He thought it a pity to burn something that still had value.

From one of the windows he heard his wife's voice. "What's the matter, aren't you changing? Do you want to ride the way you are? Hurry."

He did not answer. The gypsy child had returned to the yard, and for a moment the old man felt jealousy—of the child's laugh, of the way the young man had laid his hand on her shoulder, of the intimacy between the two. The child took a few steps toward him, but then stopped, waiting.

"Where you come from?"

She pointed back mutely to the place where gypsy trailers stood in a field.

He took out his roll of bills, but the child only shrank back several steps. He put the money away. "You're a friend of his?"

He saw the girl's eyes flash. She came closer again. She still did not say anything, though the confessional seemed to interest her. He watched as the girl stepped closer to it, touched the wood, timidly pulled open the door, then giggled as though a thought had come to her.

"Is it a theater?" she asked, still giggling. "It must be a theater."

He understood; she thought the box was the stage for a puppet theater. Maybe she had been to the Prater, where they still put on puppet shows on Sundays. Perhaps the sailor...

"Did *he* take you to see Punch and Judy?"

She nodded eagerly, looking up at him, and he realized that in saying this he had won her confidence.

"Did you like it?"

"Oh yes. Can I..." She toyed with the confessional door.

From close up, he noticed that the child was older than he had assumed, twelve maybe, and her breasts already somewhat developed. For a moment he was overpowered by the idea of himself in the confessional, perhaps even draped in the heavy black cloth of the cassock, with the curtain drawn, and this girl to one side of it, kneeling, speaking through the grating, confessing. To what? He would see her face, her moving lips, her downcast eyes—the sinner! He would be nothing more than a shadow whose breath she would feel when he pronounced absolution...

He opened the door for her. "Go on in."

The child hesitated, then slipped into the confessional. She sat down on the bench and closed the door behind her. Now only her head and shoulders were visible.

From some distance away he heard footsteps, and in a

moment he would hear the sound of the garage door opening. He did not have much more time.

"Why did he leave, if he was your friend?"

The child's face set. He saw how wary she was: he was only reviving her suspicion. By now he realized that what she had been gripping in her hands all the while was one of those kerchiefs the young man wore.

"That's a present from him?"

She nodded, and then unexpectedly slid down from the bench and vanished. He heard only a few noises, the rustle of her clothes, as she knelt properly, then a clearing of her throat like an actor, then silence. Above the top of the door appeared something particolored, a head, outstretched arms, and a voice, still very uncertain, that said, "Hello, are you all there?"

Because he was standing so close, he could look down at the child, at the part that divided her black hair down the middle; and since this seemed to him somehow unfair, he took a step back.

"Yes, we're all here."

The puppet vanished for a while. There was a whispering, as though the two were conferring, and then the puppet's head appeared above the edge of the door again.

"I'm Golliwog." The child was trying to disguise her voice, but she was not very good at it.

He recalled something from the dim past, when he had been a very young man and *she* a young woman.

"But Golliwog is a dance."

"How silly," the puppet said. "That's a name. My name is Golliwog. The great ballerina." Again the puppet disappeared, again the whispering could be heard, and then the puppet returned.

"Who's this now?" the junk dealer asked.

"The girl who spits to all four winds—east, west, north, and south."

"I see! No name?"

"How silly! Puppets don't have names, not till they learn how to behave, anyway."

He was by now convinced that she had got all this from the young man. In time he might find out what it meant if he gained the child's confidence.

"Did *he* teach you all this?"

The dark-skinned face appeared over the rim, heated, flushed, the large, dark eyes sparkling.

"Yes!"

In the garage the motor started, and he said, "I'm sorry, but I have to go now. Maybe you'll come back sometime and tell me more. I'd like to know everything about puppets. Of course only till your friend comes back."

"Is he coming back?" the child asked in surprise.

He did not have time to answer. Maybe she will actually come and I'll find out more, he thought. But then he saw the surprised expression on her face, and suddenly felt sure that he'd never see the young man again.

8

The big living room was full of smoke. It hung in front of the floor-to-ceiling bookcases filled with leather-bound editions, and it drifted toward the windows with their heavy red velvet drapes. No one in their family smoked, and there were no ashtrays, but for high clerics who smoked, and for them alone, something was always found in which they could deposit cigarettes and cigars.

The vicar-general rose from his armchair. Cigar in hand, he greeted the priest.

"Well, here you are at last, Zuckermann. Come, sit down here with us. I was just praising that great dinner your mother served the last time. No one in the whole city that can cook like your mother."

He was in high good humor. After a few drinks, his face, thin in proportion to his stocky figure, radiated well-being. He wouldn't even need drinks, the priest thought; every man behaved this way after being exposed to his mother for a sufficient time. He'd often had occasion to observe it; almost all of them succumbed to the charm of this woman, and members of the clergy were especially susceptible.

"It must have something to do with this place as well," the vicar-general went on. "My predecessor also used to dine splendidly here. He was the nuns' confessor, very popular with them, cock of the walk, so to speak. After confessions there was always an opulent meal. Great cooks, those Ursulines. Those were the days! When I think of the way our sisters run around nowadays. Won't take much more and they'll be wearing miniskirts. Come now, Zuckermann, come do sit down. I suppose you'd rather like that, sisters in miniskirts?"

His mother answered for him.

"I'd have nothing against it—provided they have beautiful legs. I still remember those first American soldiers, right after the war. Tight trousers as if molded to them—when you looked from behind! I must admit I enjoyed the sight. Up to then I'd seen nothing but men in horrible, drooping trousers. Not everything has deteriorated."

The vicar-general deposited his cigar on a plate.

"So who says the church isn't keeping up with the times?"

His coarse laugh suited his heavy body, but it sounded somehow false, too hearty, and it did not divert attention from the stern, hard lines of his face and the small eyes that suggested how nasty he could sometimes be.

"You are truly lucky to have such a mother, Zuckermann."

Again it was his mother who smoothed over the ensuing silence.

"You ate on the plane?"

"Yes, on the plane."

"Still the grand ascetic," the vicar-general said. "How is your oratorio going?"

"Very well."

"The church must have a part in everything human, eh? And what is worthier of the human being than a beautiful voice. Let them who sing come unto me! Maybe it wasn't written that way, but it would certainly fit." He glanced over at the record player. "The bells of Bethlehem—what a story!"

"I played him that old recording," his mother said, not by way of apology, merely as an explanation.

He did not mind; she had frequently told the story: how on Christmas Eve 1933, for the first time ever, the ringing of the bells of Bethlehem had been transmitted directly to the entire world by radio. And he, a boy of twelve at the time, had been so impressed that from that day on he knew for sure that he wanted to be a priest. So her story ran, though in fact she had invented it, just as she invented stories about her own life. He had never objected. In fact, in the course of years the tale of the bells had come to seem possibly true to him.

For a moment there was a silence. Then voices could be heard from the hall. Kropik was admitting the ladies, showing them into the small parlor. His mother rose.

"My bridge ladies. They are always a bit impatient if we don't begin at once." She intensified the smile she turned on the vicar-general. "You won't be severe with him?"

She swept out of the room, erect in her long violet dress, a grande dame, the raven hair twisted in a chignon at the nape of her neck and held in place by a large ornamental comb. The Pekinese followed her.

"Truly a remarkable woman, your mother." The vicar-general seemed to mean it, although almost everything that fell from his lips tended to sound mocking. "With such a woman..."

Whatever he might have meant to say, he did not finish the sentence. Earlier he had observed the pills that had been laid out on a table with such deliberation that he could not help suspecting she wanted to suggest she was a sick woman. Probably she was in excellent health. She looked—the skin on her hands and face led him to the comparison—like a lizard undulating in the sun. Were lizards unusually long-lived? She had held out hopes, spoke of a foundation grant to the archdiocese; but whenever he had tried to pin things down, she cleverly evaded him. Probably someday this son of hers ...would get all the money... The thought reminded him again of the purpose of his visit.

"You have been in Rome, I hear? Have they found out what kind of vandal it was who damaged the *Pietà*?"

That was still the talk of Rome, but what was the point of it here? So he kept silent. He had taken a chair, sitting as far away as possible.

"They'll say it's a madman. But I doubt it. Playing insane to get off with a light sentence. That reminds me"—his voice took on a sterner note—"your chess-playing club of convicts. That's one of your activities you will not continue!"

"I have your permission."

"Yes, but since then, I happened to look at the files ... That man Oplatka, for example...isn't he your favorite? How vividly you've described him to me! A pitiable boy, really, who's just had a great deal of hard luck. Fundamentally decent. Unfortunate circumstances. I read the file differently...a refractory, corrupt criminal."

The priest sat stiffly on his chair. He took pains to listen—to listen in silence. He tried to picture Oplatka's face; oddly, he could see only the back of him in his prison jacket, stooped over the chessboard. He remembered how much concentration was expressed by the boy's back, under the perfectly straight line of hair at the nape of his neck.

"That sentence he was given...five years, that's disproportionately long."

"There's our Zuckermann!"

"Five years for a boy who's barely nineteen because he..."

"Because in order to obtain narcotics he committed all these outrageous crimes! I prefer not to discuss that any further, really not. What you are doing is just plain pastoral adventurism, no more, no less. Please forgive the harsh language, but that's what it is to me."

"Would you mind speaking more plainly?"

"Oh, I can indeed speak more plainly, my son. You will stop this club! You will discontinue your other activities, if that is the proper name for them. For all your good intentions, which we have never overlooked, which we do not overlook now, your good deeds have caused more vexation than they have done good. The Church cannot look on while it is being harmed, nor while one of its priests is harming himself in a very personal way. Dabbling. Well, let us drop that. All we want is that in the future you restrict yourself to your proper duties."

"Otherwise?" At least now it was coming out in the open.

"Now, Zuckermann! Surely I don't have to spell that out for you. And going to Rome, over our heads... Surely you know as well as I what that can mean."

On the return flight he had let the consequences run through his head. He did not imagine they would dismiss him from the diocese. Perhaps he would be temporarily relieved of his post; perhaps he would be threatened with transfer to some obscure country parish. For a moment he actually had the wild hope that in order to get rid of him they would accede to his request after all and send him abroad to a missionary station.

He stood up. When it was still, the house was full of noises, a crackling in the wooden coffering of the ceiling, in one of the doors. He still could not hear any rain. He opened a window. Outside a slight wind had risen, but it still was oppressively hot.

"Is it going to rain?" The vicar-general had followed him. "I hear that your weather predictions are more reliable than the meteorologists'."

"Yes, it's going to rain."

As if on command, a few heavy raindrops fell, but nothing more.

The vicar-general smiled.

"You have many talents, Zuckermann. Sometimes that is a cross."

The priest thought, None of this really matters to me any more. I only want him to leave.

With a certain malice, he said, "If it's really starting to rain, it'll be hard to get a cab."

"Yes, they seem to vanish from the surface of the earth." The vicar-general retained his faintly amused smile. "So I thought it gracious of your mother to offer to have the chauffeur drive me home."

"Tell me when I should call him."

"And you'll let me know your decision? Shall we say Monday?" He paused. "I mean, this cassock—it does still have significance for you after all."

"That's why I don't understand how I have anything to decide."

"I knew you would take it sensibly. I'm very glad. You expected this, didn't you, my son?"

This was pure flourish...the vicar-general was hardly older than Zuckermann.

"Yes, I've expected it."

They stood side by side at the open window, the cigar smoke drifting out from the room.

"I hope nevertheless to see you soon," the vicar-general said. He turned from the window as if he were on the point of leaving. "You didn't by any chance read our local papers while you were in Rome?"

"No."

"Of course they played the thing up. It is truly deplorable. The less they know, the wilder their imaginations... 'Swindler in Cassock'..."

"I haven't seen the local papers."

"Someone got himself a cassock and went around in it collecting money from old ladies. And I assure you it was no amateur. He worked only the classiest residential neighborhoods, only large, unattached houses. Called only when husbands were at the office and the ladies at home alone, or even better, he called on lonely widows. The man must be a good observer. And these ladies still actually go on defending him. Such a nice young priest, they say, so dedicated."

Why didn't he leave? Why was he telling him all this? More than ever the priest wished to be alone.

The vicar-general seemed to be considering whether to take another cigar, but refrained. "He always used the same story: Become a foster parent for a little girl who's been orphaned. Or else the father was dead, the mother worked in the rice fields, and the child was only five and dying of poverty. Save little Doan Thi Wu—or whatever name he used."

"He collected money for that?"

"A cleverly cooked-up story: *Your* money will feed, clothe a child, ensure that he's tended to by doctors, taken into homes, taught in schools. *Your child, ma'am!* Very cunning. The children always came from the usual areas: Bangladesh, Honduras, Vietnam, Chile, the Sahel, Tanzania."

For the first time since entering the room Czepe Zuckermann seemed genuinely concerned; perhaps the names of those foreign lands had stirred him, names that were connected with his own dreams.

"How do you know the man was a fraud?"

"We would have known about it. He would have needed

permission..."

"Of course. And did he succeed?"

"Charmed by him, none of the ladies was willing to come right out and say how much she had actually contributed, let alone offer to testify against him. Seems he hit the wrong person just once, and that woman reported it only after considerable hesitation."

"Can I talk to him?"

"Just as I thought! Now, there is a case for Zuckermann. No, you cannot talk to him, unfortunately."

"You mean he hasn't been arrested?"

"Would I be telling you all this otherwise? Didn't want to push his luck, possibly. Anyway, the collecting suddenly stopped. It was only chance the press found out, from one of the detectives who was investigating."

"He wore a cassock?"

"I suppose a whole slew of them are lying around the old-clothes shops. Another of those things that cause me to ask whether the Church was right in 'keeping up with the times'."

"You said I could help you on this?"

"Did I? It was just an idea I had, so that you'll keep your ears open. A fake priest—that's the sort of story the people you know would surely be talking about, eh?"

"If you catch him—what will be done?"

"You mean about the fraud? Oh, you know: our kingdom is not of this world. We have no interest in punishment. All we want is to see that no fake priests go running around in this city making a mockery of the Church. Otherwise, the whole thing ought rather to be played down. We don't want to create a stir."

"Does he have a name?"

"He used several false ones, of course."

"No name? Any other clues?"

"Yes, one thing—a tattoo."

The priest raised his eyes and examined the vicar-general's face. He seemed to be looking for something specific there, but the expression was the same as always, a mixture of geniality and hardness.

"What kind of tattoo?"

"That's one more reason we want no fuss about the affair. It's a—crucifixion of Christ."

Czepe Zuckermann's left shoulder drooped somewhat lower; the movement would have been almost imperceptible to anyone not looking directly at it. Many years ago—just before he had left the seminary—he had contracted tuberculosis. There was an operation in which sections of his three upper ribs were cut away. This had resulted in making his left shoulder sag; but as someone who had always put great stress upon looking hale, he usually offset this by an especially erect posture.

"A crucifixion—as a tattoo!" The vicar-general's voice was filled with true indignation. "I call that blasphemy."

"It's nothing especially new," Czepe Zuckermann said in a suddenly gentle voice. "There's a great Christian tradition for it, in Loreto, in Jerusalem. Many pilgrims returned from those places with tattoos. All sorts of Christian motifs, doves, the Virgin Mary... Christ on the cross was one of the commonest."

"Blasphemy, if you ask me." Now it was the vicar-general's turn to study the other man's face.

"It goes straight back to Holy Scripture," Czepe Zuckermann said, undeterred. "Shall I quote St. Paul to you? *Henceforth let no man trouble me; for I bear on my body the marks of Jesus*." He flashed a smile, the first time he had smiled all evening. "Galatians six, seventeen."

"Good at the weather and good at Scripture, those were always your strong points, Zuckermann." The vicar-general listened to the noises in the house, to his own voice. "Well, I really will have to go now."

"I'll tell Kropik." He left to look for him. On Saturday the chauffeur always stayed to wait on the ladies and later to drive them home. The priest knocked on his door, asked him to get ready, and then went to tell his mother that the vicar-general wanted to say goodbye. She came from the room where a light illuminated the green card table. She had kept the cards in her hand, new, gold-rimmed.

"How did it go?" she asked softly.

"Quite well." Somehow it even sounded convincing. "And

how is it going with you?"

"Poor cards so far. But the game is young yet."

The vicar-general came out into the hall, and she turned to him.

"I hear you have had a good conversation."

"I take it that was a *private* trip to Rome. The expenses are being covered privately, I assume?"

"Of course they are," the woman said, her tone suddenly reserved.

I treated him much too leniently, the vicar-general thought, and said to the woman, "I hope you'll think about that... I mean, what we discussed. This foundation you suggested..."

"Why, of course, I shall give it serious consideration. I am sure we'll take a step ahead next time."

"You ought to consider the tax advantages also. If I can be of any help in that respect..."

"We really must discuss all that at our leisure, not when you're on the point of leaving and my ladies are waiting impatiently. Really at our leisure. Is Kropik coming? Good... Well then, *nemsokára*, as the Hungarians say. And don't forget your hat this time." She returned to the other room, closing the door behind her.

"About this foundation," the vicar-general began, "I wouldn't want you to think I..."

Czepe Zuckermann waved that aside. "It's *her* money. She knows what to do with it."

The vicar-general took his hat. Kropik appeared, in brown livery, wearing gloves. "This way, please, Your Reverence."

Zuckermann accompanied him as far as the door. Kropik had preceded them; his footsteps echoed in the high stairwell.

The vicar-general extended his hand. "I hope you won't misunderstand my motives. Obedience, my son, must be one of the pillars of the Church."

"Of course."

"Don't take it too hard. After all, what are you giving up? Certainly, God has presumably greater love for tempestuous young priests, our comrades in arms with flaming swords ...

But you're no longer young. Neither am I. What God requires of us two, Zuckermann, is no longer great deeds, it is merely fidelity. Drop in on me whenever you feel in the mood."

"Gladly." Czepe Zuckermann was only slowly beginning to realize what this man had taken from him.

"Do you fish by any chance? Come with me sometime. I know a good lake, very out of the way, not fished out, with a few pike in it, fine fellows. I always say, standing out there at five o'clock in the morning with rod in hand—that's my early Mass."

He descended the broad marble stairs that were saucered in the center from the shoes of so many nuns.

9

The young man walked along the dusty path, green duffel bag in hand, windbreaker slung over his shoulder. He walked close to the fences that separated the various junkmen's yards. Most of these were deserted by now. Dogs that had been left behind to guard the places ran along with him, inside the fences, without barking at him. The thought passed through his mind that it was fortunate dogs liked him; it seemed a trifling matter, but for him it was vital. It was better to have the dogs on his side. And children.

He turned around, but the little girl had long since vanished. Odd; he had never asked her to watch out for him, nor would he have been able to tell her precisely what to watch for. There were always so many different signs that told him it was time to change places. Sometimes he himself would have been unable to attribute his decision to a specific fact. It was a canniness he had acquired in this one-year AWOL—just as a sailor knew from long experience what a certain wind meant, or how to tell the depth of water just from the color of the surface. And yet he wondered whether it was not just instinct that told you where you were safe and where not.

He walked slowly. So they were looking for him—that was nothing new. They probably did not know that he had abandoned the role of priest. Still, he was somewhat uneasy. Broken-Glass Island had been such a safe place, one of the best he'd had recently; if they were looking for him *there*, that was a bad sign. Not too bad, but a sign that should not be ignored.

But though he was uneasy, he was definitely not alarmed. There was no reason for alarm. Alarm would have been in order if he had not packed his things at once and left. Vacillating, thinking it over, postponing because he was attached to something, anything—to a Land Rover, for example, or a gypsy girl he'd taken to a Punch and Judy show—that would be grounds for real alarm. That was what he had to be on the lookout for, more than any official. Getting used to any one place, becoming attached to people, meant in itself giving himself up. If that happened, he'd be sunk. He smiled at the idea, As long as I'm alone I can walk on water!

He broke off his reflections and stepped to the side. He had heard the motor, and without looking back he could tell it was the junkman's diesel and by the driving that his wife was at the wheel. The gray Mercedes passed by him. Through the cloud of dust it threw up, he saw the embroidered cushion on the rear ledge: a flowered border with the car's license number in the center. And he saw the junk dealer, just an outline, his head twisted as he tried to look back. Sometimes, at sea, when he'd been sailing a long while, he'd think every cloud on the horizon must be land. That's what had happened to the junkman, but undoubtedly he knew by now it had been an illusion.

Actually he would have liked to take that trip with the junkman but his passport was not good enough for that anyway. The car vanished in a dense cloud of dust, and the young man discarded another idea he had toyed with for a moment: to go to the church and wait for Milli to talk with her.

He had allowed himself this thought for a while because changing places also involved considering all the other possible places you might go—and most of all it meant deciding who was trustworthy. Little as he knew about her, he was sure Milli would never do him harm. Blurting out his first name—he couldn't blame her for that. She had never asked uncomfortable questions about his past. Nevertheless, he had a feeling it was better to avoid her, and he trusted this feeling.

Certainly, he felt the craving for a woman, but he smiled

at that: it was always that way when he changed places, as though he had earned a reward after a long voyage. He would have a woman, perhaps today, perhaps tomorrow. That was no problem; this was a big city and in big cities there were always women...

There was one place, where the houses had not yet grown together so densely and the traffic was not yet so heavy, that offered a panorama of the city. He always paused there and he did now. The day was as sultry as ever, oppressively hot, but at least there was a wind now and beyond the river it was already raining, long, straight streaks in the white light. The city was still swaddled in its smog; only the landmarks reached above the haze. Although in reality the young man was looking down on the city, from the point where he stood it seemed to him to be on higher ground so that he would have to climb to reach it.

He put down his duffel bag and looked closely at the city, like someone seeing it for the first time. He needed this pause anyway because he had an important decision to make. He knew that it was about six P.M.: at sea, bells struck every half hour and on the hour; on land he also managed without a watch. There were other kinds of bells you could guide yourself by, and then, of course, there was always the sun and the sky, although in a foreign city you could go wrong on that, even if it lay in the latitude—48.12 degrees north—that ought to be familiar to him.

Six P.M. was an especially good time to change places. Leaving in the middle of the night was the worst. There were only a few places you could go to then: the railroad station, for example, and that was one place it was better to avoid. The morning was better, but only when you were new in a city and needed time to get acquainted with it and decide what places were safe and what not. But for that purpose you had to move about a good deal and ask questions, and that was the disadvantage.

Beyond a doubt, late afternoon or evening was the best time of all, like now. You didn't have to rush things. You didn't spend a lot of time running around with a green duffel bag; a green duffel bag always attracted attention, but he had been unable to bring himself to part with it. Most of all this was a good time because everybody was at home. Even if you turned up unexpectedly, people were readiest to help out at this time of day. They had a hard day behind them and a few pleasant hours ahead, and that put them in a friendly mood.

I really am lucky.

He again turned his entire attention to the city. Far off at the end of it he saw the river, or imagined he could see it. He liked cities with rivers best of all. But this one had disappointed him in that respect. It was a city that got nothing out of its river—its two rivers if you counted in the canal. The river was not even a good escape route, which rivers ought to be, because you could use it in only one direction—west—although he was at the moment not thinking so far ahead.

He was not yet finished with this city. What experience did it have waiting for him? There were always reasons for him to stay, beyond the ordinary, accidental ones, reasons that did not immediately appear on the surface, and he was concerned to find out what these were before he left. He stood looking sharply down upon the massed buildings, as though he had only to stare long enough to obtain an answer, or at least a hint. But perhaps he was transfixed only because he still had to decide where to go.

He recalled what the junkman had said this morning: that he knew the city as well as though he'd been born here. Yes, he was good with cities, he, a young fellow from a small island. He could fix a city in his mind, its structure, its access routes, its central squares, its transportation network. Even before he set foot there, he had learned the names of streets, squares, important points. It was true, of course, that this city was especially easy to fix in mind, with its ring around the center and with the other neighborhoods grouped around the ring like a snail's shell. He would remember that—a city like a snail's shell. In his head he had already drawn diagrams of many cities. And there would surely be new ones to add to the old.

Where he had been born and raised, the sea had governed everything. But even then he had dreamed about cities. When he was asked what he wanted to be when he grew up, he never answered like the other boys, "I'll be a fisherman... I'll be a sailor... I'll build boats... I'll join the Coast Guard... I'll be a bird-watcher... I'll take over my father's seafood restaurant... I'll work in the Dolly Shop"—the general store at the port on the island, so called because, like many stores that sold seamen's goods, its sign featured an old doll. His own answer had always been, "I'll be a taxi driver in Seattle"—Seattle because it had such a pretty name and was the nearest big city.

At the age of ten he had memorized every street in Seattle. He taught himself from a map of the city; and in the evenings on the beach, when it was dark and you could imagine that the glow to the southeast along the coast was Seattle, he would drive his cab, drive his customers through the city—one hundred thirty-nine miles of waterfront—customers who often tried to catch him out by giving him the name of some small alley consisting of only a few houses, or by asking for a warehouse on Pier 39 whose name they did not even know.

The young man continued to look at the city. In its pillow of haze it seemed to him denser and more impenetrable than usual, almost without streets, as though it had only a few narrow thoroughfares, twisting, misleading, like an oriental city built to confuse foreigners but offer security to the natives. He didn't mind. He picked up his green bag. He had made his decision. If it was no longer safe out here, the answer was to plunge into the heart of the labyrinth.

He reached the new place he had decided on in half an hour. It was not far from the church or the wholesale flower market. The area had been badly damaged during the war, and there were still ruins behind board fences. But you could not always tell whether the fence was hiding a house that had been destroyed by bombs or one recently torn down to make room for a new building or for the highway that was being brought into the city from the west.

The houses along the street might still be inhabited, but they seemed to have resigned themselves to demolition in the near future. They had gray, crumbling façades, dirty windowpanes, and on the ground floors shops closed off with rusty grilles. As he walked he noticed the cranes, their long, steel-girdered arms outstretched, motionless now, but it was easy to imagine what they really were: advance scouts who with a single movement would mark out the next victim among the houses.

The young man had reached an oblong building, a textile plant with a series of glass roofs at ascending levels. He turned into a narrow street. At the end he saw the building that was his destination: a former brewery. It was a three-story structure, originally painted a light color, now dark. The brick chimney towered over it, and the neon sign was still in place, although letters were missing. During weekdays, the street was lively, but now it was deserted. It had started to rain.

He entered the abandoned brewery through a wide, high gateway. The ground was paved with thick, square cobbles. The young man moved slowly, keeping an eye out, ready to turn back at the slightest alarming sign. Old barrels still stood around in the big inner courtyard; they were falling apart because the hoops had rusted through. The smell of beer still hung in the air.

He turned toward another, narrower passageway that led to a further courtyard. Once again his manner underwent a change. He abandoned all signs of caution. His gait was different, each step shorter, lighter, springier. He began whistling, less a melody than a brief signal.

He came to a low wooden ramp. Beyond it was a row of windows, painted white so that they were opaque. A short flight of stairs led up to a blue door. He repeated his signal and waited. When the door opened and someone appeared in it, another change came over the young man, this time in his face. He wore a broad smile; a high-spirited grin erased several hard lines and made him look even younger.

"Is that you?" said a voice.

The yard was narrow, the walls high, so that not much light entered, and in addition the man at the door did not seem to see well. He squinted, his eyes much too small for his massive skull, which was bald but for a few sparse hairs and his thick black eyebrows. He wore a loudly striped, short-sleeved shirt; his powerful arms were covered with dark hair.

62

The young man tossed his bag up the ramp, then climbed the steps himself, again with that new elasticity.

"Really you!" The man extended his great arms. "It's the pinball champ!" He hugged the young man. "The champ himself. Whistling and cheery as ever!"

He picked up the duffel bag; in his hands it suddenly looked small.

The door led into a large room that was filled from wall to wall with flippers, slot machines, and what were called arcade machines. The room was so choked with them there was scarcely enough space to move about. In spite of their bright colors, the machines looked numb and dead. Only one device in the back of the room was working, producing a penetrating tone: the high, sharp beep-beep of a spaceship's signal.

From there a voice now complained, "He's too early. I don't have this damned thing ready."

The man in the striped shirt called out a name. His voice echoed from the walls.

"Come here! Come over here and see who's back."

The shrill noise stopped. A man approached them, laboriously threading his way among the machines. He closely resembled the first man, but he was smaller, frailer, and he moved with a slight limp. He was wearing overalls, right next to his skin, with screwdrivers protruding from the pockets.

When he came up closer, his face brightened. "It's the flipper champ! The champ is back!"

He waved a hand at the machines. "These damned arcade machines are too damn complicated. Condom dispensers and candy machines, nothing wrong with them."

He gave a nearby machine a kick, and the machine actually responded with a sound.

"See! Too complicated! Electronics!" He cast a triumphant look at his brother as though he had just provided conclusive proof. Then he turned again to the young man.

"I'm damn glad you're back, Champ."

Outside the rain had become heavier; it beat audibly on the sheet metal shielding the roof.

10

"Milli? Are you there, Milli?" The door was unlatched and the radio was playing, but Czepe Zuckermann hesitated. Once he had gone in without knocking and without waiting for her reply and had found her naked, out on the small balcony, stretched out on the chaise in the sun. He had not forgotten that white body in the blazing sun.

She was a sun worshiper, or should he rather put it, a sun fetishist? Oddly, her skin remained white, and the doctor had warned against these sunbaths after she had once fallen asleep in full sunlight and awakened with a fearful headache. For weeks thereafter she had had to stay in a darkened room. But even in the evening it was not safe to go barging into her room. Milli might be sitting outside in a light, transparent negligee, especially when the moon was shining. As a girl, because of these "moon baths" she had been expelled from the nuns' school. A child possessed by the devil...

He knocked again before entering, still cautious.

The doors to the balcony were wide open. The rain poured in. It had already soaked the curtains, which the wind tugged outward, and at the threshold the white carpet was dark from the water it had absorbed. The light was on. He did not see Milli, but that did not mean anything. He could enter a room, especially her own, and think she was not there; nonetheless she would be sitting somewhere, perhaps on her bed in the corner, knees drawn up, so motionless that it was easy to overlook her.

It had something to do with the colors she wore. Her clothes always blended with the colors of her room: some pink, some green, a great deal of white. It was a young girl's room, with its white furniture, the profusion of pillows on the bed, the phonograph records on the floor. The only black item was the radio beside the bed, an extremely old and rather clumsy model with a round dial.

"Milli?" He looked around once more, then went to close the doors. The balcony was not very large; it was enclosed by a blind and roofed by a wire trellis with vines growing on it. They were already fairly thick; later in the summer and until deep into the fall the entire balcony would be wreathed in them, forming a blossoming bower.

He folded up the chaise, placed it along the wall, and likewise closed the parasol. He stepped back into the room. He looked around once more, as though Milli might after all be hiding somewhere. On the secretary stood a few books, a photograph—it was himself in a priest's robes. Then he noticed something lying on the floor by the bed, a white object that looked like a small, crude doll.

He stooped—one of his idiosyncrasies was that he could not bear any litter; everything had to be in its place. As he picked up the white thing, he saw that it was not a doll, just a kerchief with a knot. He laid it on the bed by the pillows. He gave it no more thought; with Milli you grew accustomed to oddities. Leaving the room, he closed the door behind him and climbed the stairs to the attic.

She was waiting for him up there; he knew that at once from her perfume. Milli almost never used perfume, but if she did it was usually their mother's, which on her smelled too sweet and too strong.

She was sitting on a hassock in front of the big map of the world that nearly covered the entire wall. He went over to her, stooped, and kissed her on both cheeks; the perfume smelled even stronger.

"I was looking for you. You left the doors to the balcony open. A while longer and your room would have been under water."

"The doors? Is it raining? I've been up here a long time. It will do the plants good if it's raining. Watering them—it isn't the same."

In an odd way she resembled their mother. She was blond, but she had Mother's complexion and her eyes, even her somewhat too long nose. And yet the effect on her was altogether different, like that of the perfume. Everything that fitted together in their mother did not form any sort of unity in her. And then, he thought, she has never had Mother's toughness—no more than I have.

"You don't mind my coming up here?"

"No," he said, although all he wanted was to be alone.

"Did you like the flowers in the church?"

"Oh yes, thanks. Did you pay for them?"

"Don't worry, I'll get it back. You really don't mind my being here? I'll leave in a minute."

This was his realm, to which he admitted nobody. Milli was the only person who could come up. She was not interested in his shortwave station, but she often sat looking at the postcards he received in response to his broadcasts. She removed the foreign stamps and asked about the places with strange-sounding names with which he kept in radio contact: with the priest in Ankázoabo on Madagascar, with the Franciscan monk of Mount Poinsur near Bombay, with the many amateurs in Africa and Latin America.

She went on sitting and looking at the wall map. She was wearing a white jersey dress whose low neckline was partly covered by a long, faded pink scarf.

"Are you looking for something?" he asked.

It was a maritime trade map showing the principal routes between the great seaports of the world. It was a good twenty years old and outmoded; in the old days he used to buy the latest maps, but after he became a priest he had given that up.

"Milli? Can I help you?"

"Just wanted to see how well I can still play Father's game. Remember? *How do you get to Benares, quick!*" She closed her eyes, as though that would help her concentrate. Her lips moved and she whispered a few names. "Trieste... Venice... Brindisi... Gibraltar... along the ..."She opened her eyes. "Is it the west coast of Africa?"

He smiled, remembering how weak she had always been in geography. "Yes, the west coast—if you want to go to Benares."

"Yes, something easy. I'm still not very good at the game. I haven't played it in such a long time."

He had almost forgotten. His father had always asked such questions: "What's the fastest route from Genoa to Benares?" Or he would merely say: "Amsterdam-Melbourne via Colombo, return by way of the Panama Canal. Quick!" You had to answer him without the aid of a map or globe. He was very proud if you knew the answer and he would hand out prizes; the faster you answered, the bigger the reward.

He could not recall his father's trying the game on Milli. He had left them before Milli's birth, returned once for a year, the year Milli was born, and then vanished again, this time for good.

"You'd rather be alone, wouldn't you?" she said.

"Tomorrow is Sunday—you know. And it has been a long day for me... I've brought you something from Rome."

"A scarf, green chiffon?"

He looked at her in surprise.

"Mother unpacked your bag; I saw her when she came from your room." She laughed like a child. "She didn't see me, but I saw her, and she was holding the green scarf." She stood up and kissed him. "Thanks, anyhow."

He always felt slightly embarrassed when she kissed him, not on the cheek but on the mouth—though it was just a light, fleeting touch. He would have liked to tell her not to use Mother's perfume.

He asked, "Did she give it to you?"

"She thinks it's ridiculous that I wear these scarves. She thinks, 'What did I spend all that money on all those operations for, and she still goes on wearing those ridiculous scarves.' You think the same thing?"

He felt her eyes watching him closely, those big almost black, burning eyes.

"I was surprised when I heard you were back," he said.

She laughed softly, and again it was the high-spirited

giggle of a child. "And how surprised *they* were!" Her face changed abruptly; her eyes took on that hard look his mother's could have.

"They wanted to be rid of me, dump me in that horrible sanatorium."

"It's a hotel, Milli."

"I don't care what it is. I solved the problem my way." Her voice dropped to a whisper. "You know what I did?"

"I've heard about it."

"Kropik really doesn't know. I went into someone's room and simply stretched out on the bed and went to sleep— *pretended* to go to sleep! I had stumbled into others' rooms before *by mistake*, but after that I knew they wouldn't want me to stay. You won't betray me? I know you won't."

He tried to read her expression, and when she smiled he thought he understood what she was saying. Her strategy was essentially the same as his when he felt he had to defend himself against the excessive solicitude and domination of their mother. Mother was a woman who had always wanted to protect her children against everything. It seemed she was always warning, "Don't ever pick up anything from the street, children... Don't use the soap in strange toilets... When you go out after dark, put on something bright so drivers can see you at a distance... Czepe, never go out twice with the same girl... Milli, don't get involved with men." But then, when Milli was twenty-eight and still unmarried, the line had changed: "This is unhealthy, Milli. Are you aware that most nuns die of abdominal cancer because they haven't led a normal woman's life?" Whereupon Milli had abruptly married. He, Czepe, had found an escape by going to sea, and later his becoming a priest had made him independent to a certain extent. But Milli's efforts, above all her marriage, had hardly helped her.

But, he thought, there was something else, a more important explanation for her distraction, her absentmindedness, her *isolation*. Just like him, Milli wanted something out of life that could not be had: perfection. And by the time one found out this was impossible, that the world didn't want what one was prepared to give it, wasn't it altogether natural to simply withdraw from it, to isolate oneself? One invented one's own self-created port in which to anchor one's dreams...

But he could not talk about it. All he said was, "You've always gone away in summer."

"This one is different." Before he could ask why, she said, "What did the vicar-general want?"

"The vicar-general?" For a moment he had forgotten. "Oh, the usual thing."

"What was that about the fake priest?"

At first he was taken aback, but then he laughed involuntarily. "Tell me. How do you always manage that?"

"What?"

"Listening at doors so that nobody ever notices?"

"It's easy. And then, of course, I've had lots of practice. What did he tell you?"

"If you were eavesdropping...."

"He said something about a tattoo—he said the man had a tattoo?"

"It really is late. I have to prepare for tomorrow."

"You're not going to turn him over to the police? I mean, if you find him."

"There was never any question of turning anyone over to the police."

"I couldn't really imagine you would. Good night. I'm glad you liked the flowers."

He stood for a while at the door. He listened, but her footsteps were light, almost inaudible in the flat white shoes. They were called ballerinas, she had once told him. When he could no longer hear a sound, he turned back into the room.

11

The rain had stopped. It was hot up here, sultry, because the room had not been aired for days. He could hear a low stirring on the sheet-metal overhang of the roof—probably the pigeons emerging from their shelters. But undoubtedly the rain would soon begin again.

He opened the window built into the slant of the roof. Removing his jacket, he hung it over the chair and sat down in front of the table on which his rig was assembled. He switched on the transmitter and waited for it to warm up. The storm front was coming from the southeast and he might have difficulty with reception from that direction, but the southwest would scarcely be affected. He had had a rather expensive rotary beam installed up on the roof; he could turn it in any desired direction by means of a control on the table.

When the transmitter had warmed up and was giving off its peculiar faint odor, he forgot everything, the days in Rome, his defeat, Kropik waiting at the airport, the vicar-general and the things he had had to tell him...

"CQ at forty-four, four, from OE 1NBX calling..." He called the man in Kabete, Kenya.

He had placed the padded earphones on his head. Nothing existed aside from his moving lips, the microphone in front of him, the illuminated dials, the knobs for tuning the various frequencies, and the sounds his ears caught.

"Calling fiveZ2SevenGH... Do you read, Kabete?"

With the earphones on, his hair seemed even sparser. His forehead looked naked.

In the years after the war he had been a radio officer on the *Mariano*. She was an Italian freighter, a three-thousand-tonner over forty years old at the time and not fit for ocean crossings. The *Mariano* plied the Mediterranean and the Red Sea, always the monotonous route. In the course of this service he had become familiar with most of the port cities from Izmir to Tangiers, and the ports of the Red Sea as well: Jidda, Massawa, Al Mukha, Bab el Mandeb.

"Kabete? Yes, I can hear you now... Hello... Seems I have a moon bounce... Hello, hello... Kabete? Come in... Confirm."

He had entered the cities, bought presents, and visited the brothels, but the *Mariano* had never stayed in one port long enough for him to undertake a trip into the interior of Africa.

"Yes, I've got you...it's fine...go ahead with your message...now..."

Just twelve years ago he had had his first look at the continent during a Lower Sahara Tour, to which his mother had treated him in celebration of his consecration as a priest. By plane to Timbuktu, from there by jeep and camel to the Mountains of the Moon. The Cook Tour had differed greatly from the way he had imagined this same journey years ago: crossing the Sahara on foot, a test of his endurance and toughness.

"*Rien à signales*...no more...love and kisses..."

"Wait..."

"Too much interference..."

He had gone on a second African trip eight years ago. A spring tour that was supposed to have taken him through all of central Africa from Accra to Nairobi. But a severe case of dysentery had forced him to abandon the tour halfway. Since then he had had nothing but his collection of maps, which he kept in the table drawers, the dictionaries of the Kukuyu dialect, the many notes he had taken when he began a translation of the catechism and parts of the Bible into Kukuyu. When he thought it over—his connection with Kabete had broken down and he turned some of the knobs, altered the direction of the antenna and the transmission frequency—he had been slightly disappointed by Africa. During the second tour in particular there had been endless, senseless delays, thefts in the hotels, arguments with natives about tips, and, of course, the oldest planes imaginable, flown by pilots who took the greatest pleasure in making reckless landings on impossible sites. Perhaps this was one reason his interest and his imagination had in recent years been turning to another continent, South America.

"Calling OAAthreeN. Pisac... CQOE 1NBX calling Pisac... Confirm."

A moment of selective fade, and the signal was garbled. He increased the power on his receiver, and for a moment he picked up the station in the Peruvian village in the Andes and heard that it was occupied. He had to wait for the end of the current conversation, but in any case felt his luck was good in that his partner was already at his set in spite of the five-hour time difference.

For a moment he removed the headset because it was pressing too hard against his ears; then he pulled it down over his head again.

"Calling Pisac..."

He imagined a picturesque church—he had been sent a snapshot of it—tumbledown, high in the mountains, built into a steep mountain ridge. It was as if he were standing there himself, outside the church door, in glaring sunlight, to be sure, but in an airless cold that made breathing hard.

"Calling Pisac... Pisac, come in... Confirm."

There was an imploring note in his voice, and when nothing more than a rough alternating current tone still came, he briefly consulted his notes and switched the transmitter to another band.

It wasn't going the way it did on other nights. He seemed to lack patience, concentration, that absolute devotion to the apparatus that was essential. And he knew well that the whole thing was basically a variant of his father's game: How do you get to Benares, quick!

Yet he had spent years at it. He had all the certificates that existed, including the highest distinction: *Worked all countries in the world.* Often it had been more than a leisure-time activity; often for long nights he had been one of those priests, a Camilo Torres—the name that stood for so many others.

He knew the names, the stories of these men. He knew what successes they had scored, where they had failed. And sometimes, as he sat here in front of his set until late in the night, sometimes it happened. He would be leading them into the mountains of Bucaramanga, whole armies of poor landless peasants—he would be the true priest engaged in the struggle against hunger and injustice. He would lead his armies out of their hiding places, forward, in surprise attacks, then back by secret paths to a prepared shelter. He lost a few of the men in his army. He gained new ones, lost them, and once more won new ones...

"OE 1NBX calling XE1P1... Come in... Confirm."

He was calling a station in Sierra Madre del Sur, Mexico.

But he could not make a connection. Nothing happened. He had no luck tonight. And there was something else, a noise that did not belong. He removed the earphones. Now he could hear her voice.

"Czepe! Don't you think it's about time... Czepe! Why don't you answer?"

He left the room, but he remained at the top of the stairs. "How is the game?"

"Cards are improving. The main thing is not to lose patience, to bide your time and make use of your opportunity."

"You still playing?"

"We'll probably go on for another hour. But you ought to call a halt for today. Is there anything you'd like?"

"No thanks."

"You really did eat on the plane?"

"Yes."

He had taken nothing on the plane, and he was hungry, but he could not give any other answer. Sometimes he would go for days scarcely eating, finding the very thought of food disgusting. Then again, when everybody was asleep, he would creep downstairs to the kitchen, devouring all he could; or he would go to a certain Yugoslav restaurant down by the river and order roast mutton dripping with fat, and later become sick from such unaccustomed food.

"Really, there's nothing I need."

"Good night, then. Remember not to have any food after twelve o'clock. Don't forget. Good night, Czepe."

"Good night, Mother."

He went back into the attic room and switched off the transmitter. For a while he sat there listening to the low murmurs from the rig as the various instruments cooled.

Czepe! Czepe Zuckermann!

What could a man do? With such a name? He would never become a Camilo Torres, never be a man like that Buddhist monk—a picture that frequently flashed before his eyes—who poured gasoline on himself and burned himself to death in the streets of Saigon.

He was only Czepe Zuckermann. A man with an odd name, a man like any other, a feeble, weary, burned-out case.

He opened the side compartment of the desk and looked among the maps and notes until he had found what he was looking for: a small, cheap portable altar. Some time ago he had found it, dusty and dirty, in a secondhand dealer's shop. He had kept it, always hoping that someday he would be able to use it in some remote, lonely place where there was no church. He stood it on the desk and thought, Please, please give me one more chance, one more opportunity. The thought was simultaneously accompanied by alarm at his weakness and the immoderate nature of his wish.

He unfolded the two side panels of the altar. He stood for a long time looking at the small and extremely crude wooden statue of the Crucifixion. Then he rolled up the left sleeve of his shirt.

In the cold, hard light of the desk lamp the tattoo on his forearm showed distinctly. The figure of the Crucified One on his skin was no more than four inches long, but the tattooing had been executed with such precision that the abdominal muscles were visible, the pain in the profiled face, each of the nails, the loincloth. The design had been done in three colors: the deep blue of the outlines, the body, the cross, and the nails;

the light green of the loincloth; the tiny splotches of blood in red. The tattoo was old—how old exactly, thirty, thirty-two years?—but on his white skin and in the cold light it still seemed radiant.

He thought of the man who had done the tattooing. He tried to recall the day, the hour, the room, and most of all the motives that had prompted him to choose that picture. Had he really chosen it himself, or only agreed to the tattooer's suggestion? A sense of challenge, boldness? But was his recollection right? The only thing he recalled with any assurance was the hum of the apparatus, the burning sensation of the needles on his skin. But was that important? What was important to him was that there was another human being in this city who bore the same tattoo, the same sign.

He closed the panels of the altar and put it away. Rolling down his sleeve, he went to the window. He looked out. All he could think at the moment was, I must find him.

Under the cloth of his sleeve he felt the tattoo, as though it were only a few hours old, as though he could still feel the prick of the needle.

Part Two

12

Once again the morning was too cool and damp. Nevertheless, it held promise of being a warm summer day, the first in a long while. And high time it was. At this season a vendor ought to be putting money by; but during the past weeks—first with the unbearable heat, then with temperatures that dropped twenty-five degrees within an hour, with thunderstorms, showers, and hail that smashed the glass roofs of the nursery gardens—prices at the wholesale flower market had soared.

How can I make any money at such prices, the flower vendor wondered.

It was shortly after seven. He had bought his day's supply and was pulling his cart through the tangle of people and vehicles, through the din of the square that surrounded the main hall of the flower market.

By this time most of the vendors had made their purchases, but the streets around the market were still choked with vans. It was hard to imagine how any of them would ever get out of the traffic jam. Vehicles were parked on both sides, in front of the shops and cafés on one side of the square, and in front of the wholesalers' shops attached to the great market hall on the other. The traffic lanes were filled with hurrying pedestrians and vendors.

There were dozens of them pushing their laden carts ahead or pulling them behind. The noise of the wheels on the rough pavement mingled with the tooting of auto horns and the shouts of the drivers to make room. But to him all the noises sounded muted; his hearing aid again was not working, and the button sticking uselessly in his ear actually made him all the deafer.

He had bought the roses cheap—some of the outer petals had already been plucked off. It might well be that he would have to remove others; that would make the flowers smaller, but at least they would look fresh. He did not feel good about this; he would try to sell the roses only to strangers whom he was not likely to see again, not to his regular customers.

He found a narrow gap between two parked trucks. One of the boys who were offering their services all over the market helped him to pull the cart up to the sidewalk. He left the boy guarding the cart and walked past the bank. It was still closed, but in another half hour the lobby would be jammed with wholesalers depositing their money. It was said that this branch bank had one of the biggest turnovers in the entire city, and although ordinarily he did not give that a thought, on this particular day it made him even more melancholic.

The café, little more than a booth, stood adjacent to the bank. It leaned against the massive, substantial building like a weak, crippled plant in need of support. At this hour the shabbiness of the interior was scarcely noticeable because the room was filled with men from the market, drivers, and a few prostitutes from the night before.

The flower vendor went to the table at the window, behind the door. He did not have to wait long; the owner came and set a tray down on the marble tabletop, a cup of light coffee and a croissant.

"How about a couple sausages and gravy? You're getting skinnier every day."

"Thanks, not today. I'm not feeling very well." He answered a question from another man at the table. "I don't know what the devil it is—incubating something. First I'm in a sweat, then I'm shivering; maybe I'm just getting old. Not younger, anyhow." He coughed, and the others at the table observed him, listening to his coughing as though they could learn more from the sounds than from his words.

The flower vendor drank his coffee, broke off a piece of

the croissant, and ate listlessly. He had moved his chair so that he could watch the main entrance to the big flower market.

The men around him chatted in hoarse morning voices—from eating too little, smoking too early. They laughed, greeted new arrivals. To the flower vendor the words all merged into a general roar—after all, he knew what they were talking about, what they were laughing about, whom they were greeting. For more than thirty years he had been coming here, sitting at this table; and he would go on coming until the place closed down, perhaps soon, when they tore down the wholesale market. Whenever talk turned to the new market out in the suburbs, almost beyond reach for small peddlers like himself, he listened intently, trying to catch every word, but without losing sight of the entrance across the street.

He stood up at once when he saw the girl. She was looking around, and seemed indecisive. Hastily, the flower vendor took out some coins and laid them on the table. Outside, on the sidewalk, he had to wait until he found a gap in the stream of traffic. He waved, called her name, but by the time he edged into the stream of vehicles she had already stepped inside the big hall of the wholesale market.

She had dressed much too lightly for the coolness of the morning, a white linen dress with a thin rain cape over it, one of those transparent plastic capes. Inside the hall Milli immediately felt warmer.

Perhaps it was only the soft light that flooded in through the high glass roof. The glass was greenish and seemed to stretch overhead like a broad sail; sustained by nothing at all, it floated there like a big kite of green India paper.

That was one of the reasons she liked coming here: the big green kite that cast an unreal light on all the plants and flowers, as though they would remain forever just as they were at this moment, fresh and bedewed, never withering.

She paused for a moment, then turned to the left and walked along the double rows of stands where the cut flowers were arranged in successive tiers, mostly emptied already. She also liked the fragrance of the freshly watered flowers; that too made her feel warmer. It was a fragrance entirely different from the ordinary scent of flowers, more like a greenhouse. Certain types of flowers with certain smells dominated the hall at different times, like the geraniums in May or the asters later in the year. Right now the lilacs overwhelmed all other scents.

The stands formed small streets within the hall. For a while she wandered about with a lost feeling till the scent of the foliage plants told her that she was on the right path; everything smelled heavier and earthier here. She came upon the first orchids in the decaying heaps of humus, then the others, the dangling ones, and finally those that had already been wrapped in white tissue paper and packed into long, narrow boxes.

Here, too, there was an air of departure. Young men were closing the cartons, piling them one on the other in stacks that frequently reached over their heads as they carried them away. They all moved swiftly in spite of the stacks of cartons, and made a game of dodging each other at the last moment.

She had been coming to the market long enough to know the meaning of the gaps in the tiers, of the changed noises, of the voices no longer crying prices, of the men who stood around in knots, chatting. The market would be closing soon, and she chided herself for having come so late. She always woke very early in the morning, especially in the summertime, but then she would completely forget about time. She never knew how late it was, simply had no feeling for the time; she would look at a clock and the next moment forget what it said. Even the clocks played her false. She had owned many, but they always either told the wrong time or did not run at all. Czepe would invariably laugh at her when she ran to the telephone, dialed one-five-zero-three, and listened to the taped voice: *In ten seconds it will be...*

She came to another intersection that, it seemed to her, she had already passed several times. Then she saw the young man, khaki shirt, bright kerchief. He had his back to her, was kneeling on the floor about to pick up a stack of those orchid cartons. She was surprised, but then again not really. She had always counted on finding him here. She even thought, as she hurried toward him, that she must take care not to address him by his given name in the presence of others.

"Hello, Orchid Man…"

She found herself staring into a stranger's face as the boy turned and straightened up.

The stranger smiled, holding the delivery slip between his lips. He knew her, as did most of the people here, knew whom she was looking for. They had become used to her. She came three or four days in succession, then omitted a day, returned, always looking around the big hall for the Orchid Man. At first she had constantly asked for him, but that had stopped a long while ago. Now she simply came and looked for him.

The boy knew, and he could not resist temptation. He piled the white cartons, five of them, on one hand, used the other to take the slip out of his mouth, and, balancing the cartons, performed a dance, chanting rhythmically, "Anyone seen the Orchid Man? Anyone seen him today?"

Balancing his cartons and dancing, he went on with his chant: "What has become of him, where can he be? No more orchids, no more orchids for me! Nobody knows…" Catching her look, he stopped abruptly.

"I'm sorry…" he began, but she had already run away.

The flower vendor caught her at the side entrance. He had heard the boy's verse, heard the silly chant, and had traced her by that. Though he had taken a shortcut, he was out of breath. He gripped her arm and held her back. This was the first time he had ever touched her, and he wondered at how thin her wrist was. She must weigh very little, he thought.

"Hello, Milli."

He had to hold her hand tightly.

"What's all this? Don't waste your tears on someone like that. That bunch have one of those stuck-up flower shops in the center; you know: water running down the window… They take two hundred percent on the orchids 'cause they got a little running water on the panes. Not worth your tears. You don't mind me calling you Milli? You once told me I could."

"Sure."

"I've been waiting for you."

He changed sides so that he had his good ear turned toward her. They were standing in the shade under the overhanging roof of the market, beside one of the shops built right up against the wall. The shop had already closed. A pile of empty crates was waiting for the garbage truck.

"I think I've found something."

She looked around in all directions. "Something about him?"

He nodded, and because he hoped that as many people as possible would see him standing here with her, he said, "You look prettier than ever this morning. That rain cape's becoming; it wraps you up like a flower."

He thought it really did make her look like a long-stemmed flower—the white of the dress, the green of the long, dangling scarf, and the transparent rain cape floating around her like cellophane. He suddenly felt better, because for one thing he was reminded that he had always compared his women to flowers. Although he'd never been drawn to the thin, long-stemmed kind. He preferred the plump ones, girls who were like peonies, a heavy, full blossom and all that rich, firm greenery...

"Where is he?"

"Didn't I promise I'd keep my ears open?" He felt he had a right to enjoy the moment for a little while longer.

"I asked around, *confidentially*, like you told me. That's why it took time. Nobody seems to have seen him since he disappeared from that junkman—never could understand what he wanted to get mixed up with *him* for anyway."

"You said..."

"This is a big city. But I know people that get around. One way or another word was bound to reach me. I was beginning to think he must have left the city... Do you know what the junkman called him? 'Sailor.' You know what they're like. Ships that pass in the night."

"Please tell me! What have you found out?"

A fit of coughing stopped him for a moment. He pointed across the street. "See that little shop? You ought to be able to read the sign; can't quite make it out from here."

"'Notions'? Gold on black."

"Yes, that's it. You'll find a man there with a clubfoot. That's how he got his name, Sweet Devil. Everyone around here calls him that." Again he coughed hoarsely, perhaps because he had talked so much; he was ordinarily a taciturn man, noted for confining his remarks to his customers to the minimum.

"He knows where...he is?"

"He should know, yes."

"You're not certain?"

"This Sweet Devil—if I got a name like that it'd make me madder than hell. Anyway, he's a wholesaler. Supplies candy for slot machines. Know what I mean? Those machines with hard candy and little surprises mixed in with cheap rings and plastic teddy bears, the ones you mostly find around schools. It seems one of the fellows who puts out the machines...well, you'll get the whole story out of him."

"You haven't spoken to *him*?"

"You said it had to be confidential..."

"Thanks a lot."

"Nothing to thank me for. You really look terribly pretty today. I think the weather's improving too."

She looked across the street. Suddenly she seemed doubtful about what he had said, or else just the fact that she'd been disappointed so ofter held her back from crossing the street.

"I'm late already," he said, as though he were trying to help her. "Have to get to my spot or I'll lose the morning business. I have lovely lilacs today, double white ones. Or won't that do, lilacs in the church?"

"White, always. Perhaps with a few roses."

"Oh no, you don't want to mix them with roses. White lilac is always loveliest by itself."

Then save the lilacs for me..."

He watched her cross the street, which had suddenly emptied. The last shops outside the market hall had closed, the old rusty gratings been lowered. Most of the trucks were gone; empty, crushed crates lay about everywhere. The street pavement itself was covered with discarded remains of trampled flowers. Soon the men would come along with their long brooms and carts, and after them the spray truck, to wash away the last wisps of greenery and scattered petals.

He watched as the girl entered the shop, while he too crossed the street to his handcart. When she came out again, she seemed unsure of which way to turn. She stood still and looked around, first to the left, then to the right. When she caught sight of him, she waved; obviously she had found out what she wanted to know.

He watched her until he could no longer see anything distinct, only something long-stemmed, white.

The bank doors opened. The wholesalers in their smocks, carrying their leather moneybags, poured into the building. The last of the men, mostly drivers, left the cafés, and along with them the tired, sleep-starved prostitutes. Now the big iron grating over the main entrance of the market hall was also closed.

He paid the boy who had guarded his cart, slung the leather belt over his shoulders, took hold of the handles of the cart, and began to pull it. It was a heavy cart, but he found it lighter now.

Maybe I'm not incubating something after all, he thought.

13

The two men sat over breakfast in the kitchen. The third, still under the shower, which was farther back along the narrow corridor, tried to take part in their conversation. Now and then he leaned out from behind the flowered plastic shower curtain, his massive head and even more massive shoulders steaming and red. His sparse wet hair hung down over his forehead.

"Don't you believe anything he says, Champ."

The man at the table, who closely resembled his brother, except that everything about him was smaller, shook his head.

"You ought to tell him it's no use spending an hour under the shower every morning softening himself up. He has this idea it's going to get him back in shape. But he'll never be back in shape, not good enough to wrestle again. He won't listen to me. All his life he hasn't listened to me."

"What's he saying?" the man under the shower called down the corridor. "I hope you'll stick with me, Champ. You know the rule: always stick with the underdog."

"It's just ridiculous," his brother at the table said. "He'll never go in a ring again. He's too old. With that shoulder he can't do it. Besides, we have this business, and wrestling's a dead issue. The days are over when women would scream for him."

He jerked his thumb at the walls. They were covered with newspaper clippings and photos, all showing the same man, a huge, hairy colossus, naked except for tight black bathing trunks, wrestling with other men. In most of the pictures he had them in such holds that they were blinking into the camera with pain-narrowed eyes.

"What's he saying about the women?" The steaming head emerged from the curtain again.

"Come and have breakfast with us," the young man said.

They fell silent, drank their coffee, and ate. The hum of the shower stopped. Instead they heard the sound of wet bare feet on the shining floor of the corridor. At the end of the corridor was a window through which daylight fell, but in the kitchen they had to use artificial light even by day. There was a plain table with a few chairs around it, an old sofa on which the young man sat, a king-sized refrigerator, a stove, and the drainboard, where the dirty dishes were piled.

The big man appeared in the kitchen now, clad in a blue bathrobe which did not cover his bare, hairy legs. As he toweled his thin air, he made a movement with his left shoulder. It was evidently habitual: a twisting of the shoulder forward and backward in its socket.

He sat down, poured a cup of coffee, added hot milk, and dropped five lumps of sugar into the big cup. Holding it in both hands, he drank, pausing between sips to jerk his head in his brother's direction.

"You want to know the truth, Champ? He's the one the women go for. Hard to believe, bald as me and a game leg besides—but the girls are crazy about him." He leaned back. He had eaten nothing, only drunk the coffee. From the bathrobe pocket he took out a pack of cigarettes and lit up. "Don't let him kid you, Champ. I've never even thought of returning to the ring."

The young man listened with a smile; he had often heard variations of this morning conversation.

"I'm glad enough if I can move this arthritic shoulder just another day. That's why I stand in the hot shower so long. *Me,* I'm glad that torture in the ring's all over with."

"You don't say!"

"I tell you, Champ, he's the one who's got a hankering for the good old days, my little manager here. Did I ever tell you this game leg here was my manager? I did the fighting up there, sweating and aching—I was the one that had to take on all those bruisers—but did I get the girls? Not on your life! They were all crazy for little brother. Go figure that out. Just wild about him, like there was something special about a guy who limps. Explain that to me. What's he got that I don't have bigger..."

The frailer brother shook his head with a pretense of earnestness.

"Don't talk that way in front of our little monk here! He must have taken a vow, don't you know?"

"Really?" the ex-wrestler asked. "Have you, Champ?"

"Of course he has," his brother replied for the young man. "Three weeks holed up here with nothing to do but repair these damned machines—if that isn't a vow."

The wrestler looked around the table. "How about us bringing a couple of ladies along tonight, okay?" He indicated the unwashed dishes. "For them too. He's a real wonder, Champ, this little brother of mine. And the best of it is he gets them for a one-night stand. They're not hanging around the next day. I don't wake up one morning and find their dresses hanging in my closet. *That*, Champ, is when you get the message: when they start leaving their clothes hanging. Makes me nervous. Can't stand having a lot of things collecting around me, owning all those goddamn things... You must know that feeling."

"The Indians—they'd just hold a potlatch."

The wrestler leaned forward, intrigued.

"What's that again?"

"Potlatch. It's an Indian custom. They'd throw a big feast where a man gives away everything he owns. The more potlatches an Indian gives in his lifetime, the more his fellows think of him. They say Chief Maquinna, chief of the Nootkas, gave nine of these potlatches in his life."

"Hey, you hear that?" the younger brother said. "He knows about Indians too."

"Where I come from is old Indian country."

"Thought you grew up by the water? On an island?"

"It was all Indian country, islands included."

"Indians on an island?"

"They were supposed to be good fishermen—cedar canoes and handmade hooks and lures. But back then there were plenty of fish. Halibut, salmon, gray and black cod..."

"Why don't you ever tell us about that? If you know good stories, you ought to tell them."

The wrestler stood up. He consulted the slip of paper on which the day's route was noted. "I'd better get ready."

"That okay about the girls for tonight?" The smaller brother had also stood up. He carried the dishes over to the drainboard.

"Will they really do the dishes?" the young man asked.

"They all know if they come to the wrestler's they wash dishes. Don't you want to come on our route? You've done wonders cleaning up the backlog these past weeks."

The young man had begun placing the remains of breakfast in the big refrigerator. They both seemed to have their jobs well organized.

"I want to get the rest done," he said.

"You've got persistence, Champ, that's what I don't have with those machines." He suddenly gave the young man a grave, searching look. "Tell me, did you really win that championship? What was the name of it again?"

"The U.S. Open Pinball Championship."

"That's it. Is there really such a thing?"

"I wouldn't make it up, would I?"

"You ever met anybody in this town who doesn't make things up? Doesn't imagine things that never happened? It's something about this city. It's totally made up, Champ. This city doesn't really exist, none of it. What kind of cities you like best, Champ? I suppose you've seen a few."

"A few, yes."

"Tell me about it. The cities you like, the ones that really exist."

"I like cities with water." The young man answered hesitantly.

"Tell me one city with water you like, Champ, just one."

"One? It's one directly on the water, on a sound. There're more than a hundred shipping lines that go out from there to the whole world, and sailors like it for a special reason. When the ships come in with their hulls covered with barnacles, they bring them in through a canal into a freshwater lake in the heart of the city. The barnacles don't like fresh water; they die and fall off the hull."

"That sounds like a good city for sailors."

"Not just for sailors. It's a good city altogether. And beautifully situated, on seven hills."

"You don't mean Rome?"

"No, not Rome. We don't have cities that old. It's named after an Indian chief."

"You must know lots of other cities, Champ." He saw his brother returning. "You have to tell me more about that sometime..."

The wrestler was wearing sandals on bare feet; a striped shirt in loud colors dangled out over his slacks. In one hand he held the canvas bag he used to collect coins from the slot machines he had put out all over the city.

"Damned long route today. We'd better get started."

They switched off the light and left the kitchen. The big warehouse contained far fewer machines than it had three weeks earlier. Crossing that room, they entered another where they kept supplies for the slot machines: paper bags with the mixtures for the candy machines, cartons of peppermints, packets of rubber contraceptives. It was Monday, and that was an important day because all the slot machines had to be refilled.

They worked in silence, carrying the bags and cartons out to the ramp and loading them into the panel truck outside. Finally they brought out two slot machines and the tools they would need to install them.

"Two new spots—that's all I could find," the onetime wrestler said. "They used to go for rubber dispensers like mad. I used to average a thousand a week—gross, that is. A week, just think of that. Try to market a machine like that today, they're horrified: 'What, a thing like that in my rest room?'"

He slammed the back door of the panel truck. The sound reverberated loudly in the yard, surrounded as it was by abandoned buildings. The wrestler folded the slip and tucked it into the breast pocket of his shirt.

"It's all the pill. I always say the only person left on my side is the Pope. He's our only backer. And he's fighting a hopeless fight, just like me."

He clambered in behind the wheel of the truck, started the motor, and raised his hand in salute. His smaller brother sat next to him.

"Don't work too hard, you want to be in shape tonight! And tomorrow, tomorrow we'll have a potlatch. See you tonight, Champ!"

The truck started off. The noise of the muffler echoed from the walls. The muffler was hanging by a wire; the young man mused that it was time he fixed it. He had been meaning to do so for days, but he suddenly had the feeling that he would never have the time to do it. It was a curious feeling; it came over him, out of nothing, a kind of mood. But of course there were reasons; moods didn't come over you just like that.

I'm telling too many stories, he thought. And they're asking too many questions. It was natural enough for them to ask, but did he have to be all that cooperative?

His hands were busy untying the knot of his kerchief and tying it again. Finally he shrugged, climbed the steps to the ramp, and stood among the slot and pinball machines. He spread out a green cloth, laid out his tools, and went to work.

14

He worked for hours with quiet concentration. He was used to being alone throughout the day. Unexpected visitors hardly ever turned up. Those who wanted repairs generally telephoned, and he would note down the information: name, location, and number of the machine. Such calls were rare because everyone knew that the two brothers were out on their route by day. So when he heard someone tapping on the windowpane, he immediately had the feeling that it could only be she.

He had thought of her often during these past weeks, had been preoccupied with her. He had even considered letting her know where she could find him, but then had always decided against it. She was, he thought, the type who would become attached to men, who would make them foolish presents. But most of all he had speculated whether she would manage to find him. He had tossed coins: heads, she finds me; tails, she doesn't. As he laid his tools aside and crossed the room, he felt troubled, but at the same time he was proud of her for having accomplished this almost impossible task.

He walked slowly and softly, still undecided. Because the windows were painted over, and because it was lighter outside than in here, he could see her, while presumably he remained hidden. Her knuckles rapped against the glass, and he saw—or thought he saw—her face pressed against one of the panes. Recollection conjured up for him a hungry face: the face of a child seeing things it craves and knows it will never receive. The expression on her face had always roused a certain uneasiness in him. Now it stirred yet another memory.

He remembered himself on the night he had entered the city for the first time. The three of them—the "Professor," his wife, and he—had been sitting in the circus wagon, which was securely fastened to a railroad car. As the train slowed down, he had pressed his face against the windowpane and tried to get his first view of the city's lights, as though he could tell from them what to expect. He remembered particularly how intensely lonely he had felt at this moment when he should have been filled with curiosity and excitement.

"Hello. Hello, David... David."

She was calling in a whisper. He opened the door for her. She glided in, closed the door quickly behind her, remained standing in front of it.

"I've been very careful. Nobody saw me." She looked around the room. "You're alone?"

"Yes."

"I'm certain nobody saw me."

"Why should nobody see you? We're old friends, aren't we?" He tried to toss that off as casually as possible. "How did you find me?" That was the question that interested him the most.

"Didn't I say I would find you? I'm good at finding. You're good at hiding—and I'm good at finding."

She took a step toward him, as though she expected him to kiss her, but when he made no move to, her expression changed; it became serious and reflective from one moment to the next.

"It was pure luck," she said. "I'm not really good at finding, you know. Constellations, yes—I'm even better at making out constellations than Czepe. But in the city I regularly get lost. We've been living in the same place now for nearly ten years, but when I go down into the street I never know what direction to take. The flower vendor on the corner—is he on the right or the left? I have to think it over every time. When I go to the cinema, which is right nearby, after I come out of the show I have to ask myself—right or left? And when I decide it must be right, that's sure to be wrong. The thing is, I simply can't remember the names of streets. Cassiopeia, Andromeda, Pegasus, Aquarius, the Whale—I can always find them, but never streets. That's one of my most dreadful dreams: I won't find the right street."

She had followed him across the room, back to the machine on which he had been working. She was wearing the plastic rain cape. In her hand she held a package, a rather large one, wrapped in green paper and tied with a green ribbon. It looked like a present she had brought along for him, but she seemed to have forgotten about it. She looked at the garish machines, went from one to another, touching them cautiously, as though afraid her touch might set them off.

"What's all this?" She laid the package aside and began unsnapping the rain cape.

She had difficulty with the snaps, and as he observed her hands, their peculiarity struck him. At first glance they seemed quite all right, thin, well-manicured hands. But there was something wrong with the fingers; they seemed bent, oddly crooked, as though they had once been broken by force and had not grown back together properly.

She laid the cape aside and pointed at the machines. "What does one do with them?"

He went over to a bank of switches and pulled several of them. Some of the machines came to life; a few, like the pinball machines, simply lighted up, while others, like UFO Target, suddenly began sending out signals. She turned on her flat-heeled shoes first to one and then to another, with her scarf fluttering behind her, as though she were being controlled by the signals.

"You must show me how to play!"

"Whichever you suggest."

"What is that one?"

"Flying Circus."

"That sounds interesting."

He had her sit down on the black leather stool, dropped coins in, and explained the mechanism. With one handle you could govern the trajectory of the small biplane covered with camouflage paint, guiding it up or down, so that it flew through five rings that stood in a deep-green, fluorescent, unreal landscape.

"Slowly! Just a light touch."

Under her unpracticed hand the biplane dipped and staggered, and because the electronic machinery of the apparatus gave out dark, crashing, uncanny noises whenever the rings were touched, it sounded as if the plane were shattering into a thousand pieces.

She started, really frightened, and said, "I'd rather you did it."

He leaned over her, placed his hand over hers, and guided it. Watching the landscape and the plane, he made it rise and fall. It dived through the rings, rising and falling, until the machine stopped. For a moment he left his hand resting on hers, surprised at how well it fitted into his.

Twirling around on the revolving stool, she looked up at him. "Are you as good with the others? Where did you learn that?" When he delayed answering, she smiled. "Oh, I know. No unnecessary questions. Shall I tell you what kind of games I'm good at?" She waited. "I'll tell you all the games I've played, all right?"

"Okay." The feeling he had had when he touched her hand warned him to be careful. He would let her talk, would accept her present—if that was what it was—and would get rid of her as soon as possible.

"Do you really want to hear about them?"

"Sure. Tell me your favorite game."

"The best games were my father's, ones he invented himself." She remained seated on the stool. "All games for at home. I wasn't ever allowed to play outside. Dreadful thought to Mother: a daughter of hers playing on the street."

He looked at her in surprise. All his games had been played outside, by the water, on the beach. Aside from the pinball machine, he could think of no games he had ever played indoors. Or was there one after all? A second earlier he had found it baffling that anyone could want to talk about such things, and now he too was infected with the desire to recollect games he had played in his youth.

"One of them was Head, Body, Legs. You ever played it?"

He shook his head, silent because he was busy with his own thoughts.

"Everybody's given paper and pencil. One person starts, draws a head, folds the paper so that the next person can't see it. Then that one draws the body, and the next person the legs. Nobody knows what the other person has done, you see. You can't imagine what creatures come out of it... Of course, you don't do just human forms. Father would draw a captain's head, I'd add a lion's body and Czepe a toad's feet. Such weird creatures..."

"Tell me some more." It seemed to him he had known such captains, with the feet of toads and the bodies of lions.

"He—I mean Father—was good at imitating voices, just as you are, only he couldn't do ventriloquy. He'd do takeoffs on famous people, uncanny how real he could make them sound, scary. Sometimes he'd play out whole scenes, things he'd heard on the radio, especially accidents and disasters. There was one skit he always kept coming back to, but I don't know whether I..."

She stood up, suddenly nervous, and began walking among the machines.

"In those days people were crazy about zeppelins. One, the *Hindenburg*, burned up in America, at Lakehurst, I think, and he used to do a skit on that, pretending he was a reporter who'd watched it all."

"Give me an idea."

"Really? But it's scary."

Her voice changed as she began to speak: "Oh...look at this magnificent airship! Like a great feather, it's floating toward the mast... They're going to moor it now; only the two motors at the stern are keeping it aloft... But...there's a blast...out of the way!... Oh!... It's burning...burning... Nothing but a sea of flames; flames shooting a thousand, fifteen hundred feet into the sky."

She threw herself into the scene more and more. Her voice became choked with tears.

"What a calamity!... Oh, has the world ever seen the like?... What a ghastly sight!... Oh...it's collapsing... Sheets of fire falling to the ground... Oh...it's unbearable!...

Oh...the humanity..."

He had been watching her with growing alarm. There was something strange about her behavior that disturbed him. She was no longer acting this scene. He saw tears starting from her eyes. In the silence that followed her outburst, the signals from the machines sounded excessively loud, and he went to switch them off. By the time he returned, she was calm. She had dried her tears with her scarf, and was already smiling again. For a moment he had lost all sense of time and place.

"You certainly do remember things!"

"That was what Father was like," she said, as though nothing had happened. "Of course, our favorite was always the one we simply called 'Father's game.'"

"What was that?"

"He invented it for us, or for himself, I don't know which. It was very simple. 'Tell me the quickest route a ship takes.' He would have us come close, Czepe and me, and then he'd start: 'From Trieste to Benares via Cape Town. You, Milli, quick!'"

"Know the answer?"

"Trieste, Venice, Brindisi, Strait of Gibraltar, *west* coast of Africa, Cape Town, Durban, Mombasa, Karachi, Bombay, Benares."

"That's very good."

"No, I was never very good at the game. Czepe was, but not I. Though I always tried hard because I wanted to please Father. That's why I studied up on it, these last weeks—so you'd enjoy it."

"From Seattle to Kobe. back via Manila and Honolulu—quick, Milli!"

She looked at him. "That's a route you've sailed?"

She's clever, he thought, clairvoyant, to guess that right off. He had often sailed that route, yes, sailed that and others many times.

"I take it your father was a sailor?" he asked.

"Oh yes, of course. A captain."

He looked searchingly at her. It would never have occurred to him that she might be a seaman's daughter. Whenever she did not wear that hungry child's look, she gave out the aura of a world that was alien to him, one he would never penetrate: large houses, many servants, big gardens, limousines; he did not even know exactly how he ought to imagine her world.

"'I've sailed around the world forty times,' he used to say. Imagine—forty times around the world. That's why he was always coming and going, coming home and vanishing again." She looked at him, smiling. "Almost like you."

"Your father? Is he still living?"

He had asked casually, but she reacted violently. Her face turned pale, her eyes darkened; it was those eyes of hers that made him think she could become dangerous, ragingly so, in anger.

"He's dead," she said, almost tonelessly, and as if she meant that his death had been directed deliberately and solely against her.

Her moods shifted abruptly, ran cold and hot, hot and cold.

"Won't they be wondering where you are?" he asked.

"Me? Oh no."

"Have you had lunch?"

"Lunch? I can't remember. But I am hungry."

"Would you like tea or coffee? We have nothing but tea bags, but the coffee is very good. We buy the beans green and do the roasting ourselves."

"Who's we?"

"Two brothers. This is their business."

He led the way to the kitchen and switched on the neon tube, which took a while before it lit up the room. She sat down on the sofa, which was upholstered in black. She indicated the newspaper clippings on the walls. "Those the two men you work for?"

"Only one, the one who's always on top."

He busied himself for a while setting out lunch things, and finally joined her. "Will you have your coffee black or with milk?"

"Just milk, please, no sugar," she said. And a little later: "It's good, your coffee, and so is the chicken. I really was hungry."

Here, in the isolation of the kitchen, not a sound from

outside could be heard. Once the telephone in the warehouse rang, but he ignored it. He sat facing her. Her dress was white, and even her hair seemed silvery-white against the black sofa back.

"You never tell me anything about yourself," she said.

"Maybe there isn't much to tell."

"But there is always something."

"Maybe I'm not very good at telling things."

"You don't trust me?"

"That isn't the reason."

"Then I understand it even less. It's perfectly natural for people to tell each other things when they..." She did not finish the sentence. "Couldn't you tell me what kind of games you played?"

"We played ball."

"You see!"

"We had no balls, except old tennis balls that sometimes drifted up on the beach. There was a naval station on the mainland with a tennis court down near the water, and the officers' wives knocked a lot of the balls into the sound. In the summer, when there was a west wind, they washed up on our beach, heavy and pretty much done in by the salt water, but still they were balls."

She nodded attentively.

"We played baseball. We had no bats, so we used broken oars from the fishermen's boats."

"What's the name of the island?"

"I never said anything about an island."

"No? I can't remember your saying it, but I was always sure you came from an island."

"We hunted rabbits. There were thousands of them. We went out at night with a flashlight and caught them in the nets the fishermen used for salmon. And we played Echo. All those islands—well, all right, it was an island."

"Tell me about the echo game."

"A lot of the islands lie close together. Sailing around them in foggy weather is dangerous because of the rocks. The fishermen manage in fogs by using echoes to steer their boats, since they don't have any modern equipment. They can tell exactly where they are by the length of time it takes for their voices to echo from the rocks. We played echoes: we'd set up big plywood sheets along the beach, or in the dunes, and sometimes even out in the water at low tide. Then at night we'd practice; one of us would be blindfolded and we'd lead him to a place, and then he'd have to say just from the echoes how far he was from one point or another."

"I'm sure you were good at it."

"My father always used to say that some people are born with a feeling for echoes and that sort of thing."

"Was it a lonely island?"

"Depends how you look at it. It was small, but not lonely. There are so many of them, you know, almost two hundred if you count them all. Some are nothing more than sandbars, and others are moss-grown rocks."

"Did your island have a name?"

He smiled at her question. "The Spaniards who discovered the islands gave a name to the whole group. They called them the Islas Bonitas, the beautiful islands."

"No other games?"

"I don't think so. But we heard lots of stories. We boys helped the fishermen tar their boats, and ran to the store to get them their tobacco, and they paid us back by telling stories. The old guys used to tell stories about Indians, and the not-so-old ones about smugglers. The islands were a paradise for smugglers. There are so many of them, with hundreds of small, hidden bays and narrow, dangerous passages where it's hard for a pursuing boat to follow. Most of the stories were about ships that came in toward shore in darkness and fog, on moonless nights, and unloaded their stuff into small, fast skiffs. A lot of the fishermen remembered Prohibition, when they smuggled in Canadian whiskey and Puerto Rican rum... Oh yes, I remember another game. Pinball."

"Pinball, like the machines you have here?"

"On the island there was a restaurant down by the fishermen's wharf. It had a pinball machine, and the owner'd let me play it free if I washed dishes for him. It was the only pinball machine on the whole island, and I never did find out how it had got there. But there it was, and I had it all to myself, all through the mornings when the fishermen were out in the sound."

"What about your father—was he a captain too?"

The young man kept silent for a while. Young as he was, he had already found out one thing: love always began with talking, and the last thing he wanted was to fall in love with this girl. And yet he liked talking with her. She had made him say things he had kept to himself for a long time, and as he talked he realized how deeply rooted he still was in those things.

"Was he?"

"He would have liked that, anyone calling him a captain. All his life his one wish was to own his own boat. That was his dream, a fishing boat and one great catch. But every fisherman dreams about one great catch, one great voyage, one great season."

"Then he was a fisherman?"

"He and his partner sailed out and fished, yes."

"Was he a good fisherman?"

"I think you could call him that. But he wasn't so good at the rest of it."

"What else does a fisherman have to be good at?"

"At selling fish, for instance. That part didn't interest him. He always argued with his partner, even about the fishing itself. There're lots of fish in the strait, cod, sea perch, halibut, and of course in the summer there's salmon. Salmon was Father's favorite. There are all kinds of ways to catch salmon, hand nets, gill nets, dragnets, or just with hook and line. My father always used to say that the only decent way was the hook and line. But at the same time it's the hardest way to catch salmon. You should have seen his hands, scarred right down to the bone in places where the line ran through them."

"Are you like him?"

"I hope not, not that way, anyhow. The time I'm talking about was right after the war; there were lots of fishermen and not enough canneries or fish dealers or fish restaurants. Out in the strait my father sometimes did better, although he only fished with hook and line, because he knew the right places, the currents the salmon followed in the summer, and the depths where you had to fish for them. But he always lost out on the marketing end. So he was forever quarreling with his partner, and that was another reason he wished he had his own boat. I have a hunch if he'd ever gotten one it would have turned out pretty bad. He would have sailed farther and farther out to sea, just to catch fine fish in the decent way, and then he'd have sold even less. You can say he was stupid—my mother used to say that often—but that's how he was."

"He never did get his boat?"

"No," the young man said, and dropped into silence.

He would have liked to tell her more, at least the rest of the story. At the end of September when the first typhoons from the southwest Pacific ruffled the waves of the Juan de Fuca Strait, the salmon fishing stopped. During the winter his father worked in the ocean fishing fleet, belowdecks, cleaning the fish with knife and scraper—the hardest work there was. From one of those voyages he did not return. They had made a great catch that year, had radioed home that they had three hundred thousand pounds of fish in the hold. But the great catch was their nemesis. It was February, extremely cold, and the ship became coated with ice. The breakers that crashed down on deck froze before they could run off, and the ship sank with its heavy cargo.

There were no survivors; not even the corpses were found. But his mother had set her heart on having a grave, planting flowers... The young man would have liked to describe how he had looked for flowers to plant on the grave... The only kinds that could stand up to the island's cutting winds were wild roses, cattails, and dandelions.

Yes, he would like to tell about that, sometime, to someone like her...

15

He had been far away in his thoughts. The girl in the white dress with the almost white hair against the black upholstery of the sofa had said something...

"You must have been very fond of it. Why did you leave it?"

"Ever since I was a boy they were always saying we'd be leaving the island."

"But..."

"My mother talked about nothing else. She's Italian, very religious, and there wasn't a Catholic church or a priest on the island—and no bingo either."

"Bingo?"

"A game of chance." He smiled. "She had her way finally. She married a sheep rancher on one of the bigger islands, and now every other night on the dot of eight she shows up at her beloved bingo game."

"I hope she wins."

"Oh, I'm sure she does. She's the kind who always wins at bingo."

"What about your father? Did he also want you to leave the island?"

"He had two brothers on the mainland. They amounted to something, and he always wanted me to go to work for them."

"Did you?"

"A few times. One of them had a big poultry farm. He talked about nothing but chickens, especially about one of his hens that laid over three hundred eggs in three hundred sixty-five days. She was the state champion—but other poultry farmers also claimed to have birds like that. I liked my other uncle better. He raised bulbs. He had acres and acres of land, and in the spring you couldn't see anything but fields of tulips, snowdrops, narcissus, and hyacinths."

"So that's why you know so much about flowers. And when did you leave the island?"

"After my father died. The spring after that."

"How old were you then?"

"When I left—fifteen."

"And what did you do?"

"I found a berth on a ship... I was strong and I guess I looked old enough."

"From Seattle to Kobe and back via—I've forgotten the rest."

"Manila and Honolulu."

"I could listen on and on to your stories."

"That's all there is to it."

She had listened all along with serenity and close attention, motionless, without so much as changing her position on the sofa. Now she leaned forward and extended her arm across the table to take his hand. He withdrew it as if by chance. She pretended not to notice, and said, "When you love someone, you'd like to know everything about him."

Never before had he felt that the light in the kitchen was so glaring, that the pictures on the walls were so obtrusive; he thought he could see all the dirty dishes behind him. What a place to talk about love!

"Some more coffee?" He stood up.

"I suppose you don't believe that I love you?"

What was he to reply to that?

"Because I'm—so much older?"

"No." He felt he could say that with a clear conscience: when he looked at her he thought she was really not much older than he was.

"I'm talking nonsense?" She also stood up. "And I forgot

all about the present. I did bring it, didn't I?"

"You came with something wrapped in green paper."

"Yes, that's a present."

She followed him back to the hall filled with machines, where she had left the package, and looked around.

"It's for your room."

The wall telephone rang. This time he took the call and scribbled notes. When he returned, he found her standing at the foot of the iron staircase that led up to a kind of gallery.

"Is your room up there?"

He nodded, no longer surprised by the way she seemed to know things through a kind of clairvoyance.

"Do you know, I've never seen a room in which you've lived."

He hesitated. He was trying to recall why she had come. He had meant to ask her a question, an important one, but he had forgotten that too.

"Please show it to me."

She climbed the stairs. He thought it simpler to follow her than to try to stop her. There were a number of rooms along the gallery. The smell of them suggested that malt and hops had once been stored in them.

There was not much furniture: a steel closet, a brass bed covered with a red quilt, a small table on which stood a Philco radio. He always kept his things packed, so nothing lay around. Aside from the radio, the room contained nothing personal. The window looked out on broad, flat roofs. The young man had stayed in a good many places, and he had found out one thing: rooms you liked were the worst because it was hard to leave them behind. This room was one you could turn your back on at any time, without a twinge of regret.

With his toe he pushed the green duffel bag farther under the bed. She lingered at the door, looking for a while at the small black radio as though it represented the one thing in the room that she could grasp. She had carried the package, and now, as though she were only just remembering it again, she held it out to him.

"If you don't like it, don't bother opening it."

"How can I tell whether I like it if I don't know what's in

it?"

For a while she struggled to untie the ribbon, but finally gave up and handed it to him still wrapped, with the ribbon dangling.

As soon as he held it, he knew what it was.

"It's a pillow, isn't it?"

"Yes. I know it's a silly present."

It was: a small pillow covered in green velveteen; its size made it absolutely useless. He did not know what to do with it and so he laid it at the foot of the bed.

"You once told me that there's nothing you hate more than those pillows filled with foam rubber at cheap hotels. It's ridiculous, but at least it has real down in it." Tears were flowing from her dark eyes. Her hair hung loosely, unkempt. In spite of the tears she tried to smile. "Say it! It's ridiculous and useless."

"Yes, it does look sort of ridiculous."

And yet at this moment he wanted very much to embrace her. It seemed the most natural thing in the world, because at this moment she was beautiful. As though nothing more were needed than tears to make her face perfectly beautiful. He felt a craving to kiss her face, to make love to her body. And there was another reason: for a brief moment it seemed to him that with her he could find his way back to the island, or at least to a place comparable to the island.

She had slumped onto the bed, still in tears about the silly present, or about something that only she knew. He untied the kerchief at his neck and shaped it into a puppet. He crouched on his heels at the side of the bed. He looked at the puppet in his right hand and asked it, "Tell me, is a pillow worth crying about?"

"Of course," the puppet replied in a puppet's voice.

"Really?"

"That's the first thing a puppet learns. Crying and laughing—that's what puppets learn first."

"Tell me more," he asked the puppet. "Tell me a good reason for crying."

The puppet on the hand of the young man seemed to hesitate. Then it looked at the girl on the bed, studied her carefully, and then said, "I don't have to tell *her*. She knows all the reasons for crying, the good ones and the bad ones. She could even tell *me* a few reasons."

"What about me?" the young man asked.

The puppet now studied the young man. "Maybe you knew good reasons once upon a time. But you don't any more. You turn your back on crying girls."

After what seemed a long silence, the young man said, "I didn't turn my back on her."

"All right, so you didn't. All I can say is, *that* surprised me. You must love her."

"Do I really?"

The puppet in the young man's hand turned toward the girl on the bed. "How ridiculous! To think of saying anything so ridiculous. We see what we see, don't we? He loves her and can't manage to say it. Only men can be like that. But we see what we see, don't we?"

The girl on the bed looked up. "Is that right? That you simply can't manage to say it?"

"That's possible, yes," he said.

In the silence thatat followed they could hear all the ordinary sounds again: the pigeons outside the window, the sheet metal of the roofs expanding in the heat, and then as Milli stood up the creak of the metal bedsprings.

"Will you give it to me?"

He handed her the puppet. She held the kerchief in her hands; it was now no more than that, but it apparently seemed something more to her.

"May I keep it?"

"Yes, of course…"His craving for her was greater than ever, but he said, "Don't you have to go?"

"At least tell me I can come back."

"Any time."

She went to the door and paused there. "I did tell you why I came, didn't I?" She looked at him, suddenly confused and useasy. "They're looking for you. Did I really not tell you? That was the reason why it was so important to find you."

"Who's looking for me?"

"Who? The police, the vicar-general, I assume, and

Czepe."

"Your brother? Why him?"

"It's all so confusing. I think Czepe's looking for you because he wants to help you. The vicar-general..."Her face lighted up. "It's about the priest's clothing, my brother's cassock, the one I gave you."

"You never gave me any cassock."

For a moment that perplexed, disturbed expression returned to her face; but then she laughed. "Oh, I see, you want to test whether I remember rightly. It was only the ticket from the cleaner I gave you, right? You wanted the cassock for—what was it, a costume party?"

"I didn't give you a reason. You said you had to pick it up from the cleaner and I asked you for it." That was something he did not like to remember. It had been such a foolish idea, getting money that way. Or rather, the idea hadn't been so bad, only what he had done with it. "Did they ask you about the cassock?"

"Only Czepe asked me. I pretended I didn't know anything about it. I just happened to hear the conversation—not the whole of it, but enough, and I wanted to let you know right away."

"How did you find me?"

"It wasn't easy." She sounded proud.

"Are you sure nobody followed you?"

"Followed me?"

He looked searchingly at her, speculating. "If they're looking for me, like you say—all they had to do was follow you. You are the only person who could lead them to me, don't you see?"

"But they don't know anything about the two of us."

"Maybe they do."

"Oh no, I swear they don't. And I'd never tell them anything. Never. It's not kind of you to think anything like that."

"Tell me how you found me. If you could do it, others can."

"Nobody else could." She looked up at him. Then she told him about her visits to the market, the flower vendor, the man with the clubfoot; she omitted the scene with the boy loading the boxes of orchids.

"I believe it now—nobody but you could have managed that. But be careful in the future."

"Of course." He could see how happy she was about this conspiracy that forged a tighter link between them.

"There's something else." Her hands were toying with her scarf. "Do you really have a tattoo?"

If she had known him better, or if he had been less skilled at controlling his feelings, she might have recognized how this struck home. He didn't answer at once, so she had to ask again.

"Do you have one?"

"Most seamen have."

She nodded.

"It's just a custom."

"A kind of trademark?"

"Possibly." His thoughts were elsewhere.

"You've never mentioned that you have a tattoo."

"Where did you hear about it? Who said I had?"

"They were talking about it—the vicar-general and Czepe."

"Did they talk about what it was?"

"Yes, but I wasn't able to hear that. I asked Czepe about it, but he wouldn't tell me." She looked at him a moment as if considering whether there were any point to asking him, but then decided against it. Instead, she said, "Do you know that I have a tattoo?"

"You?"

"A mark, a mole—that's a kind of tattoo, isn't it?" She loosened the long scarf that was wound twice around her neck, but did not take it off, merely drew it down so that the very white skin of her throat was exposed.

"Here."

For a moment he did not see anything, thought this must be one of her strange notions, but then he saw the scars. There were several of them. some almost invisible, others more apparent, including the delicate dots where a wound had obviously been sewn up. It looked like a skin transplantation, but he could not be sure of that. He felt a craving to touch the spot.

"What is it?" he asked.

She laughed and tightened the green chiffon scarf. "Someday I'll tell you."

They left the room together. At the steep iron staircase she faltered, extending a hand to him for support. He remembered how easily she had climbed the stairs. What she said was barely audible.

"I...can't... I'll never make it...going down those."

"What's the matter?" She had shrunk back from the stairs, and as she averted her face from them and leaned against him, he could feel her whole body trembling. Her face was white, and because she used a heavy red lipstick and she was so close to him, it seemed chalky, almost like a clown's face.

"I can't... It's a...fire escape, isn't it?"

"But Milli. What's got into you?"

She was slow to calm down. After a while the color returned to her face and her body stopped trembling. "I think I can do it now. May I have your hand?"

She let him lead her down the stairs. There was hardly room for two side by side. When they reached the bottom, she leaned forward and kissed him quickly, almost casually. Then she took the end of her scarf to wipe the lipstick from his lips.

"Where will I find you again?"

"Come here any time."

She looked around the room as though she were seeing it for the first time. Them she smiled, understanding. "I may not find you here."

"Who says so?"

"I know you. I know my father...he did the same thing to me, ran away from me. That's why I understand, a little. Once he tried to explain. I remember he said, when it hurts, run away, change places, that helps. Or something like that. Just give me something, some kind of hint that'll help me find you." *Cop. 2*

"You found me this time."

Again he was struck by that understanding smile. "But next time you may make it harder for me. Please, just a hint, so I have something to begin with."

He thought for a while. Then he said, "You find me at the

royal fish."

"Royal fish?"

"That's what sailors call the whale."

"Is that really a hint?" But then she seemed to understand. "Of course, the whale! And when?"

Again he took time before replying. "In the evening when the show goes on."

"Do you have a name there? Have you noticed that I've called you David only once?"

"You'll find me there."

"The royal fish!" He seemed to have touched a chord in her imagination, and she took her rain cape and went to the door repeating under her breath, "Royal fish..."

At the door she kissed him again, once more casually and lightly. Then she said in a whisper, "No, don't come out with me. I'll find my way alone."

Involuntarily, he smiled again. The smile banished the tension that had been printed on his face ever since her mention of the tattoo.

He stood watching through the half-opened door. She did not turn around once. From the length of the shadows in the yard he saw how much time had passed. He closed the door and returned to the machine he had been working on when she arrived.

He had enough time to make up his mind before the two brothers came back from their route. In the big hall he climbed the iron staircase once more, took a new kerchief from his duffel bag, and tied it around his neck. Then he returned to the hall and went over to one of the pinball machines. If I reach the 100.00 mark with five balls, I stay, he thought, otherwise, I'd better move.

He started a ball and stood there, his hands resting on the front corners of the machine, watching as the silver ball struck the ellipse at the upper rim of the playfield and then passed through the middle of the three gates. Flippers doubled its speed, round kickout holes hurled it back into play, stoppers made bells clang, lights flare, and numbers blink on the backglass. The racket of the pinball machine at times seemed nothing but an explosion of light and sound. Only when the fourth ball slipped between the two flippers that guarded the runout slot at the bottom of the playfield did he look at the score. The machine was an old Gottlieb, and on this kind 40,000 points with five balls was a good score. The score on the backglass now stood at 66,500 points, one more ball to go. He rested his hands on the corners of the old Gottlieb, shifted his weight from one foot to the other, moved closer, putting his right foot under it, adjusted the other foot—all this to find the right position. He seemed like an athlete mildly nervous before a tryout. He worked the ball, absorbed in his game, only looking now and then when the bell clanged, the lights flashed, new figures appeared on the scoreboard: 70,000...80,000.

He played a fast, risky game with this last ball. It jumped about crazily, crisscrossed the playfield, was deftly caught by the flippers, thrown back rapidly into the field; it repeatedly climbed into the upper regions to accumulate more points against the bumpers, the bonus gates, the eject holes. The minutes went by; the stillness in the big room seemed to increase. He continued to keep the ball in play, working, it seemed, under some special grant of immunity that could not expire. When the ball finally dropped out of the game, quite suddenly and unexpectedly—it did not slip between the two guarding flippers, but rolled with fearful slowness into the long dead lane on the left side of the Gottlieb, where nothing could prevent its disappearance into the runout slot and it vanished with a dull thud—he held his breath and took a step back.

The score had stopped at 98,700. It was not entirely clear when the young man turned away whether he was proud or disappointed.

Of course it was absurd to make such a decision depend on the outcome of a pinball game. But then again, a game was as good as anything else: counting buttons or tossing a coin. Better, because you always had a chance to beat the machine yourself, so at least you had the feeling that matters were in your own hands. Maybe it was nutty to set the target so high—100,000 points on an old Gottlieb! But he would have felt he was cheating if he'd set the figure lower. He had taken that dare of his own free will, and near the end there he'd been full of confidence that this time he would reach the 100,000 mark, which he'd never done before on the Gottlieb.

16

She did not stop until the shop suddenly appeared right in front of her. She could not remember how she had come here. She did not know why she was standing here, or what time of day it was, or even what day in the week. But the shop, the glittering and fantastic things in the window, struck her as familiar.

A red neon sign inside the window blinked. MAGIC, the sign said. That seemed like a message intended specially for her, a message that she alone could understand.

The neon sign gave no indication of time, since it blinked on and off all day long. She came to this shop often, sometimes early in the morning, so she knew that. For a moment the fantastic objects in the window engaged her full attention: the masks that stared at her, all those false noses, big red noses with glasses, mustaches; the wigs, whole faces made of rubber, weird heads, faces of animals and people...

Heads, bodies, legs, she thought. Yes! But what did it all mean?

Heads, bodies, legs.

The things disappeared from her sight abruptly, as though someone had plucked them out of the window display. She saw only herself, rather indistinctly, a dim mirror image in the glass pane. She shook her head as though she did not like what she saw.

Heads, bodies, legs.

Somebody had mixed everything up, put the wrong head on the wrong body. Of course, that was it. This head no longer belonged to this body, and the body did not know what to do with the head it had on. Everything mixed up. Czepe or her father...

I was telling someone about Father—who could it be?

She knew that much now. She had been talking to somebody about it, had told about their games, remarked that he had sailed forty times around the world... He was never there when she needed him most, as she did now.

I need you now!

Were people noticing that she was talking to herself?

Maybe talking to oneself was more common than anyone thought. Father always used to talk to himself. He said it came from watching at the bow all night long; it was a lonesome job. The bow was the stem, the prow, the front part of the ship, the cutwater that the big waves broke against... How did that go? Oh yes, the big heavy waves, bow waves, hundreds and hundreds of tons of water—in time they actually twisted the prow, even though it had special reinforcement. You didn't realize it until you saw the ship in drydock, a real dent.

When they bring me into dock someday they'll see all my dents and bruises from the thousands of tons of water that have spilled over me.

Heads, bodies, legs.

She could not see her legs in the glass pane; the shopwindow went down only to knee level. The things in the front part of the display caught her interest now: rockets, firecrackers, Catherine wheels. And all the novelty items: cigars that exploded in your face; strange birds—ducks?—that perched on the rim of a glass and dipped their beaks into the water; glass eyes on the bottom of a glass filled with water; a ring that would not come off your finger...

She extended her left hand and studied it. There was no ring on it. It was her mother who wore all those rings. That mother of hers who could have all the men she wanted, who could even afford to turn them away by the dozens.

Dear, good Mother. You who shooed all men away from me and afterwards found fault with me for not having any and wondered where they all could be.

How much well-meant advice she had always given her: Don't run after them, don't flatter them, don't force yourself on them, don't give them any presents—control them!

You loving mother!

She suddenly laughed as she recalled the Pekinese. Was it possible that this was the day she had let the dog slip from the leash? It had been a hot, sultry day—the weather was always a great help in remembering particular days.

Kropik had not trusted her when she had offered to take the dogs out. "Now, don't let them off the leash, Miss Milli!" *Miss*—what cheek! "Both of them see so poorly, they're almost blind." She knew that Kropik did not trust her. But then he always had so much else to do, was always busy doing things for her mother. Mother...

But Kropik couldn't prove anything against her. No one had been watching when she loosened the collar. She had made sure of that. Maybe the dog was the only one to suspect anything, at the moment he felt liberated from that narrow band. He had been so surprised that he stood still, then he dashed off after all. Perhaps the driver had suspected something. But no, he had been just as surprised. Maybe he would never have realized what had thumped dully against the fender if the dog hadn't yapped so loudly.

A pity Mother hadn't heard that!

And Kropik. How he'd come running. His probing eyes on her. But what could he do? In the future all he could do was trust her even less. Let him know how dangerous she could be, what a devil...

A devil.

In the shopwindow lay a devil mask, but the thought had stirred another memory: a tiny, sweet-smelling store, whose pinewood shelves were filled with cartons that gave out a sugary odor, and tall, narrow jars displaying samples of bright-colored candies—the shelves reaching all the way to the ceiling and far back into the darkness at the rear of the shop. Out of that darkness a man had come. She had heard him before she saw him, the sound of his clubfoot on the wooden floor.

Sweet devil...

When she entered the store this morning...

This morning. Now she remembered! Oh yes, of course. *She had found him.* She suddenly remembered everything up to the moment she had fled down the fire escape.

But wait. Hadn't he said it wasn't a fire escape? He had taken her hand and helped her. That was certainly right. And they had discussed something else, something very important. He had given her a hint. But what had it been? She needed it now; she must remember.

Right now all that she could remember was the streets. So many streets. Cars braking sharply in front of her; drivers shouting after her. New streets, different ones, so many of them. She had tried to find her way back and had finally ended up at the flower market, in front of the shop with the sign NOTIONS...

One hint, anyhow. She had begun anew, at the end of the thread. When she again failed to find the way back, she had returned for a second time. She had intended to ask the Sweet Devil, but the shop had been locked. Face pressed against the windowpane, she had seen all those brightly colored glass jars—or had it been slot machines?

She looked around and saw that it was already turning dark. On the other side of the street was the illuminated window of a wig shop, full of white, expressionless faces that had masses of curled hair heaped above them. Another shop-window was full of cuckoo clocks. Next to that was a movie theater with a floodlit still shot in front. There were tall open doors, and crowds of people going back and forth in front of them, eating ice cream.

Ice cream ... It had been such a lovely day, the first in many weeks when it had not rained. Very early in the morning—no, it had not been all that early—she had gone to the flower market and...

She lifted her right hand, and the puppet was there!

She turned around toward the window, pressing the puppet firmly against her breast. MAGIC, the sign blinked. She smiled and thought, *I kissed him.*

It's true, I kissed him! *She remembered!* He had traces of lipstick on his mouth, or at least on the corners of his mouth. I told him I love him, not quite like that, but very plainly, and he told me the same, though less plainly. But then there was another thought: love that never came at the right time. She pressed the puppet tighter against her chest: Is that a good reason to cry, puppet?

Before the puppet could answer, she heard the commotion behind her. A car almost skidded as the driver braked quickly. At the same time a woman's voice cried out, "There she is!" When Milli turned around, she saw a gray limousine, highly polished, with a tall, narrow back seat and a long hood. Then she caught sight of Kropik in his brown livery with the double row of buttons which seemed to glow as he approached her.

"Miss Milli?" He called out to her. And the other voice, the voice of the woman who was leaning out of the car window and pointing in her direction, rings flashing, called, "Stop her, Kropik! Quick!"

But this time the puppet had reacted even faster.

Run! the puppet had whispered, *run!* And she had not hesitated a second...

17

The young man studied the hotel from across the street. He had stepped back into the entrance to a store, his green duffel bag on the ground between his feet. Since darkness he had been inspecting places, and had finally returned to this one. He looked calm, relaxed, not even deeply interested, but he had been watching very closely, taking note of everyone who entered or left the hotel, every light that went on or out behind the windows of the small, four-story building.

By now he had a good notion of the hotel's clientele. A few strippers, some elderly, tired-looking musicians, a number of smooth-talking waiters with slicked-down hair, an old man in a worn swallowtail coat who was undoubtedly a has-been magician with a bag of tricks, some other music-hall performers. Most important, there were no prostitutes— the one who was walking up and down the street in front of him had left her beat only once for a short turn with a customer, and she had taken him to another hotel. There were no tramps, no drunks, and so far as he had seen, no junkies or pushers.

A hotel with down-at-the-heel artistes, musicians, and magicians was the best place he could find. No one took any interest in such people. They themselves preferred to be let alone. As for the strippers, they were almost never prostitutes, and the police knew that. The young man was satisfied, but he continued to wait.

The owner had picked, out of all possible names for the establishment, the unremarkable one carried above the entrance: Hotel Austria. Small flags had been placed along the marquee; they were dirty and tattered, but the national colors and insignia could still be distinguished. The flags hardly added to the hotel's distinction: in fact, they looked rather ridiculous against the dark, battered façade and the dirt-encrusted shutters. The small hotel's appearance suggested a convention site for has-beens.

Such a place promised anonymity, and right now that was critical to the young man. I'm where I started out in this city, he thought. I circled around it, moved out farther and farther from its center, and now I'm back almost at my starting point. The Praterstern freight station, where the freight train had come to a halt that first night, was close by. And so was the river.

This was the Second District, which had always been a cheap, rather despised neighborhood. It was situated on an island between the two waterways—the Danube and the canal—and was notably damp, even now in the summertime. In the old days Jews from Galicia had settled in this neighborhood, and unless they managed to get rich, they had remained there. For that reason a good many of the city's inhabitants still called the neighborhood Matzos Island. The Jews were long since gone, and there were no matzos, but it was still damp.

One could tell the hotel stood on a damp foundation. Up to yards above ground level the masonry was dark, oozing moisture; and the foundations of the buildings to the right and left of it had the same leprous look. The young man had also closely studied the adjacent buildings; other hotels, strip-tease bars with display cases showing photos of strippers discreetly pasted over with white tape, an amusement arcade whose doorway was hung with bright strips of plastic kept constantly in motion by boys entering and leaving. There were many cafés and night spots, dreary and small. From time to time the touts and doormen of the striptease joints went through one of these doors to have a quick drink; they were huge, strange figures in fantastic uniforms, with epaulets and white gloves. And then, as though the street would not be complete without the smell of fat and burnt meat, there was a tiny frankfurter stand, jammed between two buildings.

The young man seemed to have made his decision. He stooped and picked up his duffel bag. The whore who had been parading up and down the street in her miniskirt and white, tight-fitting boots came over to him, her cheap, shiny white bag swinging from her shoulder. Seen from close up, her face, though still very young, seemed to hold little curiosity: little more than the sleepy instinct she needed to choose her customers. A single earring dangled from her left ear. The other ear was unadorned.

She did not speak to him. Perhaps she did not regard him as a likely customer. Perhaps she was only showing caution. She simply stood beside him after he emerged from his niche and then hesitated for a moment because someone across the street was approaching the hotel.

They watched the man together, as though they had the same interest in him. He was dressed in dark clothing, a lean, middle-aged man with thinning hair. The odd thing about him was the way he moved, with long strides that nevertheless did not seem to carry him forward very far, much as if he were walking in the wrong direction on a moving sidewalk. He paused in front of the hotel, looked up at the sign and the small flags, then went on with the same long strides.

The streetwalker followed him with her eyes. "Odd, the way he walks."

"Business bad?" he asked.

"Not exactly booming."

"Even with all the tourists?"

"Can't depend on the tourists any more." She was not looking at him; her eyes kept surveying the street while she talked. "They come for the Lippizaner and the opera. And they have wives with them. It's better in winter, even in the fall, because then the men come alone."

Farther down the street the man in dark clothing was now talking with one of the doormen; then he vanished from sight.

"Don't waste any money on *that*," the streetwalker said. "Those striptease places are a swindle. The girls are just hideous, real freaks."

She demonstrated what she meant. She tilted her head to one side, pulled down an eyelid with one finger, twisted her eyes, and let her tongue hang out of the corner of her mouth. As though all that were not plain enough, she performed a kind of wildly twitching, crazy parade in place, pulling up her miniskirt and tossing her slender legs in their white boots as high as possible.

"I get it," he said. "You do that well."

"Yeah, I'm pretty good at it." She moved away, and without another word resumed her beat.

The young man crossed the street and entered the hotel. The reception area was small; the cubicle for the night clerk was not much bigger than a telephone booth. The man in front of the board of keys was apparently young, but there was no swearing to it. An ashtray stood on the narrow counter in front of him, with a burning cigarette in it. He did not look up as he rattled off, "One night, a hundred ten schillings; one week, six hundred fifty. No rooms by the hour."

The young man counted out the tab for a week. The black-haired clerk with the peaked face ignored the money.

"Passport?" His voice was surprisingly high. He extended his left hand, still without looking up.

There were three violet dots on the ball of his thumb, so small that they could easily be overlooked, but the young man's senses had sharpened the moment he set foot inside the hotel. Of course, the spots might have come from one of the ballpoint pens the clerk had clipped to the breast pocket of his white shirt, but they looked more like a tattoo. Pimps carried marks like these for mutual recognition. The young man was on the point of taking back the money he had laid on the counter. Apparently he had not yet decided what new role to slip into, and this was only the beginning. There was much more still to do, more important decisions to make than the choice of a hotel. And then, of course, he did not like pimps.

"Don't you like my face?" he asked.

"Of course I like it. Nice honest face. But I still need your passport."

The young man took a passport out of the side pocket of his windbreaker.

The clerk leafed through it. "Dudic, Petar, twenty-eight. Sailor, eh?"

"You can read it," the young man said. "Riverboatman, not sailor."

"Of course, riverboatman." He pushed the passport back across the counter, together with a registration form and one of his pens.

The young man filled out the form carefully, without haste, and signed it. The passport was a danger. It was made out in Serbo-Croatian, a language he did not know, and so he used it as seldom as possible.

The black-haired night clerk took the money and the form. He looked at the board and after long reflection chose a key. "This is the best room—what they call the best here."

The young man read the number and shook his head.

"Give me one on the second floor and up front."

"Those are the worst. You won't sleep much there on account of the street noise. And if you close the window you suffocate." He handed him a new key.

"If you ever slept belowdecks next to a ship's engine, any room seems quiet in comparison to that." The young man tucked the passport back into his windbreaker. "Are you here all night?"

"Yes, every night. If you need anything... Girls?"

But the young man had already gone toward the elevator, a narrow, glazed wooden cage behind a fancy iron grating.

The room looked exactly as he had expected, possibly just a little worse, but he would not be lingering here long. Everything was green: the door, the rug with its burn holes, the walls, the bedspread, and the curtains. A dull green that reminded him of military gyms and ships. There was even a shower tiled in green, with a green plastic curtain.

He laid the duffel bag on the bed and stepped to the window. Holding the curtain aside, he looked out. The prostitute in her white boots was still strolling up and down the street, but he was more interested in the street itself. It was a one-way street; cars were a rarity. Every car that drove up to the front of the hotel would be audible, especially a police car.

Policemen could never resist bolting out of their cars and slamming the doors loudly as they did so. He opened the window a crack; immediately the smell of the frankfurter stand poured in.

Closing the curtain over the window, he began his inspection of the room by opening all the drawers and wardrobe doors. It was odd how often people left things in hotel rooms, just as though they expected to return to the same room sometime. He found a single sock in the wardrobe, and two cheap ear clips in the drawer of the night table. He wondered how long they had been lying there.

He unpacked only a few things: razor, soap, towel, toothbrush, and toothpaste. Then he placed the Philco on the night table beside the bed. He switched it on and waited until the round dial glowed red and green, then he turned on the volume low so that it would not drown out the noises of the street. The set was too big and clumsy for a man who traveled light, but he had owned it for a long time. In fact, nothing had been longer in his possession than this Philco. It was as old as his tattoo. He had acquired both the same year and at the same place, Kobe, both purchased with his first wages as a cabin boy.

He sat down on the bed to change his shirt. The tattoo on his left forearm was entirely blue. Since it had been done when he was a little more than fifteen, and since he had grown afterward, it had become distorted. But that was not the sole reason for the extreme oddity of the face. It was a Japanese Christ.

He studied the figure, trying to recall why he had chosen that one among the many patterns and symbols the Japanese tattooer had offered. Perhaps he simply wanted to set himself apart from the other men aboard his ship. Their tattoos were always the same: the anchor, the helm, the life preserver, gulls, lighthouses, broken masks, sunrises, inscriptions such as "Ship Ahoy!," the names of various girls, with or without hearts, and—in rare cases—entire scenes: *The Sailor's Grave* or *The Last Man before the Mast.*

The Christ on the cross had turned up in the Japanese tattooer's book of samples. He had pointed to it, instantly resolved to have this—until then he had been unable to decide. At the time he did not know why, and to this day he could not have explained to himself why it had to be that one. He recalled only that he had been afraid of the needle, had turned his head away so as not to watch the procedure. But then the pain had been only slight. On the way back to the ship with the Philco tucked under his arm and the fresh tattoo, he recalled, he had felt like a man.

But the tattoo had not been the success he was counting on. Some of the crewmen had laughed, others had gravely shaken their heads. And girls frowned when they saw it. They thought it very peculiar, but seldom made remarks about it. And of course it had been impossible for him to conceal the tattoo in the army... This was the thought foremost in his mind as he looked at it now. Someone who knew about that must also know about his desertion...

None of the things Milli had told him that afternoon worried him more than this. For it could only mean that they were on his trail, that they had tracked him as far as Vienna.

He stood up and unbuckled his canvas belt, laid out a clean shirt and his laundered chinos. Then he showered and shaved. For a moment he stared into the mirror as though it would be possible to find traces of her lipstick. The longing for her suddenly returned, stronger than ever.

He took the pillow, her gift, out of the duffel bag. In this dreary room it looked even more incongruous—and yet curiously touching. He placed it at the head of the bed, trying to persuade himself that the only reason he had taken it with him was that he never left anything behind. It was different with this room; here no one would think anything of it if he left the pillow when he departed.

He put on the clean clothes, slowly and with care, as though this were an important ceremony that increased the number of his few possessions. He tied a new kerchief around his neck and then stepped into the middle of the room. His eyes passed searchingly around the room, over the walls, the ceiling, the corners, the floor. He checked the lock on the door. It was cheap and easy to open. He returned to the center of the room and once more let his gaze roam around it.

He took a screwdriver from his duffel bag, moved a chair

over to the wall next to the door, and climbed up on it. Carefully he loosened the four screws of a large junction box and removed the cover. He nodded contentedly and began pushing aside the dust-crusted wires to make more room. Then he climbed off the chair, uncoiled the canvas belt which earlier he'd been wearing under his shirt, and removed bundles of money from its compartments. This was the whole sum he had collected in his disguise as a priest. So far he had not touched a single bill. At the time he had actually persuaded himself that he would use the money for the alleged cause. He divided the bills into two equal piles. One of these he pocketed; the other he carefully rolled up. He fastened it with a rubber band, stuffed it into the junction box, and screwed the lid back on.

Once again he returned to the window, threw a glance out at the street, another glance around the room, and then left. He switched off the light before going out, but left the radio playing softly. He liked returning to a room and seeing the round, illuminated dial of the Philco.

18

The streetwalker covered her beat like a sentry: ten steps forward, about-face, ten steps back, bag slung over her shoulder, hands on its loop as if it were the strap of a rifle. When the young man passed her she nodded to him, almost imperceptibly. He returned her greeting in the same mute fashion.

The street was livelier now. The hour when the nearby Prater closed was approaching, and the striptease joints were starting up for the evening. There were still fifty minutes before the first program, but the touts were already luring passersby with "Curtain time" or "Hot show." They seemed to regard the fellow with the clean chinos, freshly ironed shirt, and light windbreaker, hair still damp and neatly parted, as a prospective customer. He exchanged a few words with these men in their fantastic livery, dropped into one and another of the cafés, took part in a conversation or merely stood listening in silence, then went on to another café, asked the proprietor something, went over to one of the tables, sat down with some man; now and then he gave a burst of laughter, played a pinball machine, then again whispered a few words to someone. Once in the course of his wanderings he stepped into an Instamatic Passport Photo booth and pulled the curtain behind him. Then he resumed his tour, his prolonged zigzag back and forth in the same small group of streets, describing a circuit that was not very large.

Suddenly his seemingly aimless wandering was over. His

step speeded, he checked the street signs once or twice, and finally turned into a small street and entered a building by a side door.

Before him was a long, narrow corridor whose walls had once been painted blue. A single bare light bulb dangled from the ceiling. A medley of noises sounded at the end of the corridor: voices relaying orders, running water, the clink of glasses being washed, the ring of a cash register, and, more muted, music. A row of doors lined the corridor. The young man listened at some of them until he apparently found the one he wanted.

In contrast to the dim corridor, the dressing room seemed glaringly bright. It smelled of smoke, cosmetics, perfume, and the long, frilly, sweaty dresses that hung on a metal rack. The four girls barely had room to sit at the narrow counter cluttered with jars and makeup materials. The long mirror in front of them, which took up the entire wall, doubled the number of persons. Eight girls made the room seem even smaller.

The young man closed the door behind him. Only then did he see that there were only three girls—or six. The fourth at the makeup counter was a man—still a man, although already wearing a long, tight-bodiced dress, and with his dark hair taped down at the edges to keep it from escaping through the wig. The man said, "No men allowed here!" His voice was neither male nor female.

"Are you Sally?" the young man asked.

"Sally, the uncrowned queen of the night." Now the voice was distinctly a woman's, with a pleased and flattered note in it. "I've always known it—one day fame will walk in through this here door."

"I'd like to talk to you. Alone, if possible."

The man turned. He had dark, flashing eyes. Whatever he saw in the young man's appearance, fame or something else, he signaled the girls with a wave of his hand. They seemed to understand and left the room. The man who called himself Sally turned back to the makeup counter again.

"On stage I put them all in the shade," he said. "Did you ever see me?"

The young man sat down on one of the stools. He took the batch of passport photos out of his jacket pocket and laid them on the counter without saying anything; he was giving the impersonator time to respond.

"You're looking for a job?" Sally turned to the young man and studied him with eyes that despite their pasted-on lashes still seemed very masculine. "Yes, you might do. But we're full up. We only have room for one star here."

The young man indicated the photos. "I'd like something around one of these. I've heard you handle that sort of thing."

"You heard that?" The man continued to apply his makeup. He was certainly not much older than the young man. His face looked girlish, but his eyes were remarkably alert.

"I've been going around and heard a few things."

"New in this neighborhood?"

"In a way, yes. But I won't be staying long. Could be I have to get out of the city fast."

The hands were once again working over the face. In contrast to the man's eyes, his hands were the most feminine part of him, with their delicate fingers and long fingernails. It was impossible to tell whether the fingernails were genuine or fake. On stage his hands certainly would not betray him.

"All right," he said at last, using a full man's voice now, and a surprisingly deep one at that. "I'll risk it. What do you need?"

"What can I get?"

"That depends. A Yugoslav passport would be cheapest. Those Yugoslav sailors are always losing their passports."

"Riverboatmen," the young man said, smiling. But the smile did not linger.

Late in the afternoon, when he had set out before the two brothers returned home, he had still been undecided where to turn. As he walked through the city, he had been repeatedly struck by the big white directional signs at important intersections: Bratislava, Prague, Brno, Budapest. All the main thoroughfares that led out of the city pointed to the north or southwest. It didn't matter who used them; for him they were useless. He had suddenly felt as if he stood with his back to the wall, as if this city itself stood with its back to the wall. Whatever his reason for coming here—he had so far not fathomed it, probably would never fathom it—he had made a poor choice. At least this was one new lesson: never again choose a city that had an escape route in only one direction.

"I have to travel west," he said.

"How far west? Is Germany west enough for you?"

"It may be I'll have to go farther."

"Then ideally that means a British or American passport, right?"

"Right."

"Do you know what that means? Somebody has to 'lose' one first. Somebody has to 'find' it. Somebody has to bring it to me. I have to work on it. A lot of people are involved and they all want their share."

The young man took out all the money he was carrying. He smoothed the bills and laid them on the counter beside the photographs.

"I have this much to spend. I have more, but I need it."

The man in front of the mirror glanced at the money, then at the young man. "You're about—twenty-five?"

"Good guess. But anything between nineteen and thirty-five will do. I can adapt."

The man nodded. "I believe you. It simplifies the thing if we don't have to make too many changes."

"And I'm not choosy about the name," the young man said. This time the smile lingered a little longer. "I'll be content with any name."

"When do you need it?'

He took his time replying. Suddenly he felt strangely at home in this room, which, when you looked at it closely, had a shabbiness like that of some minor limbo where sinners were taught to abandon all hope. "Probably soon," he said at last. "I can't say exactly. In a week, maybe sooner. It sort of looks like sooner, but there wouldn't be much use my ordering it for right away. Or would there?"

"You seem to know the game." Sally lit a cigarette. For the first time he too was relaxed. He had finished his face; all he needed now was the wig.

"Yes, sort of. How long is the passport *safe*?"

"The first forty-eight hours after it's lost. Maybe twenty-four hours more, but then not so absolutely safe. I can guarantee you two days to pass any border. Of course, you can use it longer than that, but not at borders. If you're lucky, the loss won't be reported at all. Americans especially tend to go to the consul rather than the police."

"What kind of notice do you need?"

"Twenty-four hours is enough for me. In special cases twelve'll do if we're lucky, but you're better off counting on twenty-four."

"I'll come in time. Will I find you here?"

"Every evening. Where can I reach you?"

"I'm in the neighborhood."

The man nodded contentedly, as though that was the answer he preferred. He took the wig into his slender, feminine hands and leaned his head forward to put it on. "If you stay around awhile—will you be working?"

The young man had also given that some thought. It was always better to have some kind of occupation. Someone who stayed in a hotel all day long, who had time to sit around in cafés, attracted attention; people asked questions about him, talked about him. Someone who worked would be ignored; he came and went like everybody else.

"Yes, I'll be doing something."

"May I ask what? It's just that I'm interested."

He had also decided that, during the last hour of his circuit. "I'll be working for the Professor."

The man, or rather the woman now, turned around. The wig had completely transformed him. Even the eyes seemed brighter; they had suddenly become the inquisitive, amused eyes of a rather too loudly made-up woman.

"Really, for the Professor?" The voice was now Sally's. She took the photos, opened a drawer, and deposited them in it. Then her slender hands began counting the money, with rapid, practiced movements, thumb and forefinger cooperating smoothly and merely flicking the corners of the banknotes. When she was finished, she handed some of the bills back. "Sally gives a discount to anyone who works for *him!*" She winked coquettishly, deliberately giving the words a double meaning, as though she were now completely in her role.

There was a knock on the door and one of the girls looked into the room. Sally gestured, rose, gave a last look in the mirror, and touched up her lipstick where the tip of the cigarette had left a slight trace.

"And this," she said, taking the remaining banknotes, folding them carefully, and thrusting them into the deep decolletage of her dress, "goes where all naughty girls put their savings for their old age."

They went to the door. She waited there until the young man opened it for her. She swished by him, holding up her dress: Sally, Queen of the Viennese Nights, as it said in English under her photos in the showcase outside.

"Be seeing you," Sally said out in the corridor.

"Maybe soon," he replied.

He took his time about going back to the hotel. The humid, rather tropical heat was once again swathing the city. The room would be stuffy and hot. He had done everyting that was to be done; the fact that he had taken care of it all in a single evening gave him a reassuring feeling. In the past few weeks he had been showing weaknesses.

Those were over and done with, he hoped. If he could stay in this city a while longer—good; there was more to be learned always, everywhere. If not, he was ready for the next voyage. He had set enough canvas to move quickly into the wind. That was something he believed in absolutely, unreservedly: that a new horizon made up for all mistakes.

He found the streetwalker still at her post. He could not understand it. She was young, clean, pleasant and yet not obtrusive. Perhaps she was still standing there because she treated every strange man to her crazy St Vitus's dance, scaring him away with that eyelid pulled down, that dangling tongue, that twist performed in place.

He went over to her, thinking of his room, of all the greenness, of the pillow in the corner and the Philco with the glowing dial. "A tourist in the city," he said, "and not interested in Lippizaners."

She merely nodded and went with him.

He gave her the money Sally had given him back. She took it and without counting it tucked it into her white plastic bag. He asked whether she could stay the whole night, and she merely nodded, already undressing. He did not watch her as she did so, but before he crawled under the green blanket where she lay, he noticed that she had placed her clothes neatly over the chair. She was still wearing that single earring, a child's earring, a daisy.

He normally slept lightly, but when he awoke she was gone. He got up and looked the room over. She had rummaged through the duffel bag, and because she had found nothing in it she had taken the Philco. The windbreaker was gone too—probably to wrap the radio in—and with it the Yugoslav passport.

Really brave—this was his only thought. To slip out of his arms and out of the bed, dress, search the duffel bag, and get away with it: and he a man who ordinarily woke at the lightest disturbance. She must have sneaked past the night clerk with the Philco under her arm—*brave*. He was not angry, not even disappointed; he wasn't even sorry about the radio. She had had a much worse evening than he, tramping back and forth alone, perseveringly, and finally running into a man who asked her to spend all night with him and paid her no more than, probably, she ordinarily asked for an hour.

Of course she wouldn't be there this coming night, and that was something he regretted. The street would lose something. He wished he could let her know that everything was forgiven and forgotten and that she could come back and resume her beat at her old place, ten steps forward, ten steps back. He would miss seeing her. If you were going to call a room like this home, you tended to cling to such little things.

There had been no need to turn on the light. It was already daylight outside the curtains. He went over to the window, parted the curtain, and opened the casements. The street lay deserted. Even the smell of the frankfurters was gone. The air was damp and heavy, but then he felt a touch of coolness, just a breath of fresh air.

The river, he thought. The breeze came from the river. Someone had said that this city did not do enough with its river, or something of that sort. He had forgotten who said it. Standing there and feeling the fresh breeze on his bare chest, he felt for a moment that this was about all anyone had a right to expect.

19

The priest stood by the river. He had come much too early. The tattoo shop would not be opening until later, and so he had walked down to the water. From within the city there were only a few points of access to the riverbank; almost everywhere it was blocked by the railroad tracks that ran along the shore, by pumping stations, refrigerated warehouses, coal chutes, and oil storage tanks.

He stood on the bank, a solitary and rather forlorn figure in black, and looked at the water. The day was already hot, but no sun could be seen, only a light-gray mist overlying the darker gray of the water. Through it the river looked broader than it really was and seemed like something solid, permanent. Czepe Zuckermann imagined the water flowing into a sea, the sea into another sea, and that in turn into the ocean, the big Aqua, as sailors called it.

I might be a good deal happier if I had never left the sea, he thought; and then a recollection bobbed to the surface of his mind; something he had heard or read about an old superstition of Peruvian Indians: when a man was deathly ill and all other remedies had failed, he would be carried to the bank of a river. The flowing water alone, the Indians believed, would make the life within him flow again... Perhaps I should heve come here sooner, he thought.

He turned his back on the river and slowly walked back to the tattooer's shop. He was too warmly dressed for the day, with his black suit of heavy cloth and his black turtleneck sweater. In the past that would not have bothered him. He could no longer tolerate heat so well, he reflected; it was as though his body had not realized that it would never be going to Africa or any other such faraway place.

He had never devoted much thought to the question of how he was to find that young man. He recalled how hopefully he had set out into the city that first evening. And how disappointed he had been when he returned home, very late, without having been approached and spoken to by any such young man... Yes, that had been exactly how he had imagined it—it would happen in just such a mysterious way.

Nothing of the sort had occured. And from day to day he had grown more disappointed and disturbed. He had prolonged his nocturnal tramps, extended his radius. During the first few nights he had talked with old friends, asked questions; but then he stopped that. He began simply to wander around, more or less aimlessly...

He crossed a small rectangular park. The district might be regarded as a kind of atrophied waterfront. The rivermen from the Balkan countries bought clothing and other textiles here, and the shops carried almost nothing else. The fabric stores stood side by side, windows stuffed to the very last corner. On warm days like this, bright-colored articles of clothing were strung outside, so that it looked as if the ground floors of the buildings were made of fabric.

Czepe Zuckermann approached one of these buildings. It hardly differed from the others. The window was somewhat narrower and not quite so crowded, and a handwritten sign hung behind the glass of the front door—bleached by the sun. Some of the words could barely be deciphered.

Get yourself tattooed by the Skipper. Painless. By
hand or machine. More than 1,000 artistic patterns.
Any design you want executed.

It was just after eight; when he tried the door, he found it locked.

"Looking for Skipper?" a voice above him asked in a

foreign accent. He stepped back and looked up. A young woman with black hair was leaning out of the second-story window. She was wearing a red sleeveless smock that revealed large patches of bare, deeply tanned skin; her arms were propped on a pillow. "Shop closed for now. Skipper has a girl"—she laughed as though he might better understand the point that way—"and a boat."

"What are his usual hours?"

The woman turned into the room and said something Czepe Zuckermann could not make out. A man appeared at the window, a huge body in a faded blue undershirt.

"You looking for Zuckermann?"

"Yes." As always he was startled when the name was applied to someone else, and especially to his father—as though a Catholic priest were not only forbidden to marry and have children but also to have a father in the flesh.

"Doesn't he live here any more?"

"No." The man was now leaning out the window alongside the woman. "He's bought a boat. If you know him, you know he was always crazy about boats."

"A boat?"

"Always wanted one and finally got one."

"Can you tell me where it's docked?"

He knew all his father's stories. How he'd come by the scar on his hand—from a harpoon line on a whaling ship; how he had drifted alone in a leaky lifeboat through shark-infested waters around the Cameroons and survived to tell the tale; how he'd sailed forty times around the world—just stories. In the past his father had painted a few ships in the old Danube port; he had lettered the names on them, and that was all. He had never come any closer to the sea that that...

He had taken a cab upriver. The man had explained where the Skipper's boat was. First came the big refrigerated warehouses, then the old, now unused coal chutes and the tank parks disguised as coal bunkers—they dated back to the war and apparently were not considered worth blowing up. The waterfront road ended at the new winter port, but Czepe Zuckermann did not have to go that far. His cab reached the shoreline railroad, overgrown with weeds now, and the ship graveyards, with launches and skiffs so gutted that only the skeletons were left.

Here he told the cabdriver to turn. But after a short distance the driver stopped, shaking his head. "I can't take you any farther; my springs won't stand it."

Czepe Zuckermann paid him and continued on foot over the reddish-brown dirt. He skirted the bigger puddles of water from the heavy showers of the past few days. Around him was a desolate landscape of the wreckage of ships and parts of old small boats.

The sun had not yet come out fully, but it could now be seen at least—as a white, metallic hole cut out of the gray mist. In this peculiar light the wasteland, which most of the time undoubtedly looked utterly dreary, took on a strange beauty. And when he caught sight of the boat standing in the midst of a neglected garden full of weeds and rampant nasturtiums— the man had described it quite well—it struck him as an object of incomparable splendor; a vessel sunk to the bottom of the sea.

In the distance he heard the muted pounding of a scrap-metal yard. Out of the mist where the river must be came the sound of a ship forging upstream. The boat in the small garden was a chunky old coaler. The lower half rested on the ground at a slight tilt and was tarred black, the upper parts were painted white. An anchor chain ran slantwise down from the bow and vanished into the ground amid the luxuriant greenery. All that was lacking to complete the illusion of a boat lying on the bottom of the sea were the countless barnacles which in time attach themselves to the hull of a sunken boat.

As he walked on, he noticed another sound. Someone was scraping rust. This was a sound so familiar to him that he recognized it at once. It came from the other side of the boat, which he could not see. He ducked his head and walked through the passage under the anchor chain. Then he was able to see the man on the ladder that leaned against the hull of the boat.

He was wearing earth-stained white slacks and a white

shirt that was not much cleaner. Still, he wore his clothes with a natural dignity. His hair was gray, very long at the nape of the neck where it emerged from a dark captain's cap. He looked simply too young for a man just over seventy, too lean, too limber; but that was a thought that had come to Czepe every time he confronted his father.

"May I talk to you?"

The man dropped the wire brush into the pail that hung from the ladder. He wiped his hands on his slacks and spread his arms wide. "My precious son! My exceedingly precious son." He turned toward the boat deck. "Carola, Carola!" he called, and it was as though he were addressing his shout to the boat itself, since no one answered him "Carola, look who's here!"

He climbed down the ladder and paused there, facing his son. "Ships get rusty fast if you don't keep after them... What now— must I bend my knee? Must I kiss the *schmutzig* ground like an old Jew getting back his son?"

The priest was acquainted with that too. In spite of his name, there was not a drop of Jewish blood in the family; but with the name Zuckermann people always thought there was, and his father played along by using those bits of Yiddish. No doubt the idea appealed to his convoluted imagination: *A Jewish skipper!*

"What can I do for you? Slaughter a fatted calf? Or would a good breakfast do?"

"May I talk to you?" the priest asked stiffly.

"May he talk to me. You still ask the same stupid questions. Come on board. You're lucky. I just happen to be lying at anchor here between voyages. We'll have breakfast together, a fine, healthy breakfast, and celebrate our reunion. The way things ought to be between father and son, no? You've got time enough for that?" He went ahead to the gangway, which was leaning against the hull amidships.

Czepe Zuckermann followed him. The wood of the deck was dark, but scrubbed clean. Flanking the gangway were pots of petunias. The middle of the ship had been remodeled; a broad staircase led down into the hold. The priest saw rugs, a table covered with magazines, two bunks, painted red and hung with red curtains. In the upper berth a woman was sleeping. Only her hair could be seen—long, thick blond hair—and one leg that half dangled out opf the berth. There was bright-red polish on her toenails.

His father had paused at the top of the stairs. Hands funneled to his mouth, he shouted down, "Wake up! All hands on deck! Breakfast in fifteen minutes. Carola!"

The woman stirred, slowly raised herself, yawning. She sat up, her bare legs dangling over the rim of the bunk. Her face was hardly visible under her mane of hair, but it was evident that she was very young.

"Fix yourself up a bit. The priest is visiting us, my precious son. We want to make the best possible impression on him."

He went on to the galley. A table and a few chairs stood there, screwed firmly to the wooden deck. He sat down in one and stretched out his long legs. He was wearing old tennis shoes but not socks; the skin of his legs was tanned and very smooth.

To make some kind of beginning, Czepe Zuckermann asked, "How are you?"

His father made a gesture, stretched out his arms as if to say that this was an unanswerable question. "You know the proverb: old skippers never die!"

The mist had been steadily dissolving, but all the same it came as a great surprise when the sun appeared. It emerged as though from a thin white shell that was dropping away from it. Suddenly it was there: big, round, intensely glowing. The man in the captain's cap looked over at the river, which could now be seen flowing by very close to them.

"Sometimes I sit here early in the morning, and I think my boat is really out there on the river. What am I saying—on the ocean. The big Aqua, son! Sailors—they're the last inveterate dreamers, the last men in this world, son. Wouldn't you have been happier out there?"

He has not changed, Czepe Zuckermann thought. He will never change. Milli told everyone her father was dead, and whether or not she herself believed it, in her way she was right. For him, too, this stranger had long ago ceased to exist. It would always be an enigma to him why his mother had taken up with this man, for he despised exactly what she valued so highly: a regular life. Perhaps she had imagined she would be able to convert him. But she had not succeeded in changing him; he left her and went on his "voyages." He always did only what was barely necessary, and only the things that occured to him at any given moment, that suited his capricious temperament. All his activities were delusions pure and simple, one more impossible than the last. He imported leeches from Izmir, rosaries from Spain, toys from Hong Kong. He started all kinds of enterprises and quickly abandoned them. And somehow, somewhere, he had obtained tattooing needles and inks, along with a catalogue of designs, and so was able to open his tattooing parlor. That was the only thing he had stuck to with something approaching perseverance.

Still, once upon a time his father had impressed him: all those made-up stories, the stories themselves and the way he told them, his voice, his laughter. Czepe knew that his own love of the sea, of distant lands—his own delusions too, of course—had been instilled by this man, and they were as permanent as the tattoo. For that reason he had never forgiven his father for simply stealing away, stealing out of his life.

20

Carola had appeared on deck so unobtrusively that Czepe had become aware of the fragrance of the coffee before he realized her presence. He had been struck by her youthfulness when she was still in the bunk, but the impression was even stronger now. She was surely not much over twenty. Her long hair was gathered into a ponytail and tied with a ribbon. She wore faded jeans with flowers embroidered along the seams, and a close-fitting T-shirt that revealed a good deal of her tanned skin and the tawny hairs on her arms. She moved lithely and rapidly, barefoot, her toenails glowing red.

She gave him a nod, without saying anything, and began setting the table with those same deft movements. She poured coffee for the two men, unfolded a cloth napkin and handed it to his father. Then she moved off, silently, but returned shortly and sat down on the deck. She had brought a number of things wrapped in a cloth, and now spread them out before her. She began removing the polish from her toenails. The sharp but not unpleasant odor of the solvent mingled with the fragrance of the coffee.

His father had laid a hand on her shoulder, not possessively but casually, as though that were the proper place for his hand; Carola sat there at his feet, as natural as a silent animal. From the moment she appeared on deck, Czepe Zuckermann had felt jealousy; that bitter, gnawing feeling in his breast could be nothing else. And as he looked at his father's hand with the multitude of blotches from the sun and from age, as he saw this hand lying on the girl's delicate skin, he felt as if he were watching something altogether obscene.

"Sinful thoughts?" the man opposite him said. "That's the problem with you priests! You have the same sinful thoughts as every normal man."

The girl at his feet seemed not to be listening. As Czepe started to talk with his father, the priest too began accepting her presence as a matter of course.

"Have you done any tattooing lately?" He noticed the way his father looked at his left arm.

"You still have it?"

"I asked you a question."

"It would be a pity to remove it." His father leaned forward. "I'm not certain I could do that design as well today. The *Cross on Golgotha*—how farsighted of the two of us to choose that one way back then, wasn't it? And what pains I took with it. My hands aren't so good since that harpoon line..." He smiled. "I think I'll spare myself that story. There are sons who like it when their fathers repeat the same stories again and again, but you've never been one of that kind."

"So you haven't done this design recently?"

"The Crucifixion? Even if I could still do it, nobody would ask for it any more. Who wants tattoos these days? The British and American soldiers after the war were my last really good customers. Besides the ones who wanted swastikas removed. Business really flourished then. The Americans were so keen on it they even brought their girls along. There must be quite a few ladies in this city still running around with 'Joe' and 'John' tattoos."

"Would you mind answering my question?"

"You mean recently. A few railroad men still have tattoos done, and a few Yugoslav riverboatmen. No real customers."

"You wouldn't be concealing anything from me?"

"Would I conceal anything from my own son, from my own flesh and blood?"

"Is there another tattoo place in the city that could do that special design?"

"I don't know any. I think I'm the only one left in the city anyhow. And certainly no one else would use that design. That was my own specialty. I brought it back from a trip to Jerusalem. Only the best tattooers settled there. Greeks, Syrians, Frenchmen, even a few Jews. We all sat together in the Suk-el-Sakham bazaar..."

The girl had applied fresh polish to her toenails. She now looked up for the first time. It seemed as if she would have liked to hear more. But when he said no more, she leaned back against the wicker of his chair, closed her eyes, and raised her face into the sun.

"...Of course that's all over with. Why are you asking?"

"There is someone who has this tattoo."

"Someone else?"

"Yes. I thought I could trace him through the tattoo."

"Why are you trying to find him?"

"He needs my help."

"I see! My son still performing good deeds. Haven't you gathered yet that the world would be better off without those who confer their benefactions on others? Your mother was always inflicting her good deeds on me. Tell me, how is she?"

"I'm not sure what you're asking."

"With her everything has to be lasting. Permanence—that's what she loved more than anything else. Everything had to last forever, whether it was love or a suit of clothes. The one you're wearing does look mighty durable. I'll bet she bought it for you."

"I'd rather not discuss that."

"Of course not, my son. She's really worked on you. She fell on you when she no longer had me." He leaned back in the wicker chair. In spite of the many wrinkles, there was something childlike about his face. "And yet, we had some wonderful times together. Sometimes, not often, but sometimes when she would forget about everything having to last forever. Then we'd go out and dance. Yes, your mother and I used to dance whole nights through. We won a lot of prizes. I tell you, there was no other woman who could dance like her. It was an inborn gift. Dancing feet—that's what she had."

Carola opened her eyes and turned her head. "Who was she? Tell me about her."

He patted her hair. "There are better stories. I'll tell you all of them, better ones than this." He looked at his son. "Your mother and me—it was simply a case of destiny, but you wouldn't accept that, would you? You think everything can be made to take a turn for the better. I can only say, My poor son, there are too many men like you in this world."

Czepe Zuckermann felt his old hatred reviving. It was stronger than ever because jealousy was now added to it. He was sick of this old man who trotted out his old stories for the benefit of a young girl. And he hated him because he seemed to have been spared all the doubts he had to live with. The way his father lived, he should have been filled with despair; instead, he seemed to be happy.

The priest stood up. His father dropped his napkin on the table. The girl began clearing away the dishes. Tiny beads of sweat hung on her upper lip, and her blond hair gleamed.

The old man took off his cap, shaped it between his hands, smoothed down his long gray hair, and replaced the cap with a jaunty motion.

He looked at the girl, smiling. She made a gesture that seemed to belong to some mysterious sign language. She too smiled, so that Czepe Zuckermann felt completely excluded. She walked off with the laden tray.

They left the ship by the gangway.

"Something else you want to tell me about this fellow you're trying to find?" his father asked.

He said nothing; his hatred had silenced him—as had these two unreal persons who communicated by means of a secret language and arcane gestures.

"You came to me once—it's a long time ago, do you remember?—before you decided to become a priest. Don't you remember that any more, son?"

"It doesn't interest me to go over the past."

But the old man went on undeterred. "You were desperate at the time. I was proud that you were turning to me." He paused. "And I did give you advice, didn't I—if you recall it."

"I didn't ask you for guidance at the time and I am not asking you for it now."

"Oh sure, you weren't specifically asking. But don't you,

in retrospect, find I was giving you good advice then? To become a priest merely because you were leading a rotten life? Didn't I say, 'It's easy to jump ship but hard to get back on board'? Are you quite sure you don't need advice now from an old sailor?"

"An old sailor! A pack of lies and fantastic stories— that's all you ever served up to us."

It looked as if the old man were seriously reflecting on that. Then he said, "It was all I could do for the two of you." For a moment he seemed sad. Through the porthole they could see into the galley; Carola was there, though all that showed of her was the blond ponytail tied with a ribbon. The old man gazed at her hair for a while. Then he said, "How is my little Milli?"

The priest tried in vain to keep calm. "There is no *little Milli*—only a woman whose mind was twisted by your fantasies." But the question reminded him of what had happened the previous night.

"Aren't you going to give me some news of Milli? Is she still married?"

"She is." It seemed simpler to say that than to go into lengthy explanations.

The old man shook his head. "It's unbelievable—with such a father you ought to be able to lie better than you do." He seemed to regard the conversation as ended. He took a can of paint and a brush and began climbing the ladder.

"Could you help me out on one single point? What do you think could be the meaning of 'royal fish'?"

The old man turned halfway up the ladder. "Forgotten all your lessons? Royal fish—that's a whale."

"What if I were to say to you, 'We'll meet by the royal fish'? What would that mean?"

"My guess would be that it was Jonah—that's the mounted whale that's on exhibition near the Prater. The 'Professor' tours with it. There are posters everywhere."

"Where near the Prater is it exactly?"

"In the meadow opposite the fairground. Are you supposed to meet someone there?"

"Perhaps." He was asking for Milli's sake.

"Not much luck with a whale. Have you forgotten all that? Don't ever whistle a song on board, especially not at the helm. That brings on a storm. Don't ever talk about horses. That means bad weather too, and usually from the southwest. Don't ever go on board with a black suitcase or umbrella or you'll bring bad luck with you. But a whale—Jonah—that's really asking for eternal damnation."

He had reached the top of the ladder. Once again he reshaped his captain's cap. Then he dipped the brush into the white paint and wiped off the excess on the rim of the can.

"I know, I really ought to put on an undercoat of red lead." He smiled down at his son. "Come round again some-time when you're in the mood."

The priest departed without saying anything more. When he turned around, just once, he saw his father high up on the ladder, laying on the paint with long, sweeping strokes, so that a spray of white drops fell to the ground.

21

The fat woman was selling admission tickets, breaking them off from a yellow roll. She was smoking, and since she never took the cigarette from her mouth, the smoke occasionally wafted into her eyes. But this did not seem to trouble her. She merely squinted and tilted her head to one side, so that the rising smoke passed by her dark, frizzy hair. It was curly by nature, and no matter what she did to straighten it, it curled again, especially in this sultry weather.

Being fat had never bothered her. But the frizzy hair was the grief of her life, a curse imposed on her from birth. Nothing, neither her mother's fine phrases—'It's God who curls our hair'—nor the fact that certain men found this wild, unruly black wool attractive, had ever been able to console her. As a class of schoolchildren now approached her booth, she scanned the girls to see whether there might not be one of those unfortunate creatures with curly hair among them. She always let these in to see the whale for free. But as her gaze glided over the heads, she saw only straight hair.

The cigarette had burned down, and she tossed away the butt. Her father had always been nervous when her mother discarded cigarettes in that careless manner. His mounted whale might catch fire. But the daughter hated the whale as much as she did her hair, although the whale at least provided their livelihood.

"Forty-six," the schoolteacher said. He wore a dark-green

corduroy suit and looked distinctly harassed.

"Forty-six," she said sympathetically, "that's a big class." She shifted her weight somewhat on her chair; her bulk almost filled the narrow booth.

He looked over the children's heads, counting. "I'm always glad to get them out of the classroom for a while. How much did you say that was?"

She told him, and added, "Do you want the booklet?"

"No thank you. I can tell them all about the whale. It's a fin whale, isn't it? Or a sei whale?"

"It's all in this booklet. Age, length, weight, where it lived, where it was caught, how it was mounted..." Her husband, the "Professor," was annoyed if visitors did not also buy the booklet.

"No thanks. I'll explain it to them myself." The teacher turned to his class, nervously. In a loud voice he gave instructions to the boys and girls to line up by twos, so that he could count them again.

The fat woman left her booth. The whale lay in a wooden framework rather like a ship in drydock. Wooden steps permitted visitors to view it from above. There was an awning over the top of the exhibit and red and white striped canvas enclosing the sides, so that only the whale's huge head could be seen from outside.

She waited impatiently until the last of the children were inside the enclosure. She could never bring herself to look at the whale, could not stand its preserved skin, the mouth, and especially the eyes, which, small as they were in proportion to the animal's size, had a malignant expression. The air and the sun, but also the taxidermist's art, had changed its hide; in certain kinds of daylight the whale seemed like a huge plastic creature. And she hated the smell of it; it reeked of formaldehyde and the other chemicals that kept it from decaying.

She returned to her booth, although there was not much sense sitting there in the heat and waiting all morning. With a gold lighter she lit another cigarette, let it dangle between her lips. Here, at least, she did not see the whale; in its stead she had a view of the broad, freshly sown meadow at whose edge a path had been trampled by the many visitors. Behind her sounded the voice of the schoolteacher giving his commentary, the voices of the children, and farther away the first noises from the Volksprater, music from the autodrome and from the slot machine arcades. Otherwise business stagnated over there. The amusement park would not come to life until evening, at the beginning of twilight. Then the whale too would be illuminated and would draw in more visitors.

It had been in the family for a long time; her parents traveled around with their whale—throughout the Balkans, Poland, the Soviet Union, Germany, France, and Italy. She had been sent to a boarding school. When she was seventeen—she was forty now—her parents had an accident with the truck. Both were killed instantly; only the whale was undamaged.

And as things turned out, it was virtually all that her parents left her. Left alone in the world—a girl without parents and with a whale. Her first thought had been to sell it. But no one seemed interested in buying a mounted whale. Then she had met the "Professor," who urged her to keep it. He himself toured with a flea circus. And so, she thought, smiling to herself at the idea, here I am saddled for the rest of my life with frizzy hair, a whale, and fleas.

The schoolteacher had finished his lecture. Perhaps he did not know all that much about whales after all. Only the children's remarks could be heard now. She would not urge them to hurry; the next class wasn't due until eleven o'clock, and she preferred the whale with voices around it to the feeling of its lying there mute in its scaffolding. Usually no one came mornings except school classes and a few housewives. When she looked up she saw the man.

He was coming across the meadow, on the path where the grass was already trampled. He had his dark jacket over his arm and was wiping the sweat from his brow with a handkerchief. The woman took the stub of the cigarette from her mouth and tossed it away. She was surprised that a man like this should hit on the idea of seeing the whale, especially as he was alone and it was morning. He approached rather hesitantly, glancing over at the whale, which lay beneath its big canvas, and then over at the stall with its arched gateway which bore the inscription EUROPE'S LAST FLEA CIRCUS, then at the circus wagon, which was painted a fiery red and had Moorish windows. Finally he came over to her booth.

"Is this the whale?" He looked around again.

"Would you like a ticket? There's also a booklet that tells everything…"

"Is this the only whale? I mean the only one in the city? He pocketed his handkerchief.

"It sure is. What would two be doing in this city? One is already too much." She was pleased by the diversion, and she liked his manner. She had always had a soft spot for men who were shy and rather unsure of themselves. The Professor, twenty years older than herself, was such a man.

"Seems like the Viennese don't care much about whales," she continued. "Five years since we were last here and still business is bad. Of course, that's partly on account of the weather—all this rain the last few weeks." She was truly glad that their stay here would soon be ending. "There are better cities for Jonah, lots better than Vienna."

"This is the 'Professor's' whale?"

"Actually it belongs to me. But that's what it's called, yes. The Professor owns the fleas." She laughed. "They're more of an endangered species than the whales." She was wondering what he really wanted.

"Are the two of you alone, you and the Professor? No helpers?"

"Are you applying for a job by any chance?" She was a woman who seldom showed a trace of bad humor.

For the first time the man seemed relaxed. "I'm trying to find a young man—a young man with a tattoo."

"I see… Do young men still get themselves tattooed these days?"

"The one I'm looking for did."

"Can you tell me his name? Even a young man with a tattoo—if there are any left—would have a name, I'd guess."

"That—you see, that's the difficulty. I don't know his name. The one thing I know about is the tattoo. Thanks anyway."

"Wait! Why don't you give me some particulars? Who is

he? Why are you looking for him? Do you know anything else about him? I can ask around and you could come back."

"I... It was just an outside chance." The man brought out his handkerchief and wiped his brow once more.

"This tattoo—can't you at least tell me something about that?"

"It's..." He groped for words. It seemed hard for him to say, and finally he fell silent.

She encouraged him. "Is it something indecent?"

"Oh no, on the contrary."

"And what would the contrary be?"

"Really, thanks very much," he said, already beating a retreat. "There was just the possibility you might know him. You see, he said he would meet me here..."

"And you don't want to see the whale at least?" she asked. "Or take a booklet?"

"I'll take the booklet."

"Only if you really want one."

He paid, thanked her again, and left. She watched him as he walked away. The children, who had meanwhile come out, surrounded him; they closed the circle around him and the man seemed at a loss to find his way out of it, as if he were in a hall of mirrors that kept him confused.

The woman stood up. She gathered the roll of admission tickets, her gold lighter, and the pack of cigarettes, and started toward the wagon.

The heat was increasing rapidly now. She could feel the sweat accumulating under her breasts, where the band of her brassiere cut into the skin. On a day like today she always looked forward to the moment when she could undress and move around the van freely in a light kimono. Only at such times did one see that she was really fat. She chuckled at the thought. It was a lucky thing the Professor loved freaks. After all, he had grown up with them. His father had presided over a Museum of Anatomical Specimens, and later the Sensational Theater. He had brought to Vienna all the famous freaks of his day: Magnata, the Riddle of the Metropolis; the Snake-headed Lady; the Alligator Girl; the Dachshund Man; and the Onion-headed Boy; together with all the classical, archetypical dwarfs, giants, wild men, mermaids, and the bearded and tattooed ladies. Not to forget her husband's favorite, Sealo, the Seal Boy.

The woman had entered the van. The interior was decked out to her taste: orange fabric stretched across the ceiling, the walls were covered with green leatherette, and the curtains were heavily fringed. Evenings, when the wall lamps were lit, the room looked like a cave.

The Professor, a delicate-looking man with white hair, was sitting at a small folding table. He looked up, a watchmaker's loupe clamped into one eye. Before him lay his tools, tiny morsels of wood, thread, glue. At this moment he was fashioning two minute Roman chariots for a race between two fleas he had named Brutus and Caesar.

"Well, that was certainly an odd customer I had." The woman looked out of the window.

"Why do you have to sit out there? I've made some coffee with ice cream. It'll refresh you. You need something in between. Come, sit down." He was always very much concerned about her. "Who is odd?"

She pointed out the window. The Professor stepped to her side. The man was sitting on one of the benches alongside the meadow, his jacket beside him. He had tied four knots in this handkerchief and was using it on his head for a sunshade.

"My first thought was that he came from the tax collector's office."

"Come, rest. Why are you wearing a bra in this heat? Here, have your coffee... You should have called me. I could have told him that nobody's interested in the wonders of nature any more. Auto scooters, go-carts, calypso, and all that modern junk—that's what people spend their money on. But they've got none to spare for any kind of wonder, not even a flea circus..."

She had taken her seat at the table, before the tall glass with the pale globes of vanilla ice cream floating in the dark coffee; the concoction was topped by a mound of whipped cream.

"Remember the young man who crossed the border with us?"

He just looked at her, waiting.

"The one who traveled with us."

The Professor nodded. "Great talent! The way he announced the whale—magnificent. Believe me, he would have been able to do Seal Boy one of these days. A pity he left us. He was the first and only young fellow I'd have trusted to revive Seal Boy." As always when the conversation turned to this subject, he could not resist the temptation. He began the spiel he had recited many, many years ago, as a boy, in the Sensational Theater.

"La-dies and gents! Get down on your knees and thank your Cre-ator that you were not made like me—arf a man, arf a seal. As you see, this lo-wer part of my bo-dy is the bo-dy of a seal, the up-per part, as you see, is that of a nor-mal um-an be-ing..."

She laughed and thrust her hand into the back of her dress to loosen the clasp of her bra.

"He had the talent for it," The Professor continued. "I would have taught him the tricks." He looked up with an expression of injured pride. "I never talked to anybody about that."

"This man outside—he asked for a young man with a tattoo."

"A tattoo? Did you know about that?"

The woman looked at her glass, which was now almost empty. "He didn't want people to know. But I surprised him one day when he was letting your fleas feed on his arm."

"What a pity he left."

"He may be coming back."

"What makes you think so?"

"Why else would this man be asking about him?"

"You didn't let on we know him?"

She shook her head. "Tell me. Did he ever give you his right name?"

No...no. Sealo—he had no objection to my calling him that. In fact, he seemed to like the name. The tattoo you saw—what was it?"

Her face flushed and she fanned herself with her big hand. The chirping of a cricket could suddenly be heard; it must have crawled into the wood of the wagon somewhere. "It's terribly hot in here, don't you think?"

"More coffee and ice cream? That tattoo..."

"It was too dark to make it out. I just saw something on his left arm."

"Such a great talent. I even thought one of these days he might take over the whale from us..." They were always playing with the thought that someday they would give up the whale.

"Tell me"—the question had been on her mind for quite a while—"did he run away from something, or what?"

"Many young men are running away from something. That's normal. I myself ran away from home because I dreamt of being something grand, a real professor... Do you really think he might be coming back?"

"Yes, it looks that way."

He took up her empty glass and went over to the refrigerator. He put in two scoops of ice cream, poured coffee over them, squeezed whipped cream out of a plastic tube, inserted a spoon and two fresh straws in the glass, and set the whole thing down before her. He did all this with loving solicitude.

She thanked him with a smile. When they looked out of the window again, the man was gone from the bench.

22

This was the second time this morning that he had been surprised by the name. The man had come out of the gateway and had already passed him before recognition came and he turned around.

"You are Reverend Zuckermann, aren't you?"

"I am." After all those hours he had spent in the heat since early morning, Czepe Zuckermann was longing for the dim, quiet rooms of the convent.

"I've just been seeing your mother... We've found him."

The man was wearing civilian dress, a light summer suit, blue shirt, and dark-blue tie. Nevertheless, he looked as if he were in uniform. But perhaps Czepe thought that because of the police car parked in front of the building, with a uniformed policeman at the wheel. Another thought flashed through his mind—that somewhere on this street his mother's dog had been run over. He looked around as though traces could still be found after all this time.

"Can I see him?" He needed time to master his initial disappointment. His alarm also. But it was chiefly disappointment that they had found him after all the time he had spent on the search, after all his laborious and vain efforts. "Surely you have no objection to my seeing him?"

"He's already been identified," the official said. "There isn't any doubt."

The priest was longing for the cool house, for a bath, a

change of clothing, for the chance to put on a summer suit and a light silk turtleneck shirt.

"It's quite important to me," he said.

The official shrugged, stepped up to the police car, and opened the rear door for the priest. "I think I can arrange that for you." There was a note almost of servility. "I'll arrange it. After all, considering all the trouble you've taken with him, you have a right to see him."

Who had told him that, Czepe Zuckermann wondered. But then, in the heat of the car, which had stood for a long time in full sunlight, he fell into a kind of torpor, rather like an animal when it reduces the pace of its breathing and heartbeat and lowers its body temperature. The ride was brief, and when the car stopped he was not certain whether he was hot or in fact shivering with cold. He had scarcely noticed anything of the way they had come, nor did he know what the building they were entering looked like.

They had him wait in a room full of iron lockers, painted green, which were marked with letters of the alphabet. An enormous calendar was the sole adornment on the green walls. When the official returned, he was accompanied by a bespectacled man in a long white smock beating around the man's legs. What struck him was the peculiar smell, but he associated it with himself, with the rigidity he felt, as though he had been given a drug. The smell reminded him of the whale; it was that medicinal smell exuded by the mounted animal. The smell intensified when they showed him into another room—again green walls and those green metal lockers, but here everything was on a larger scale.

The official lagged behind. Only the man in the white smock accompanied him. He pulled out one of the lockers. It drew out from the wall on rubber rollers, making scarcely a sound on the green tiled floor—a long, narrow locker on high legs. Under the white sheet the form of a human body could be discerned, the feet, the head.

The man in the white smock pulled down the sheet. The face revealed was that of a very young man. It was a delicate, common face, except for the expression on it... But the priest did not yet seem aware that he was looking at a dead man's face.

"May I see his arm?"

The man beside him studied him through his dark horn-rimmed glasses, then looked across the room at the official, who had remained at the door and who only shrugged. The man pulled the sheet down as far as the waist.

The priest looked at the slender arms—very thin, very white. He could see no sign of a tattoo; there was only the mark of an injection and a bruised place on the inside of the left arm.

The priest shook his head. "This can't be him. He had a tattoo."

The official came across the room, his shoes slapping loudly on the large tiles of the floor. "What's the problem?"

"It must be a mistake," Czepe Zuckermann said.

For a moment the official seemed stunned; then he said, "Two prison guards have identified him. His father has been informed and is on the way here... I understand that it's a shock for you. All the trouble you took with him." He was trying to speak softly, but did not succeed. "This boy Oplatka was kind of a pupil of yours, wasn't he? Your special protégé..."

The difficulty of straightening out his confusion lay not so much in the information itself as in his inability, at least at this first moment, to overcome his disappointment.

"But how...." Slowly recollection returned. Oplatka, who either won or lost all his games, who never played for a draw. Now, looking at his face, Czepe Zuckermann could interpret the expression in those delicate, boyish features: the same expression Oplatka wore at chess when he had been careless for a moment and his opponent surprised him with an unexpected move. Now, in death, this expression was even clearer, even more eloquent.

"Are you finished?" the man in the white smock said with a definite drop in his voice. He seemed somewhat vexed about the unusual fuss being made over this corpse. And then too he still had to face the boy's father. Even though a stricken father was easier to handle than this priest. Was he a frustrated homosexual? Many a priest was. God knows, in his profession one could easily be cynical.

They had left the room, were returning down the green corridors, when a middle-aged, middle-class man approached them, dressed precisely in a gray suit. The police official whispered to the priest that this was the boy's father. That was a further shock. He had never known, never even suspected, that Oplatka had a father still living. The boy had never spoken of his parents. When Zuckermann gave any thought to the boy's background, he imagined a broken marriage: a nagging, quarrelsome mother, a father with whom no communication was possible, shiftless, a drinker. Certainly he had never visualized this concerned, grave-looking man.

"The driver will take you back."

He realized that as yet no one had told him what had taken place. "What actually happened?"

"What might have been expected all along."

The official was no longer taking the slightest trouble to show sympathy—if his earlier behavior had been an attempt to do so.

"What do you mean?"

"I'd rather not talk about it. He pulled the wool over your eyes anyway."

"What happened?"

"If you ask me, those tournaments were always a risky proposition. Especially since you persuaded the guards they didn't have to regard the boy as an ordinary criminal. After a while they forgot what type of person they were dealing with."

It seemed he had heard all this once before. He interrupted the official. "I'll be satisfied just to hear what happened."

"Oplatka took a walk." He snapped his fingers. "He must have planned it all along. There was nothing to it. After all, a chess player has to stretch his legs once in a while. He simply started running, and of course in that crowded hall neither of the guards dared to use their guns..."

"How did he die?"

"Killed himself. Oh, he would have done it anyhow if he hadn't been locked up—that's my opinion anyway. Prison didn't do him any good. The first thing that occurred to him was to shoot up, and he gave himself an overdose. We don't have the medical report yet. Either he died from the overdose or from an air embolism. Probably lost the technique in jail. Anyhow, we found him three hours ago. You should have been there..." He refrained from saying what was clearly implicit in his words: It's all your damned fault.

They had come out of the building. The police car was waiting with running motor. The exhaust gases hung in the hot air, a heavy, rather sweetish smell.

Zuckermann tried to recall the dead boy's face, but could not quite manage to. The features mingled with his own; they merged to form a face expressing utter perplexity. And he thought, How can I stop this, how can I avoid these everlasting failures? Can one kill oneself? It was really the last thing a priest was permitted to think, yet he had at one time considered the possibility, to the point of ruling out all the types of suicide he would never have been able to bring off. Loading a pistol, aiming it at his own temple, or, still worse, putting the barrel into his mouth, was unthinkable. There were people who could drive a car at high speed into the concrete abutment of a bridge. But he was certain he would be unable either to keep his foot on the accelerator or hold the wheel firmly enough in his hand. During his seminary days he had had a friend, a medical student, and it had occurred to him to ask this friend for a quick-acting fatal poison. But then the friend himself had died by suicide. He also ruled out drowning. The only feasible method he could imagine was sitting in a car and directing the exhaust gases into the interior.

The official had not taken the trouble to open the door for him. He stayed behind under the overhang of the building, in the shade. When the priest sat down on the searingly hot plastic seat in the back of the car, the driver turned his head.

"All set? Straight home?"

Czepe Zuckermann merely nodded, thinking, Where else?

23

She sat at her desk in a magenta dress, the manila envelope in her beringed hands. Kropik stood behind her, waiting, but that in no way bothered her.

She weighed the envelope in her hands. It obviously contained large-format photographic prints, and the negatives must be there too; but she was no longer thinking of the pictures for which she had paid so much, more than ten thousand schillings. She had had only the briefest look at them when the official showed them to her—excessively distinct flash photos of a young man naked to the waist, arm tied with a handkerchief, the syringe lying next to him on the floor—was it a bathroom floor? At this moment all she remembered was that she had bargained the official down to half his initial demand.

She turned, handed the envelope to the chauffeur, and gave him a red key case. "As we discussed, Kropik, this is to go into the safe-deposit box." He had access to it because it was too much trouble for her to run to the bank every time she wanted to change a few rings or other jewelry. "And cancel my appointments for today."

"The bridge night also?"

"No—we'll keep that."

She waited until Kropik had left, then turned back to the desk. It was good to have a man like Kropik around, someone thoroughly reliable. He was also a man who never questioned any decision of hers once it was taken. Of course, Milli and Czepe thought Kropik servile—and to some extent he was; otherwise they would not have got along so well for so many years. But he had a will of his own and his own way of keeping her in order. She respected men who could do that. It was the only kind of respect for men she had ever summoned up.

Milli and Czepe... She was always concerned about her two children, but this morning—Milli upstairs in her room under a nurse's care and Czepe off somewhere again—she was especially worried about them. As long as she lived she could help them, and thank goodness she was in good health. She rapped on the wood of the desk. Since she was a wealthy woman, the doctors were always finding something the matter with her, of course, but she refused to be impressed by their grave looks or the expensive medicines they prescribed. After all, doctors, too, were only men.

Nevertheless, it was only natural that she would die before her children, and the thought aroused her anxiety. More than that, it made her feel vulnerable. She had to make sure that her children would be able to cope with life when she was no longer there to protect them. She looked around her small study as though it must somehow offer proof that she could effect this.

There were no flowers in this room. At most she tolerated small arrangements of scentless flowers, forget-me-nots or pansies, never violets or lilies of the valley. She preferred to be surrounded by her own scent. For many years she had been using only one perfume and one powder, so that her special scent was in her clothes, in her handbags, in her handkerchiefs; she smelled of this even if she used no perfume for days.

In the middle of the room stood a large rectangular table, uncovered; on it were a telephone, a telephone book, a desk calendar with entries, orderly piles of newspapers and magazines. There were few books in the room, and the ones there were dealt exclusively with bridge. The secretary-desk also gave an impression of complete order. She alone knew what the drawers contained: coded notations on her bank accounts, inventories of her jewelery, her paintings and valuable articles of furniture; lists of her stocks, bonds, and loans; tables of yields. Attending to these ledgers was her favorite occupation. She took pleasure in the sight of them, went through them, worked on them, observed fluctuations, sold one security and bought another. As with doctors, she never took her bankers' advice. She listened patiently to what they recommended, then usually did what her own keen insight and calculation suggested. So far, her talent had not guided her wrong.

She knocked on wood for the second time and thought, At any rate that proves something. And there was an even better proof, right in front of her: the photographs of three of her husbands, joined in a single leather case.

Zuckermann's picture was not there. She had really loved that man. How he could dance, and how he had taught her to dance! They had danced whole nights through, the waltzes of that era. There was no denying it—he had been her first and great love, that carefree, nonchalant man. But when she had realized that he was dragging her down, she had—to use his language—cut the lines. That had not been easy. She had been forced to excise her love like a superfluous, harmful organ. Perhaps she should have gone down with him; that was exactly what love was, so people said. Perhaps as a consequence she had become the inflexible woman she was. But she had never been sorry, or at least she had no longer been once she reconciled herself to being old.

The subsequent husbands had been of no great consequence, hardly grand love affairs. Only the first of the three, a Hungarian landowner—a flier during the war, killed in a crash—had been like a second flowering of Zuckermann: a bold, life-loving, gallant man. The third and fourth had been solid, serious, hard-working types. And both of them, like the Hungarian, had been very rich. Each had left his widow a considerable fortune. Not that such money had simply fallen into her lap; she had had to fight for it—against former wives, children from earlier marriages, business partners. But she had won in every case, in court when necessary. Since she could not very well use three names—she had excluded the name Zuckermann without a second thought—she had eliminated the middle husband and now called herself Rosa Erdei-Melcher or, and this she liked still better, Madame Erdei-Melcher, without any given name.

All the while she had been listening to the sounds in the house. At last she heard her son. He used his key, did not glance into the living room, went by her room very softly. He was already at the foot of the stairs to the upper story when she opened the door.

"Czepe. May I see you for a moment?"

"I'd like to change first. I've been going around in this heat all morning."

"Of course, but then please come down here. I have something to discuss with you."

Czepe, she mused: he always has to change his clothes, twice a day, and never gives a thought to who washes his things, who irons them, who takes them to the cleaner and hangs them back in the closets. Poor Czepe, he really needs me... She returned to her desk to wait for him. She was not certain how much she should tell Czepe about the police official's visit, and above all about the photos. They had been taken by a newspaper reporter who *happened* to be in the vicinity and had managed to sneak into the boardinghouse room and take the shots before anyone could stop him. Or so the police official had said. She doubted the story, but that was really beside the point. All she had cared about was obtaining the batch of pictures. She would not show them to Czepe for the present, or only in a pinch, to remind him where his good intentions led; but she hoped that would not be necessary.

When Czepe at last entered her room—he had taken plenty of time, had changed his clothes and shaved—she saw by his exhausted expression that he already knew. She had been preparing to proceed gently and slowly, but that was no longer required.

"Who told you?" she asked.

"I ran into a police official as I was coming home. I went along with him... They showed him to me."

She stared at her son, for a moment profoundly shocked. "How could they!"

"I asked them to."

"Terrible, isn't it? Don't think I don't know how you feel." Perhaps it was just as well that Czepe had seen the boy, although she herself had a horror of such things. That had been one of the reasons she had first raised objections when he announced his intention of becoming a priest. A priest was constantly dealing with the dying, and the sight of a priest hurrying along the street accompanied by an acolyte had always been extremely disturbing to her.

But there, too, her fears had proved unnecessary, for the Church now administered the last rites differently. God knows she was against all these foolish innovations, but in this regard the Church had acted wisely.

"And don't think I haven't realized what it meant to you to be helping that boy."

He had dropped into one of the red upholstered chairs; he felt a great weariness. He did not look at her as he said, "I thought this was a way of doing something meaningful, yes... But it seems to have been the most meaningless thing I ever did. It's the result that counts, no? Isn't that what you've always said? In the end only the result counts."

"Why, Czepe! One is always given another chance. In truth it's what you do with your chances that counts. Remember the old days, when you were still children, you and Milli. I had to wait a long time, a very long time for a second chance. But when it came along..."

Only then did he look up at his mother. He was startled. Usually she never talked about her past. It had always seemed to him that she had a memory like a sieve, permitting all unpleasant things to fall through and only the pleasant ones to remain.

"Do you remember how we lived in those days, where we lived and on what?" his mother went on.

It was not easy to remember, here in this room, facing this elegant woman. At the time his father vanished for good, she had learned only one thing: to dance. And with that one talent she had carried her children through during the early years, working as a taxi girl in a wide variety of night spots, not always the most savory. She preferred working at night so that she could take care of the children by day. He could even fetch up the memory of once having seen her at a café table, beside her the telephone people used to summon her to other tables. And their one room and kitchen on the fifth floor! Oh yes, he remembered that very well: too hot in summer and too cold in winter, a miserable hole in a miserable neighborhood.

"Yes, I remember," he said at last, "but what's true for you isn't necessarily true for me. I had my chance. This boy Oplatka was one of many. The number of chances is not infinite."

She came over and sat down beside him.

"You know your main fault, Czepe? You're asking too much from life. Even someone with high ideals has got to see what the world is really like. To survive we have to be able to adjust. And sometimes we ought to simply think of ourselves. If we don't..."

"You talked to the police official?"

"Yes, I talked to him."

"Why did he come to see you?"

She hesitated and then said, "It's going to be in the papers, of course. He said he could not promise that your name would be kept out of it. The thing was simply too well known, he said—I mean the fact that the boy was your protégé. But at least there will be no photos."

"What does that mean, no photos?"

"No pictures in the newspapers. It seems some were taken... People quickly forget the things they read. A small item, a few names are quickly forgotten. But pictures are different; a photo attracts much more attention. But as I say, there won't be any; he promised me that, and I think I can rely on him."

"You always think of everything, don't you?"

"I try to, yes."

He studied her face. It was still a beautiful face, with that ivory skin under the sharply parted dark hair. But at this moment he saw something else: keen eyes, cunning and cold, that appraised people and their motives, life itself. The coolness and remoteness of that appraisal reminded him of the look he had observed in the eyes of convicts serving life sentences—and in the eyes of exceptionally pious persons.

"What have you decided?" he asked at last.

"What do you mean what have *you* decided?"

"I assume you have made a decision. Come on, out with it! A moment of rebellion, a moment of resistance, but in the end I always give in. I even became a priest because you..."

"It was your idea! In my opinion the diplomatic service..."

He laughed. "Oh yes, how could I forget! The diplomatic service. All the magnificent places we would go to. You would have run a grand household—I mean, really grand, with plenty of servants, plenty of guests, plenty of invitations. And how magnificently you would have done it. Everything would have run like clockwork. You would have kept everybody on the *qui vive*, in the house, the embassy, and me as well..."

"Czepe!"

"It's true, damn it! What a skillful and effective ambassadress you would have been. In some other country you would long ago have been appointed to the post. But as it was, you would have had to operate through me. And behind my back everyone would have said, 'But, you know, *she* is really the ambassador...'"

"Please, Czepe."

But he could not stop now, not while he was so full of bitterness. In any case, he knew in advance that his rebellion would not last long.

"But a man in the diplomatic service—that would have meant a wife as well. A diplomat has to be married. It would have been a tug-of-war between you and her, inevitably, though we all know who in the end would have won. So you were just as pleased by my becoming a priest. After all, that's a kind of diplomatic service, too. And no wife, nobody to question your decisions. All right, make the decisions, tell me what's to be done. I've accustomed myself to renunciation. So, a person should not have overly grand ambitions—isn't that what you said? Not any more. So then..."

"Try not to be cynical, Czepe. It never did agree with you. Afterwards you only feel more miserable."

God knows he felt miserable enough. He had never before talked this way to his mother. Sometimes he had dreamed of talking like this, and had thought it would make him feel better; but right now it certainly did not.

"You're right as always," he said.

She looked at the telephone on the table. "I have talked with the vicar-general."

"Does he know about Oplatka?"

"We didn't discuss that."

He knew he didn't have to ask any questions. She would go on running his life. He thought of Rome and of the vicar-general's visit, but both these matters seemed infinitely far in the past.

"Don't you think it might be a good idea if we left the city? At least for a while?"

"Is that what you discussed?"

"Not directly." Her hands rearranged the magazines on the table; the pile had been pushed askew. "Do you recall our outing in the spring? To that locality you liked so much, and the church called Maria am Wege?"

He nodded and waited.

"That beautiful old rectory, and the church, of course. A shame, the neglected condition of the building. But they do have plans for renovating the whole complex. They want to restore the old hexagonal turret to its original state, and put back its five bells. There is to be a new organ, and the worm-eaten pews are to be replaced. They've discovered some precious wall paintings in the choir; they are also to be restored. The old baptismal font dating from 1606... Am I boring you?"

"It is a beautiful church, certainly."

"Of course they don't have money for all of this. The parish has poured all the money it could raise into the old rectory, which was in such a state that no one wanted to live in it. They really have done a great deal with the rectory. Of course there are still some changes to be made—I can't imagine anyone wanting to work in such a kitchen. But otherwise..."

"You've been there?"

"I thought I'd take a look at it. I wonder whether the ivy shouldn't go, pretty though it is. Ivy attracts all sorts of vermin. But the garden is lovely. Do you remember the garden? You ought to see it now in full bloom. As I said, everything has been very beautifully restored. But they spent all their money on the house; the budget for the church is already exhausted... Well, then, I've dropped hints to the vicar-general that I might be willing to contribute..."

She has really been corrupted by all her money, he thought. She thinks anything can be done with money. He concentrated his bitterness, tried to direct it against her, but all that he accomplished was to think, And you, Czepe Zuckermann, are corrupted by the belief that you have a vocation—so tell me, which one of us is worse?

"It's something I've been wanting for a long time," she said, "a *real* house."

No doubt she had already thought out everything down to the smallest detail: what still had to be done, who would be given which rooms, where the bookshelves would go, the colors of the drapes, where the various lamps would look best. And probably she had already decided which pieces of furniture would be taken along, which left behind, which moving firm gave the best service. She was a wonderful organizer, naturally gifted in matters like these, which he could never cope with.

"So you dropped a few hints for him?"

"Don't you think it would be a good idea?" She did not tell him her other consideration: in a small rural parish such as Maria am Wege a priest could still wear the beautiful chasubles and embroidered surplices she had bought him many years ago, which he had never worn here. He might be able to say Mass in Latin, or at least now and then, for she had heard that the rural population still preferred the Latin liturgy to the modern one in German. But she did not want to administer too many shocks at once.

"'Maria am Wege'—you must admit it has a good sound."

"The post is vacant?"

"Apparently." She deliberately made the matter tentative, in order not to put too much pressure on him. Besides, she had another argument: "Of course, I'm also thinking about it for Milli's sake."

He looked around the room as though he had to take his bearings. I must talk to Milli, he thought; I must tell her what I've found out. Had she just imagined it all? Did the young man exist only in her imagination? In any case, he felt impelled to go to her, to talk with her. Poor Milli, how much more miserable *she* must feel...

"How is she today?" he asked.

"The doctor thinks she should be sent to a sanatorium." Actually, he had not quite said that, but she thought it could do no harm to suggest the possibility.

"There has never been any trouble with her since that time...I mean, she really is quite well. It's only that sometimes she's restless and unhappy."

"I didn't say I was considering a sanatorium. Of course she's staying with us. But the city is no place for her. She loves flowers, she loves gardens, and she's fond of taking long walks. She'd have all that out there. New surroundings sometimes work miracles."

"What did the doctor do?"

"Gave her a sedative, something light, just to quiet her down. And he recommended taking a nurse for two or three days, to have someone staying with her. But it's not anything really serious, and, after all, this isn't the first time." She studied her son closely. "You talked with her last night, after we brought her home. Did she say anything? You know she wouldn't confide in me."

"No, nothing special."

"I keep asking myself whether there's some man?"

"A man? Why, Mother!" He felt the same jealousy that had overcome him this morning when he watched his father and the girl Carola; maybe this was even stronger.

"She's changed somehow. Don't you think there's some man?"

"I wish there were," he said, but he knew at once it was a lie.

"It couldn't do her any good. I'm afraid, Czepe, she's living in a fairy-tale world—and there are some very odd goings-on in fairy tales! And then, the main thing is that being unhappy has become a habit with her. That *can* become a habit. Let me warn you against it, Czepe—you too have the inclination."

"You talk as if it were simply a matter of making up one's mind to be happy or unhappy."

She seemed to be seriously considering his words. Then she said, "I do think it's like that to a certain extent. There are people, and Milli's certainly one of them, who've discovered that at one time or another being unhappy can have advantages over being happy. There are a lot of people like that around."

"She has never demanded much of life, is that it?" Was he speaking of Milli or of himself, he wondered.

His mother shook her head. "She's always wanted whatever she could not have—and to my mind that is really asking too much."

"The way I have asked too much."

She reached out and touched his arm. "Out there in the country you'd have more time for yourself again. You could go back to your translations. I always thought that the period you were working on them was your happiest time."

He had risen to his feet. He knew she expected some answer from him, at least some kind of reaction that would reveal his position on the question, but at the moment he was incapable of any such reaction. And then, he thought, perhaps it was no longer necessary; in the end, things always went the way she wanted them to.

"You'll be here for dinner, won't you?" she asked as though the subject were closed for her as well.

"Yes. Although..."

"Oh, it will be something very light, in this heat. How about bilberries with milk? Kropik came back from the market with the berries. Unusually early in the season, don't you think?"

"This is an unusual summer."

"Yes. In town, of course, this kind of weather is always much harder to bear than in the country." She looked at her son's wristwatch. "In an hour?"

"All right."

She too stood up. It was always a surprise when she did,

for it made you realize how small and delicately built she was, something easily forgotten while she sat and you were aware only of her alert dark eyes and her voice.

"There's another thing," she said, "but promise not to laugh at me. I will not live forever, Czepe. And do you know what I wish?"

"No, Mother."

"It sounds ridiculous. But I've always thought I would like to be buried near where you are, so that I could always keep watch over you a little... Wait! You see, here in the city that wouldn't be possible. Where is there a church with a graveyard here? But the graveyard out there is right alongside the church; such a lovely place. I already have a spot in mind. Do you remember the plane tree? I always think plane trees are beautiful graveyard trees; they give a great deal of shade. And if this one were well pruned during the next few years..." It will be best, she thought, if I have the gravestone made during my lifetime; otherwise, who knows what names they might place on it?

Now that she felt sure that the two of them, she and Czepe, had come to a kind of tacit agreement, something else occurred to her.

"Leave it to me to talk with the vicar-general," she said. "After all, nothing is settled yet. In any case, it will be better if I handle it."

"I suppose so."

"I'm sure it's better that way." Her mind, forever bent on practical advantage, told her that there must surely be some way to shift the costs of the church's renovation to others.

24

The worst of all was that she could no longer remember what he'd meant when he said "We'll meet at the royal fish." Royal fish...royal fish? She lay outside on the small balcony, under the red parasol and racked her brains. Royal fish. The solution must be simple. Maybe Czepe would find out; but even if he did, she was not so sure that Czepe would tell her. How could she have trusted him with something so important, something whose true value only she could appreciate? How could she trust anyone at all? Could she trust her mother, who had stationed a guard in her room?

She turned her head very slowly, her eyes half closed, shaded by a straw hat drawn down low over her face, and observed the nurse who sat in the shadow of the room reading. She looked so harmless, so neat and orderly in her blue dress and starched cap. A single strand of hair had come loose and was hanging down her forehead. From time to time she pushed it back, as though she was brushing away an insect or an indecent thought. Nurses were never harmless and their thoughts were never decent!

Milli sank still deeper into her chaise. The fact that she had forgotten where David said to meet him was a greater problem than the nurse. Nevertheless, it was going to be tricky getting past this creature. Milli had already registered a few important points: the rather forceful chin, for example; the muscles of her arm when she turned the pages of her book;

the sensible shoes with flat heels. Each of the items meant little in itself, but together they indicated that the nurse could move swiftly and effectively should it prove necessary. No, it wouldn't be easy...

She could not count on tempering the nurse's vigilance by showing herself gentle and docile; that would be the wrong tactic with someone like this. But there were other ways. After all, she had had experience with nurses, had developed methods for dealing with them. The key was to decide on one's strategy and then stick to it.

She began to laugh, a kind of nervous titter. She had already exposed the nurse to this in small doses, since it was a cardinal rule not to let a new nurse settle down. One had to keep them hopping; never let them read a book in peace! So, whenever the woman seemed to become deeply absorbed in her reading, Milli consistently caused a diversion. She had begun with little things: turning around abruptly, letting something drop to the floor, uttering low moans and groans. But the best ploy of all was the nervous titter—nurses were trained to be alert to that, knew it meant trouble...

"Is anything the matter?"

"How can you sit there and read? Is that what my mother's paying you for? Read on your own time. You're supposed to be watching me." Milli pulled herself up in her chair, suddenly, with a jerky movement. "Suppose I were to jump. You'd never get here in time. That'd look marvelous in your record... 'Nurse so deep in her book that the patient was able to jump from balcony...' A nice entry!" She again produced that titter and watched the effect closely.

The nurse had lowered her book. She leaned forward, and her chin seemed much larger. "Listen, you. I'm not going to let you rattle me. None of your little devices. I'll read as much as I want! You're a nasty, sly...If you try anything like that with me, I'll..."

She's tough but I've already got to her, Milli thought. "This is only the start," she said. "It'll get worse and worse. You're mad at me already, aren't you? I can do things that'll really drive you mad." Giggle. "Maybe you'll be the one who jumps off the balcony."

"If that's what you have in mind, forget it. I'm on to your tricks."

"A little sadist like the rest of them? Don't I know that's why you become nurses? I've watched you: putting wrinkles in the sheets, keeping the dessert to yourself, and—oh, I know that what you enjoy most is scalding us just a little with the hot water. 'There, now we'll wash up a bit, Milli'—and pouring the boiling water all over us."

"You cunning"—the nurse glanced quickly at the door to make sure they were actually alone and nobody else could hear her—"cunning bitch."

Milli laughed. "Now look, you're losing your temper. Weren't you warned about me? They must have told you. They always do. But did they tell you everything? Did they tell you I once set fire to a whole sanatorium?...No, wait. It was the house I set fire to; in the sanatorium it was only one room." Titter. "I made a nice little fire there, burned my clothes in the old blocked-up fireplace. But you should have seen the room afterwards, all covered with soot. And my beloved mother! Had to pay for all the damage. She must have told you that. She always warns the nurses about my bad habits."

The nurse let the book slide to the rug beside her chair, let it drop as though it no longer held any interest for her. She stood up, and as she crossed the room and came out on the balcony, she kept her eyes fixed on Milli. But the look in them was no longer professional firmness; there was also the glint of genuine curiosity.

"Setting rooms afire," she said, trying to conceal her interest, "now, that's something you *can* call a 'bad habit.'"

"You mean Mother didn't tell you anything about that?"

"Did you actually do it?"

"Not just that. I set a whole house on fire, a big, handsome house with whitewashed bricks. How foolish to whitewash a house in that climate; too much west wind, and rain washing the whitewash off as soon as it was put on, so the house always looked shabby. And white petunias in the garden because they look so good at night. He was determined to have the house white; it gave him the feeling he was living in a regal mansion. That's the kind he was—always playing Mr. Big Shot. Awful climate and too much rain—it made no difference: the house had to be whitewashed, not stuccoed white but white-washed..."

Her thoughts seemed to drift away. It was the nurse who had to bring her back to the point.

"You said you set it on fire. Really?...May I?" She sat down at the foot of the chaise.

"What was that expression you used—cunning little bitch? Not a very nice thing to call me, Nurse, but *he* was a cunning bastard. We weren't married a year before he had another girl. She kept nibbling at him all the time, like a little mouse...And she had a real passion for that house. Kept writing him letters telling him how perfectly happy she'd be once she could live with him there."

The nurse leaned forward. Her eyes suddenly seemed wider, her stern mouth softer for she was no longer compressing her lips so tightly.

"That must have been hard on you," she said, encouraging her patient.

"Is that how it strikes you? My mother—you must know my mother a little by now, my loving and solicitous mother—she thought it was a pure piece of good fortune."

"Good fortune—I don't understand."

"Good fortune in misfortune, don't you see? My mother—she certainly has a cunning nature. She loves to manipulate, especially husbands. So when she found out—you know, she was the one who found out what was going on; I was only just a little suspicious—when she'd put the detective on him...She didn't like him from the start. She was against my marrying him at all; she said he couldn't be trusted...Where was I?"

"Your mother found out..." Although she would not descend to pumping, the nurse was prepared to help her patient whenever she seemed to be losing the thread.

"She got hold of those letters. She even had photos taken of the two of them. This was a wonderful opportunity to get rid of him and collect money from him, she said. She never trusted him, but he was rich, and that's why I was allowed to marry him in the first place. Now here was this opportunity!

She gave me careful instructions, told me what I should and should not do. 'Don't make any scenes and above all *let me handle the matter*.' You know, she'd figured everything out perfectly. Her lawyers and his lawyers, the arrangement they worked out, what I would receive if I agreed to a *quiet* divorce and he would have to pay later...Can you imagine how pretty it was for me?"

"Oh yes," the nurse said, seeming to speak from deep sympathy. "I can imagine!"

The girl in the white dress and lime-green scarf laughed.

"But I can be cunning too. I knocked all their little arrangements into a cocked hat at the last minute...by burning the house down."

It was hot on the small balcony under the red parasol. The air stood still, nothing stirred, neither the leaves nor the blossoms of the vines on the trellis. Not a sound came from the big inner courtyard. Even the pigeons, which ordinarily flew over the roofs and into the yard, beating their wings emphatically, as though especially difficult air currents prevailed in the yard, even the pigeons were gliding noiselessly now. High in the sky, the sun seemed to have spread, as if melted in its own heat.

The nurse felt oppressed by the heat. Her feet were smarting inside her sensible shoes. Under her uniform, her body smoldered as though it might burst into flames at a touch of air. The girl, stretched out on the chaise, seemed cool and comfortable. Not a drop of perspiration, not even a slight glistening, could be seen on her bare legs and arms. She seemed to have lost interest in the story she had been telling.

"The house—what happened to the house?" the nurse prompted.

"What house?"

"You were saying..."

"Oh, right, that impressive house we had. She was all ready to move in. And he thought I was in the city, because on Monday there was to be a last conference of all concerned: the two of us, the lawyers, and my solicitous mother. But he couldn't bear to wait this one more weekend."

"And?"

"I had the keys. I crept in and found the two of them in the bedroom. It was night, everything so romantic, no light, just candles burning..."

In the silence only the nurse's heavy breathing could be heard.

"And then?"

"Have you any idea how I can creep? I mean, really skulk? You could be sitting there, reading your book. I could sneak right pass you and you wouldn't even look up. It's so easy to sneak into a house when you're not expected. And how surprised they were—it was perfect! Both in bed, naked, and candlelight...In the bedroom we had those frilly curtains, yards and yards of tulle, just a puff of whiteness. They hadn't been washed since I bought them a year ago. A year in the sun—they were like tinder, dry as straw...Oh, how they burned! Oh, I tell you...The flames shot up, higher and higher. Everything was in flames...It was frightful—a sea of flames—like fire falling from the sky...Oh, the humanity...Oh..."

The nurse bent forward. She was suddenly full of sympathy, anxious to soothe the girl uttering these broken cries, sobbing, eyes drowned in tears. She extended her hand, but quickly recoiled from the mocking expression that appeared on the girl's face, and from the loud, high-pitched laughter.

"That gave you the frights, didn't it?"

The nurse abruptly stood up. For safety's sake took a step back. She was bewildered. What should she believe, what not?

"You mean you didn't set fire to the house at all?"

"There were beamed ceilings, paneling...And it was summer, no rain for ages. It burned until there was nothing left, burned right down to the foundations...Afterwards they wouldn't let me near it. As if I couldn't imagine what it looked like. The rafters charred, the windows shattered—they'd cracked and actually melted in the great heat. And that whole lovely white façade black from smoke and soot...I sure crossed up my mother's clever plan, didn't I?"

The nurse believed her. In any case, the story was plausible; it fitted this girl. Besides, she doted on such stories. This was the best she had heard from a patient in a long time. She could sympathize with the girl, given that husband. Men—they needed all the lessons they got! Tonight when she lay in bed beside her husband, she would go over the whole story, picture it to herself—transpose the scene to her own bedroom with the dingy, ancient wallpaper in violet and the curtains in the same color, and all those photos of locomotives on the walls—every one he'd ever driven—though why they had to be hung in the bedroom she never could see. He slept so soundly that he would never wake up before the whole place was on fire...

"So you whisked out of the bedroom and locked the door behind you?" The nurse blushed; sweat broke out over her body. That was hardly the way you were supposed to speak to a patient. "I mean, was anyone hurt in the fire?"

"I just gave them a good scare. Nobody was hurt, except me..."

"You?"

But Milli suddenly seemed exhausted by all the storytelling. She slid down in the chaise and closed her eyes. The nurse was disappointed, but as she went back into the room, she thought, There'll be more! It's just a question of patience. Bit by bit it will come out...

She's dying to hear the rest, Milli thought. That's good. That takes her mind off the job of watching me. Besides, I've frightened her, and that's even better. She returned to her surveillance of her keeper.

The nurse had not sat down. She looked around the room. Slowly, as though by chance, she wandered over to the desk. Aha! There lay a box of matches, and Milli closed her eyes quickly; she knew that in a second the nurse would look at her. Milli waited, counted seconds, and then, when she opened her eyelids a little, saw that the matches had vanished from the desk. The nurse was seated again, holding the book in her hand, but not reading. Her starched apron bulged slightly at the pocket into which she had dropped the matchbox.

I have her in the palm of my hand!

Milli was content. And she was genuinely tired from her effort and from the heat. She lay with closed eyes, and for the moment she forgot the nurse.

Milli had invented a game for herself for sunny days on the balcony: Making Stars. It could also be played at night, in the darkness, but it went best in the bright sunlight. You narrowed your eyes and squinted into the sun. Then, when you pressed your eyelids closer together, the red disk became darker, turned violet; if you pressed still harder, the first stars appeared, swooping like meteors; and if you used your fingers and bore down on your eyelids, you could make stars explode. They splintered into a thousand tiny particles, fireworks in an endless variety of colors.

She resumed her game, but today she did not see any stars, only weird little animals swimming in a sea of red. Swimming little creatures, strange fish, many-colored, prickly, spiny. She could not focus her eyes sharply on them. They moved with tremendous speed through the red sea, swimming into view from the right and within seconds shooting out of her field of vision. Or they came from above, their fins moving frenziedly, and plunged down to where the sea was darker, into depths her sight could not penetrate.

She did not mind that it was fish she saw instead of stars. That was rather a nice change. Still. You did not expect that you would really see exploding stars, meteors; you were content when they glowed briefly and went out before your eyes could really take them in. But fish were something else again. You wanted to see them from close up. You wished they would stay still at least for a moment, so that you could view them in all their color and beauty.

And then she thought again, Where is Czepe? Why hasn't he come to tell me what he's found out?

25

"There, just listen to him!" The Professor had brought his wife a glass of iced tea and was standing beside her booth. Darkness was coming on quickly now. The lighting had been turned on: four spotlights were beamed at the whale. There were also strings of red and yellow bulbs festooning the fence and outlining the ticket booth as well as the eaves of the wagon.

"He's got it in his blood. It's not the kind of thing you learn; either you have it or you don't." They listened to the young man's voice; amplified by the loudspeakers, it easily drowned out the murmurs of the onlookers and an occasional burst of laughter.

"...The fact is that whales, like dolphins, are some of the most talkative of all the creatures of the sea. Now, if I can have a little quiet here, I'll imitate their talk for you..."

The Professor looked at his wife and smiled as he listened to the low whistles coming from all four loudspeakers installed on the posts supporting the tent. At night, in the glare of the spotlights, the whale looked even more unreal than it did by day.

"Like a little something with your tea?" the Professor asked. "I could bring you a meringue." His flea circus was not illuminated. It would take a while for him to train a new generation of fleas, though the booth had been set up to add interest to their concession.

"The tea was just wonderful. I like it so much the way you make it with those peppermint leaves. But in this heat I hardly get hungry at all."

The evening had brought no cooling; on the contrary, the heat seemed worse than before. The air stood absolutely still, without the faintest wind. For hours a violent rainstorm had seemed imminent, and from time to time flashes of distant heat lightning lit up the sky. But the storm remained in the southeast, on the other side of the river. It lingered there, shifting back and forth, unable to cross the river itself. She wished the rain would come; it would clear the air. On the other hand, it would pour so hard that the meadow with the whale, booth, and wagon would be in danger of flooding.

"I fixed a beef salad for later. With a good dry white wine..." The Professor listened to the voice from the loudspeakers while his wife sold several tickets and tried to peddle the booklet.

"Did you tell him?" The question had been on the Professor's mind all the while, but he had held back from asking.

She sucked up the remainder of the tea through a straw and reached her fingers into the bottom of the glass to get the one red cherry. "I had to, after all. It would make no difference whether or not I told him. He's not the kind of person to stay long in any one place."

"We aren't either, are we?"

"In a way we are. We always come back to the same places."

"It would be nice if he'd at least stay until I open the flea circus again. With the fleas the whole thing depends on how you tell it. With the right slant, they think all sorts of tremendously interesting things are happening right before their eyes, while actually hardly anything at all is happening. Yes, I think he'd handle it very well."

"There'll never be anyone better than you."

"You sure you won't have something? The meringues are very delicate and fluffy...All right, I'll relieve him now."

"Maybe he'll stay longer this time," she said quickly. "I'd like to see which one of you does the fleas better. But I'm sure it'll be you." She waited until he had gone before she lit a cigarette.

Under the canvas it was even stuffier and hotter. The handle of the microphone in the young man's hand was damp. With the microphone he needed no special effort to give the spiel—he was out of practice, though. If you did the spiel regularly, you had more time to assess the audience, to watch their reactions to this part or that. Tonight he had to concentrate too much on what he was saying.

"...if necessary he can be very fast, even with his fifty tons. When he's fleeing from something, he can easily reach a speed of twenty-five miles an hour, and, even more important, he's a magnificent diver. Do I hear a guess?...What's that?...I said *deep*, really deep...*Two thousand feet?* That's better, but still not deep enough..." He noticed the Professor making his way through the throng of listeners. "We'll have a brief intermission now," he said. "Those of you who haven't yet bought the booklet, take care to repair this omission on your way out! The Professor wrote it himself and he's the one who knows the animal best; after all, he caught it himself. And he'll be here to take the podium and tell you that story himself right after our intermission. And please, notice the two exits." He thrust the microphone back into its holder.

"Very good," the Professor said.

"I'm out of practice."

"Still very good. Catching people's interest isn't easy on a night like this night, in this sultriness. The new part about the sounds was excellent. But let me give you one piece of advice: you have to take the weather into account. If it's chilly and people are threatening to drift off because they're shivering, I have Jonah swim down to the subtropics. On a night like tonight I send him into the Arctic. I do a bit about the blue, ice-cold water, and how Jonah lays his head on an ice floe to cool off. Incidentally, whales actually do that when they're resting. Many of them have been caught napping that way."

The young man looked around, watching the people, chiefly the new arrivals.

"I've made some iced tea; it's in the refrigerator. I'll carry on here for the next half hour...Say, are you expecting someone?"

"The iced tea's a good idea—thanks."

The Professor laid his hand on the young man's arm, detaining him for a moment.

"Something bothering you? The man who asked about you this morning? Can I do anything to help?"

"No, not really," the young man said. "I'll get myself a glass of that tea."

But he was uneasy, and as he went away he again looked over the crowd. It was not the man who had come inquiring that worried him. The Professor's wife had described him very precisely, and he felt fairly certain it had been the priest. And that was not the principal reason for his uneasiness.

When he had come here in the afternoon to ask for work and the woman told him about the man, his very first thought had been to "cut the line." This feeling had been so strong that he actually considered the possibility of leaving the city on the spot, without waiting for the new passport. There was no way to reach Sally before eight o'clock...

He stepped aside to let the ticket holders pour in past him. The Professor had taken the microphone, and the young man switched his attention to the recital. He liked the way the Professor worked the crowd with his fake French accent.

"La-dies and gentle-men. You may ask 'ow it come that we 'ave this majestique ani-mal, this roy-al feesh 'ere. 'Ow is it possible that 'e lets 'imself be capchaired by such a lee-tle man like me. This lee-tle professeur weighs a 'undred pounds an' 'e capchairs an ani-mal with 50,000 pounds of meat, 15,000 pounds of blobbair, 30,000 pounds of other organs, 12,000 pounds of bones...'ow did 'e do eet?"

The young man had reached the ticket booth. He smiled at the woman. "Can you really catch whales when they're resting their heads on ice floes?"

The woman had wound a gold band around her head to keep her hair in place. She took the cigarette from between her lips. He had often seen her answering visitors' questions with the cigarette between her lips, but for him she always took the trouble to remove it.

"I think that happens to be true."

"I'll have some of the iced tea."

She looked at him and then asked the same question the Professor had. "Is something bothering you?"

"Yes," he replied this time. "But I can't do anything about it. That's the worst of it. You know that feeling?"

"It really is a bad feeling." She hesitated, then went on, "You could leave with us. Just another three days. We're through with the place—these three months have been too long. I'll feel better when we're traveling again and just staying a few days in each place. The Professor would like to have you along—and so would I." She blushed slightly, but it did not show because the light of the yellow and red bulbs colored her face anyhow.

"It sounds like a good idea." But as he strolled toward the wagon he had the feeling that he no longer had that much time.

Why was he staying? He was through with the city, wasn't he? He had spent almost an entire summer here, had got as much good out of it as was possible without putting down roots. He could leave it at any time without a qualm—so why was he staying as much as an hour longer? The passport? Or was it because of the promise he'd made? Because he'd told a girl who'd given him a silly present that she could meet him here?

He climbed the narrow wooden steps that led into the circus wagon. He turned on the light. He went to the refrigerator at the back of the van and poured the tea into one of the tall glasses with the green, strong-smelling spring of peppermint and the maraschino cherry. Taking the glass, he sat down on the steps outside; it was too hot and sultry inside the van.

The darkened booth of the flea circus stood between him and the whale. He could hear the Professor's voice, muted, and occasional laughter from the public. Farther away music sounded from the Prater, oddly distorted, and from the other direction came thunder. Very close by he heard a piercingly shrill tone rising and falling. He remembered that it must be the cricket in the woodwork of the wagon.

He took a small sip of the iced tea and gazed across the broad meadow and the trodden path on its margin which the public used to get here. He would recognize her from a distance in her white dress.

It had become clear to him that the girl was the sole reason for his staying: no doubt it was Milli who'd robbed him of his ability to "cut the line."

For a boy on the island in the strait, a fishing line had been something very precious. You could fish from the pier with a short line, in the area that was dredged for the sake of the ferry that came in once a week. But from the pier you never caught much. Farther out there was a good spot, but you had to have enough line to cast over a shallow bank of seaweed and rock. That place had one major disadvantage; when you reeled in, the hook and lead often caught on the bottom. Other boys always lost a lot of their line when they tried to pull it out by force. When his hooks caught, he had reeled the line taut, then gone into the water and swum out with a knife. First he would try to dive down to free the hook. If he couldn't manage that, he'd follow the line as far down as possible and then cut it. Of course, that meant losing some line, but never as much as the other fellows. He'd learned early that it was better to cut a line that had caught than to hope to free it by pulling hard.

That's the way it is, he thought, I'm waiting for her. It's really only because of her. That had never happened to him before. For a moment his old self seemed to come to the fore. He decided, I'll drink my tea, go get my things at the hotel, and clear out of this city.

He had set the empty glass on the step between his feet. Untying his kerchief, he began shaping it into one of his little puppets. That was already close to being one of those habits one has without knowing one has them.

26

Because of the brewing thunderstorm, because of the threatening clouds and the flashes of heat lightning, he had taken a dark raincoat and umbrella with him. It was an unusually large one bought for him by his mother, who felt that such a big black umbrella was appropriate for a priest. But since it was not raining, the raincoat and umbrella made him feel like an overcautious old man.

Milli, at his side, had taken his arm. They made a strange couple—the dark-clothed man with his high forehead and thinning hair, and the girl dressed in white with her blond hair hanging long and silken, looking less like hair than some strange, fine-spun metal. Her hair was always like that after it had been washed, but even more so when the air was full of electric charges before a thunderstorm.

He had watched as she brushed it before they left. Again and again she had run the brush through her hair, for an exaggeratedly long time, so it seemed to him. He had felt jealousy because the intentness with which she did it was for another man's sake.

This was new. Never before had he felt jealousy in regard to Milli. Or had he? Sure, he had liked going out with her, liked the idea that people would never take them for brother and sister because they looked so different. He had felt good on such occasions; she looked, after all, much younger than she was, and he looked older than fifty-one. But even when she married he had never felt the jealousy he felt now; in fact, he himself had officiated at their wedding. When she returned home after a year of marriage, he had been glad. It never occurred to him that someday she might leave again. But this evening in her room, as she was brushing her hair so intently, that thought had come.

"Is it much farther?" she asked.

"You'll see it in a moment." He'd had the cab drop them off much too soon, in order to gain time.

"I'm terribly grateful to you for finding out. The whale—how could I forget? Something so simple." How is it possible to forget the most important things and remember so many unimportant ones, she asked herself. That's bad. But then, when she recalled the nurse, sne laughed silently.

"You made a tremendous impression on the nurse! Reverend Zuckermann this, Reverend Zuckermann that. She wasn't so nice to me."

"She spoke of you very nicely."

"Naturally. After I'd softened her up with all those stories. I bet I could have slipped out by myself." She pressed his arm. "Still, this way is better."

"I'm not so certain that what I'm doing is right. Really not, Milli."

A rough clap of thunder interrupted him. The storm appeared to be coming closer now, crossing the river; but it had seemed this way for hours. The flashes of lightning were behind them. Ahead of them lay the lights of the Volksprater, or, at any rate, their reflection in the dark, low, scudding clouds.

"Mother will hardly be pleased about it," he said.

"How's she going to find out? We'll be home long before she gets back from her bridge. I thought it was clever of you to wait until Kropik had driven her off."

"The nurse will tell her."

"What if she does? How can she object to the two of us going out for a breath of air in this heat? Did you find it hard to tell a lie to the nurse? Is it harder for a priest to lie than for other people?"

He was not sure what he should reply to that. Certainly it

was not harder, but it had different consequences. So he merely said, "You won't do something irrational again, will you—like running away again?"

"Czepe! Don't...misunderstand me that way. I didn't run away. You shouldn't say that."

"But Mother said..."

"What does she know about it? I was simply happy. What's so bad about that?"

He turned his head and studied her face, her smiling, abstracted face. Besides the jealousy, he felt frightened for her. He'd had time to reflect on everything that had happened on this long day, from the moment in the morning when he had walked along the river until that other moment when he stood before Oplatka's corpse. Now, barely ten hours later, he already knew that—great as the momentary shock had been—he once more had solid ground underfoot. Like his mother, he would always scramble back to solid ground. Perhaps from time to time it might be less fertile, more parched, but there would always be enough soil for them to strike root again. He was not so sure this was true for Milli. She seemed to be without roots, a plant that took its nutrients from the air.

"You'll like him," he heard Milli say. "I know you will."

"Look, Milli," he said, "you hardly know him."

"Czepe! I know him very well."

"To judge from what you've told me so far..."

She laughed, but her laughter sounded very different now. It was the laugh of a woman who was very sure of herself.

"But I've told you I love him!"

"Don't say that sort of thing!" He could not prevent his voice from sounding harsh. "How can one talk about loving a man one hardly knows?"

"I think you both will get along well. He has been to sea like you."

He seized eagerly upon this idea. "Do you realize what that means? Northing holds a real seaman for long."

She laughed again. "You're jealous, Czepe!"

"I'm telling you facts. Ships that pass in the night..."

"I've heard that before!" She laughed again, then grew

earnest. "I would still love him, wouldn't I?"

They had reached the meadow at whose end lay the tent and the spotlighted whale. Now, at night, the meadow seemed very large to Czepe Zuckermann, a vast rectangle. When the lightning flashed, it illuminated the green grass with a touch of blueness. From their distance the whale looked very small. In the morning the beast had seemed to him enormous and almost menacing, but now the entire scene—the illuminated whale, the strings of bright-colored bulbs at the booth and on the circus wagon—seemed unreal and toylike.

She too was now intent on the red and yellow lights and the brightly lit little arena. A strange voice reached them, the sound of laughter. Milli released her brother's arm.

"Over there?"

"Yes."

"It looks lovely."

"What do you find so lovely about it? A preserved whale?" He thought the odor of formaldehyde had already reached his nostrils, although of course that must be an illusion.

Her steps quickened. "That black thing under the roof—is that the whale?"

The heat was bothering him more than ever. He suppressed an impulse to wipe the sweat from his forehead. He felt he had to say something to temper her excitement.

"Wait, Milli." He groped for something, anything, that might hold her back. "The chances are he only said he'd meet you here to get rid of you."

He felt shabby, petty, wretched; but Milli seemed unaffected anyhow. She kept her eyes fixed on the site of the small show.

"It's just like him," she said. "I mean, to arrange to meet me at a place like this."

"Suppose he isn't here?"

"He will be!"

The priest felt very old, very tired, and jealous again. But this time it was not because of the man, whom in any case he could not really picture. He was actually at this moment jealous of Milli. Everyone thought she was pitiable, but she radiated more certainty and strength than he ever possessed or ever would possess.

"Doesn't it look romantic?" she was saying.

He could not imagine how she could see it that way. To him it was commercial and dingy.

"I'll come with you."

She shook her head. "That would spoil everything."

"I'm not leaving you alone..."

"You wait here," she said, very firmly. "I won't be staying long and I'll come back. That's a promise. Satisfied?"

They were walking side by side, but she was already a step ahead of him. He was still groping for something he could use to check her. Now he recalled what his father had said that morning.

"A whale—do you know that a whale means bad luck to a sailor?"

She tossed her head. "A priest isn't supposed to believe in such superstitions," she said, and rushed ahead.

27

"It's the same man who came this morning, isn't it?" He had wandered back to the booth after having his tea.

The Professor's wife took her time answering the young man. She had been expecting something, something that had been in the air like the thunderstorm, and yet now that it came she was ill-prepared for it.

"It looks very much like him," she said at last, "but he certainly didn't have that girl with him."

"That 'girl' is thirty-eight," the young man said.

She remembered the time she had found the young man sitting there in the searingly hot cabinet of the flea circus naked to the waist. She had been struck by how strong and muscular his shoulders, arms, and chest were, the body of a man accustomed to hard physical labor. There were two long surgery scars on his right side, much lighter than the tanned skin. He had not been aware of her, and she had regarded his body for some time—afterwards it seemed to her a very long time—with mingled shyness and desire, a craving so strong that for a flash she had been ready to fling herself at him, to make love with him...Of course, she had done nothing of the sort. She had merely stood there for a few seconds, asking herself what kind of women he slept with...But never, she thought, would I have imagined a girl like this one.

"Really thirty-eight?"

"Yes."

"She seems to be looking for you."

The young man did not reply. He took a step aside so that he was not standing directly in the light. The woman, who was keeping close watch on both the approaching girl and the young man, suddenly thought, He's scared of her. In the dim light his face had an expression she had never seen before—a curious mixture of hardness and helplessness. He stood there as if poised for flight, but also rooted to the spot.

The girl or woman or whatever you wanted to call this female with the mop of blond hair—no, it was not frizzy—was coming directly toward the booth. Her white dress covered a body that to the woman's eyes looked far too skinny, and the light-green scarf that dangled down as far as her thighs only stressed her tallness and skinniness.

A remark was on the tip of her tongue, but the young man suddenly regained control of himself. He approached the "girl"—the fat woman decided to stick to calling her that. She watched the two but did not see them exchange greetings; they did not shake hands, embrace, or kiss. The young man simply went up to her, fell into step with her, and together they walked toward the entrance of the brightly illuminated arena...

"Is this the whale?" Milli asked. "Can I see it?"
"Sure."
"Don't we need tickets?" She looked back at the booth.
"For you admission is free."
She smiled, very happy. "So you know all about whales too?" She spoke in a tone of great admiration. "Would you guess that I almost didn't come?"
"I was sure you would come."
"It was awful. Imagine, I couldn't think what 'royal fish' meant. I hope it'll never happen again..."
They stepped under the canvas roof and stood in the midst of the crowd that filled the gangway.
"It actually looks ugly," she said after a while, but she sounded in no way disappointed. "I mean, from a distance it looked much nicer; now it's simply ugly, and so gigantic. I would never have imagined it had such a huge head and such

nasty eyes. They really are nasty, those eyes."

"When they're in the ocean they're beautiful."

"Have you seen them there?"

"All the oceans are theirs. They've got enormous endurance, they're always on the move from the Arctic Ocean to the subtropics."

They fell silent in the oppressive heat that had gathered under the canvas roof. From time to time there was laughter from the crowd, but it was sparse and died quickly. The Professor was having a hard time with them. She had put her arm around him, and he had done the same. She drew him closer and said, "Can't we go somewhere where we'll be alone? Just for a while," she added.

"Would you like a glass of iced tea?" He felt glad that he had something to offer her.

She nodded.

He led her to the rear exit. The lightning and thunder now came in a steady succession, but still no wind had arisen and no rain was falling. They walked past the dark booth of the flea circus to the red wagon. He picked up the glass he had left on the steps. Opening the door for her, he switched on the light—the small sconces with pink shades and gold tassels. Exclamations of surprise came from her lips as she looked about the room with its shirred fabric ceiling, leather-sheathed walls, its small-scale built-in furniture, its arched Moorish windows. In the evening, by artificial light, the room looked even more exotic than by day.

"It looks like a big dollhouse." She clapped her hands. "Is this where you live now?"

"No." He had left the door open because of the heat in the wagon. "The wagon belongs to the Professor and his wife, the woman at the ticket booth."

She pointed to a second door in the background.

"That's a bedroom," he said. "This place is their home all year round."

"Wherever they go?"

"Yes." He went to the refrigerator. A television set was suspended from the wall above it. The young man filled two glasses with iced tea and brought them over to the small table.

He sat down in the seat alongside the window. When he looked up, he saw the meadow and the solitary dark figure. He considered whether he ought to put out the light, so that he would have a better view of whatever was going on outside. But he did not.

For a while they sat there silently drinking their tea. Familiar sounds surrounded them: the violent thunder, the distant, distorted music, the Professor's voice, the lazy laughter of the spectators. Then another sound began, a high, penetrating tone that was new.

"What's that?" She looked around.

"Crickets. One or a couple, it's hard to tell."

She listened to the high-pitched chirping. "It sounds as though it's right in here."

"It is. There are some types of crickets that live in houses, and this is one of those kind. It was here when I came into the city in this wagon. Apparently there's no way of getting rid of it." He smiled. "You might say they travel with their own cricket."

She listened to the chirping, which seemed to grow louder whenever they fell silent.

"Why do you keep looking out the window?" she asked.

"You did not come alone." He stated that simply as a fact, without reproaching her or implying anything.

"Oh, you mean Czepe. Yes, he brought me here."

"Why? Couldn't you come alone?"

"Mother wouldn't have liked it." She said this as though it were a perfectly natural statement for a woman of thirty-eight. "You don't have to worry about Czepe."

"Who says I'm worried?"

"I feel it. I know when someone's uneasy. I'm often uneasy and frightened."

"What makes you uneasy and frightened?" he asked.

"Oh, all sorts of things. But when I'm with you nothing frightens me or makes me uneasy any more. That's why it's so good to be with you."

"You didn't tell anyone you were meeting me here?"

She looked at him, shaking her head. "Please, can't you put it out of your mind a moment?"

"Put what out of my mind?"

"Whatever it is. Can't you be like me, perfectly calm and without the slightest anxiety? Take my word for it, no one knows about our meeting here. I wouldn't trust anyone else, only you. Don't you trust me?"

"I trust you. There's nothing more to say about it."

"That's better."

Again they sat without speaking. The monotonous chirping grew stronger, a thick curtain that shut out all other sounds. They drank the cool, refreshing tea; its fragrance spread through the wagon. Then she said, "I wish we had a caravan like this and could go wherever we pleased and carry our own cricket with us."

He looked at her in surprise, for this seemed the last thing in the world that would appeal to her. She belonged to a world which was not his, or, at any rate, no longer his; a world in which there were fathers, mothers, and brothers, and stabilities that had long been beyond his reach. He no longer knew whether he wished he were back in that world, or what he would someday want to put in its place. But then his surprise subsided and he decided that she fitted very well into this, that she seemed quite natural in these surroundings.

"Couldn't we have such a van?" she persisted. "We could drive away whenever we felt the urge."

He began to forget the solitary figure out there at the rim of the meadow.

"It's not a bad idea."

"Just the two of us. And we'll go wherever our fancy takes us. Down south when it gets too cold and up north when it gets too hot." She laid a small handbag, which could hardly contain more than a lipstick and a comb, on the table in front of her.

"Of course," she said with suddenly sober clarity, "we would need money." She leaned forward, and lowered her voice. "I have some saved."

"That would be the least of our problems."

"Still, a little money can't hurt. We would have to buy a van. I think I could get enough for that and a bit more. My mother has so much anyhow. I could..." The thought made her laugh with glee. "You know, she sometimes has very valuable jewelry in the house. We could sell it—I mean, *you* would know where to dispose of it."

Poor girl, he thought, ready to steal your mother's jewelry in order to run off with someone like me.

"I wish," he said, without knowing how it was the words crossed his lips, "I wish we had met earlier, some other time in some other place."

She nodded, serious again. "I know what you mean. Yes, I wish so too."

"I'm pretty sure," he said, "that back then I wouldn't have been looking out the window all the time and been so uneasy."

"Why is that? Does it have something to do with me?"

"No. It was…another girl, very young. She wasn't quite eleven when she died. I wish I could have met you before that happened."

"I like you the way you are." She smiled, but her seriousness remained.

"Maybe. But I liked the other one better."

"The boy from the island?"

"Yes, maybe."

"If you'd met me sooner," she said, "you'd also have liked me better." She pointed to her throat. "Did I show you the scar? I have others that don't show, but they're just as real." Again she gave that serious, somehow strained smile. "I had my first scars very early, and I'm always getting new ones."

A strange noise began, penetrating the curtain that the chirping had draped around them. It was above them, as though someone were throwing pebbles at the roof of the van. It was immediately followed by a flash of lightning that struck nearby, and then came the boom of the thunder. The rain became heavier, as though masses of pebbles were falling on the roof. The light of the lamps flickered. Then the rain stopped as suddenly as it had begun.

"Could you switch off the light?" she said.

He pressed the switch and returned to the table. The red and yellow bulbs festooning the roof of the van supplied enough light for him to see her face and hands.

"Does the lightning frighten you?" he asked.

"No. When I was little I used to run out into the garden

behind the house every time there was a storm. I undressed and ran about naked in the rain, with the lightning flashing. It was glorious; I never felt better. But they said it was sinful, like so much else in me, and that was one of the reasons they sent me to the convent school, to correct my sinful character. No, I was never afraid of storms. Watch."

She took a comb out of the small bag. With gentle, slow movements she ran the comb through her hair.

"Do you hear it?"

The hair made crackling noises. The comb attracted the fine, silky filaments like a magnet.

"See it?"

Small bluish sparks appeared around her head like an aureole.

She laid the comb aside. Her voice dropped to a whisper.

"I have a nightgown, blue, though of course it's not the color that matters but the material. It's nylon, or some synthetic—anyway it's very light, transparent. When I wear it on a night like this and go around my room in it, with the doors and windows open, it charges up, and when I take it off"—her voice had become barely audible—"when I pull it up over my head, I actually stand in flames." She added, "I wish I could show you that."

In the dim light from outside he saw that she was blushing. It seemed to him that since he had been sitting across from her in the dark, she had utterly changed. He had completely forgotten what was going on outside, had stopped looking out the window, kept his eyes fixed on her face. He felt very close to her and very like her.

In the stillness that followed the brief downpour, the chirping of the cricket began again. Suddenly he had the kerchief in his hand, and when he raised it again the puppet was there.

"Hello," Milli said, as though its appearance was not unexpected. "Hello, puppet. You're not afraid of thunderstorms, are you?"

"No... We've got a lot of rain, whole seasons when there's nothing but thunderstorms or steady rains." The young man's lips did not move; they were merely slightly parted. It was the puppet that answered in a strange, high voice that the young man had never before used for one of his puppets.

Milli looked across the table at him.

"What's her name?" When he did not reply at once, she said, "All your puppets seem to have no names."

"But I have one," the puppet protested in its strange voice. "I have a name. I do have one."

"Tell me. What is it?"

The puppet twisted its head and looked at the young man as though it had to ask his permission.

"My name is..." It hesitated.

"Surely you can remember it?" Milli asked.

"*He* knows it perfectly well, but he won't tell me, no matter how much I beg him to."

"Why do you do that?" Milli looked at the young man, and then at the puppet, which was chattering on.

"I know why. He's the one who took my name away from me. That's what happened."

"Not me," the young man said in his normal voice. "My friends did it."

"Sure, your friends. Your so-called friends," the puppet on the hand of the young man said. "You see, he admits it. At least that's something. And he still won't give me back my name."

"Perhaps he will if you ask him nicely."

"Ask him nicely...What do you think I've done?" the puppet went on, "I've begged and pleaded, but no. Sometimes he goes so far as to make promises. And then, when the time comes—nothing. Then it's the old story—he can't remember. That's been going on for a long, long time."

"Perhaps we can find another name for you," Milli said. "Maybe I'll think of a pretty one."

"I want *my* name or none at all," the puppet insisted. "He's tried that on me before. He offered me every imaginable name, talked them up, said how pretty they were, but he knows perfectly well that I want my own name back or none at all."

"But puppets are always being given new names," Milli said. "One day they're Molly and the next Dolly—I've never heard them make any objection, as long as they had a pretty name."

"Only he can answer that," the puppet said.

"Will you?" the girl asked, looking up. "Will you tell me about it?"

"Yes." He let his hand drop to the table. "I always thought I couldn't talk to anyone about it. But I will tell you, if only to prove I trust you. All these puppets...You'll have to give me time. It isn't easy to tell...She was a real girl, not one I invented, not imagined, very real...Her name was Thank Giang. In her language that means something like Clear River; they all have names like that, lovely, poetic names. Thank Giang, Clear River, that was the name on the ID card she carried on a string round her neck. She lived in a small village in no-man's-land, a place that sometimes belonged to them and then to us. I don't know how many times it was burned down and built up again.

"In the morning four of our men were killed in an ambush there. We set out to clear that village. I don't know whether you can picture the scene." He waved his hand at the room. "Telling about it here, years after it happened, makes it something different, entirely different..."

At that moment, as he groped for words to express what came so hard, he looked out of the window and caught sight of the car. Not that he was still uneasy, certainly not about what was going on outside; he broke off because he did not know how to describe that afternoon. Perhaps, too, he looked out of old habit, out of what had become an obsessional impulse.

It had begun to rain again and the car was coming through the rain with its headlights on, blue light flashing, but its siren silent. It drove right across the green meadow and stopped about where the dark, solitary figure stood, now beneath a large opened umbrella. The young man did not want to see any of this scene, and he went on rapidly, speaking hastily, rushing, because otherwise he would never say it.

"I killed her in the crossfire. Can you understand that—being scared to death...Twelve men we were, heavily armed, a few huts in the hot noonday sun, a village that seemed deserted in a flat stretch of burned grass that blackened your shoes. Twelve men fanning out but still not daring to get too far apart...How can I explain that fear? And all you have to fight down your fear with is the machine gun, your finger on the trigger, the noise it spews out, the noise that breaks the silence—silence that's the main thing that scares you...

"I could say I just shot at something moving. It even begins to seem that way to me sometimes. Or that I shot from fear of the silence? But that would only be a part of the truth. Because I see the girl running out of the shadow of the hut into the glaring sunlight—the flash from the gun suddenly glares even brighter..."

He saw the car outside from the corners of his eyes. Actually, it was just what he'd been expecting, what he had been looking for. But he did not react the way he would have at another time.

Never before had he gone so far, never spoken about that day—and never had he so keenly wished to go on talking. The desire was so strong that even now it took precedence over the reflex of flight.

"At first I was hoping I'd made a mistake. I did something totally insane, ran toward the spot—and ran directly into their fire. I made it far enough to see the girl. Her bare legs were right in front of me when I fell, and I saw her feet, her soles, black from the grass...They brought me back. When I woke up after surgery, I expected to be called to account; I thought there'd be a court-martial. But all charges were dismissed. My buddies went over after the skirmish, took Thank Giang's ID and ripped it up, and listed her as a confirmed kill. No, you couldn't possibly understand that. But it meant I couldn't be held accountable for her death. Regulations were you could kill anyone without an ID—that was called a confirmed kill, a VC kill...But I can't go on telling you about it now."

"Why not? It's horrible, but please go on. Were you condemned for it after all?"

"No—I was given a decoration—in the hospital—then I was shipped back home. Later I was transferred to Germany. And then—I was supposed to be sent back—serve out the rest of my enlistment there..." He glanced outside. "I thought, I'll never, never go back there..." He could no longer ignore the police car, no matter how resolutely he tried. For a whole year he had given them the slip. He waited for his reflexes to come to his aid to guide him as usual, prescribing the steps he must take immediately.

"What's the matter?"

"Look out the window."

She stood up and came toward him softly in her flat-heeled shoes. He too had stood up. He put a hand on her shoulder; with his other hand he pointed outside.

"You see the patrol car?"

The lightning, the thunder and fresh torrents of rain drowned out her reply. A violent gust of wind slammed the door of the caravan. During the next few minutes the two of them looked silently out of the window. In the bright beams from the headlights of the police car the long grass, laid flat by the wind, looked like a turbulent sea of an almost unnatural green color. A policeman got out of the car, and he actually looked as if he were standing in the water. The darkly clad figure of the priest approached him. They talked.

"That's your brother, isn't it?"

"Yes, that's Czepe. What does it all mean?"

"It's a police car."

"I see that. But what does it mean?" She pressed her face against the glass, then straightened up and looked at the young man.

She was, he decided, surprised, but showed no trace of alarm. Her face and her whole manner reflected the quick thinking and calm resolution which should have been his. And it was she who voiced what he normally would have thought.

"We'll get away. It's easy, in the darkness and in this weather. They'll never catch us."

She had said "we" as though that were utterly natural, and of course she was right. They had enough time. Nobody, aside from the Professor's wife, knew where they were at this moment. In the darkness, so close to the Prater with its many amusement spots and so close to the city, escape would be easy. He might even pick up his bag and money from the hotel. But there was first the question: How had they been able to locate him? If he knew that, he would be able to think out the next steps.

"Keep close to me," he said.

"You will take me along?"

He did not reply. He went to the door, held it open, and let her precede him. Already down the steps, he remembered that she had forgotten her bag. He went back and recovered it from the small table. He saw that the kerchief was still lying there, but he left that behind.

28

The storm had finally crossed the river and was concentrated above the island. Lightning and thunder came steadily in rapid series, and the temperature dropped precipitately. It not only rained, it hailed as though pieces of metal were falling from the sky. The icy granules formed large white patches on the green grass of the meadow.

Czepe Zuckermann had put on his raincoat, and in his haste had buttoned it wrongly. He was holding the umbrella high above his head. The rain hammered at the silk dome, ran down the sides, and splashed up from the softened ground. In spite of the size of his umbrella, his shoes and trouser legs were already soaked. But he seemed unaware of this. He had been waiting anxiously for Milli's return, feeling again the strong jealousy. The two had disappeared in the illuminated arena. What were they doing there for such a long time? At least half an hour must have passed. So when the police car had come across the meadow and stopped near him, and one of the patrolmen got out, Czepe Zuckermann had been relieved.

The policeman had put on a plastic rain cape. His cap also had a plastic cover. He had hesitated because just then the rain suddenly intensified. But then Czepe Zuckermann heard him say to his mate, who had stayed in the car, "I'll have a look. I just might be lucky."

"Want me along?"

"Bad enough if one of us gets wet."

Czepe Zuckermann addressed him, relieved to be able to confide in someone at last.

"She's over there with him!" He pointed toward the illuminated arena; the rain running down the umbrella soaked the sleeve of his extended arm.

"What do you mean, *she's* over there with him?" The policeman, an elderly man whose lined face looked worn from lack of sleep, stared in surprise at this fellow standing there with his outsize umbrella.

"My sister. She's there with him...She should have been back long ago. He's holding her."

"Holding her?"

"He must be. Otherwise she would have been back long ago; she promised. He must be holding her, he's capable of it..." He felt the jealousy like a real pain.

The policeman was now standing in the midst of the cloudburst and, reluctant to become soaked to the skin, he scurried back to the car. Still uncertain, still considering, he leaned in through the window. Water ran down the back of his neck, and maybe it was that that decided him. He said, "This looks more serious than I figured. He's holding a girl; you'd better call for support." He wrenched open the door and ducked inside, out of the rain.

And so they continued to wait, the priest outside under his umbrella, the two policemen in their car, the side window rolled down, police radio switched on. They watched the arena where the whale was being exhibited, though they could not see much because the windshield wipers did not keep up with the downpour and the glass was misting inside. From time to time they wiped it clear. At last the headlights of another patrol car appeared in their rearview mirror.

Water spurted from its tires as it traversed the wet meadow and stopped beside the waiting car.

The young man and the girl were standing under the tent roof near the main entrance. The audience had divided into two groups when the rainstorm began. Some deserted the whale, jumping over rivulets and running toward the street in the hope of finding a cab, or fleeing through puddles and mud toward the nearby restaurants of the Prater. The others preferred to stay, crowded under the roof of the tent.

So much water had accumulated on the canvas that it drooped low in the center. The Professor—he had first conducted his wife to the wagon under an umbrella—was trying to raise the tent roof with a pole, so that the water would run off. It poured in streams over the sides and splashed on the ground, forcing the onlookers to press even closer together.

It was a hopeless struggle to wage against those masses of water. The tent roof kept filling up, and at last the little man with his pole appeared to realize that. Perhaps, too, he had realized that the whale was in even greater danger from the spectators, who were pressing nearer and nearer to it. Two of the spotlights had been put out by the lightning, but the public-address system was still functioning. Suddenly the Professor's voice was heard from the loudspeakers, hasty and pleading.

"Please, la-dies and gentle-men, please do not press so close. Please be sens-ible! This whale is ver-ry ver-ry prec-i-ous."

Whether from habit or momentary excitement, he continued to use his peculiar accent.

"Please be sens-ible!"

For a moment Milli involuntarily smiled, but then she said gravely, "What are we waiting for? We had better go."

The whole time he had had eyes only for what was going on farther out on the meadow. The young man had observed the second car approaching, and now he looked at the girl. They had made a quick dash for it, but the short stretch from the caravan to this spot had sufficed to soak them to the skin. Her filmy white dress was sticking to her skin, and he saw her body as if she were naked, this extraordinarily slender body of hers. The long green scarf hung around her neck soaked, like a twisted rope.

"Please," she said again, "please, let's go."

"Where can we go?"

"You surely know better than I."

He thought of the green room in the hotel, of the pillow on the bed, and for a moment all that existed was the craving to take her there, to hold her tightly, to hold this wet body in his arms.

It was as if she had intercepted his thoughts, for she said, "I'll go anywhere with you." Her hair dangled down on both sides of her face. Her face was wet, and she looked at him, expectant and smiling. "Anywhere at all..."

I have to find out, he thought. First I have to find out! I must make certain. He turned around.

The rain had let up somewhat, and the doors of the police cars were now open. The men were getting out; he counted four of them. But he was not so much watching the policemen as the two dark vehicles, as though they emanated a particular fascination. From this distance, with their headlights, their flickering blue lights, and the wide-open doors, the police cars looked like monstrously large insects. The doors were their wings, and he found it quite conceivable that in a moment these would begin beating violently, with a thunderous buzzing noise, to lift the heavy bodies into the air.

He wondered whether Milli were feeling the same way, whether she understood the emotions that the sight of the vehicles aroused in him. Could she guess these thoughts also? He needed some kind of proof that he could trust her, and this, he thought, would be good proof.

"Look at the police cars," he said.

"I've been watching them all the time. They look like—birds, like dangerous birds...Please, what are we waiting for?"

He turned around, and because she had said that and because he could see her white face under the flashes of lightning, and because she was looking at him now with such desperate hope, he again thought that all he had to do was to take her in his arms and lead her away. *What other proof should I expect her to give me?* But the words that came from his lips were: "You really talked to no one else about it?"

"No."

"Then how come they tracked me down? It's taken you three weeks, and they track me down in one day. Isn't that odd?"

He hated himself for voicing this charge, but he could not hold it back.

She did not reply. Her head drooped as though her wet hair had suddenly become too heavy for her.

"I was careful, very careful. And still they track me down. After one day! That's never happened, not once this whole year. It's impossible unless..."

"Please—don't say it, please..."

"Unless somebody tipped them off. And you're the only person..."

"David..."

"The only person who knew." Only then did he realize that she could not have known about the hotel.

Her lips parted, but no words came. Her mouth remained open; her hand went to her cheek as though her face had been slapped. He saw her face before him: the crumpled face of a child, the pain, but above all the astonishment at the blow. It was not just anyone who had inflicted it, not some stranger, but the man she had trusted, who had still trusted her a moment before, who then struck her out of a clear sky.

"Be sens-ible, please..."

The world was no longer a place where one could live securely. It had seemed that way only for a moment. Only for a moment of lovely illusion...

"Oh, David..." Had she said that or not? She began running, running away from him.

He watched her go without stirring. The white figure darted through the rain. She halted once because she had lost a shoe in the soft muck that the meadow had become. Then she ran on, toward the men at their vehicles, toward the figure standing under the big umbrella.

The voice on the loudspeakers fell silent. Suddenly the Professor appeared beside the young man, exhausted, resigned. "The way people behave..." He apparently became aware of the police cars. "What's up—is this cavalcade in your honor?"

"I assume it is."

The thin, stooped figure came to life. "What are you waiting for? Get going! I'll be able to delay them. Send me a message where I can reach you and I'll let you know when we're leaving the city. I'll take care that we move at night.

Scoot!" When the young man did not react, he said, "Let me have that, I'll take care of it for you."

The young man looked at Milli's small white bag, which he was still holding.

"Thanks," he said, "thanks a lot for everything. I hope nothing happened to the whale."

"What's the idea? Are you giving up?"

The young man stepped out from under the tent roof. Very slowly he walked through the rain, which had begun to slacken. His thoughts, fixed in his mind, were still the same: I have to find out for certain.

She was still there when he reached the cars and the waiting police. The priest, her brother Czepe—what a strange name—had taken her under the big black umbrella and put an arm around her. She pressed against him, her face white, holding one shoe.

Altogether, it was an almost absurd scene: this strange brother-and-sister pair, the two cars with their spinning blue lights, the uniformed men with dripping coats and caps, and the young man, the object of this whole action, who was now coming forward to them, voluntarily surrendering. The whole fuss was so disproportionate, so inappropriate, that Czepe Zuckermann interposed.

"May I talk to him?"

"Talk to him?"

The police officer was also troubled by the scene; he, after all, had summoned the second car. It was his fault that all of them were standing in the rain, dripping wet, for no reason at all it now appeared.

"Go ahead and talk."

Zuckermann pressed his umbrella into Milli's hand. His hair, which had been dry up to this point, became wet as he stepped forward to meet the young man—with the most contradictory emotions, only one of which he could define clearly because it was thrusting all the others aside: his burning jealousy.

He was now seeing him for the first time—this fellow who had occupied his thoughts for so long. The khaki shirt sticking to the young man's skin. Zuckermann was tempted to put out his hand, to feel the muscles that showed under the shirt. That only intensified his jealousy. He imagined Milli in this man's arms, her frail body yielding willingly to him. For a moment he clutched at this image, tried to enlarge on it—but it did not last. It was already fading; suddenly it no longer mattered.

"Can I help you?" The words fell naturally from his lips. Why not? After all, he was a priest. And he even felt a sudden hope rising within him.

"If you need my help..."

Had the young man understood the words at all? He seemed rather to be listening intently to the general noises—the incomprehensible squawking of the police radio, the squeak of the windshield wipers, the music from the Prater in the distance, the rain which was producing all kinds of sounds, and only lastly this voice—as though he were not at all sure which of the sounds really concerned him.

"Are you sure there's nothing I can do for you?" The priest's voice sounded imploring.

"Are you Czepe? Milli's brother?"

"Yes."

"What kind of name is that, Czepe?"

"Properly it's Stephan, but once you've been called Czepe..."

Was the young man smiling?

"I saw you yesterday. That was you, wasn't it, last night in the Second District searching for someone?"

"Yes, that was probably me."

"The way you walked—have you been to sea?"

Zuckermann nodded. "That was years ago...I wouldn't have thought it still showed."

"That sort of thing sticks. Once a sailor, always a sailor. That's what they say, anyhow."

"I suppose so."

It was ridiculous, Czepe Zuckermann thought, that none of the many things he had wanted to say now occurred to him. During those nights of searching, on his long tramps through the city, he had imagined long conversations, formulated questions and answers; but because this scene was so different from anything he had pictured, he could not find the starting point. It had been so simple during those nights; he, the genuine priest, and this misled young man. Now he felt as if he himself were the false priest.

"What sort of ships?" the young man was asking.

"Freighters."

The young man smiled again, more freely now. "Freighters are the lifeblood of shipping."

"Oh, they certainly are." It felt natural to be talking like this.

"What lines?"

"Mostly Italian."

"I shipped on Italian boats only a couple of times," the young man said. "Too much spaghetti, but good captains. And not too much painting. 'The fore hatchway needs a paint job, Herron, take that can of red paint'—that was the order I liked least. American captains are pretty strong on that. The British are the worst of all—did you ever ship on an English boat?"

"No, but I've heard about them."

"Ever painted a coaler with black paint?"

"No, but I hated scraping the paint off the winch."

"And you gave up sailing? Are you glad you did?"

"No, not really."

"I don't know anybody who quit and was really glad about it," the young man said. "Jumping ship is easy, but getting back on is hard."

All this time it was Zuckermann who kept looking around anxiously, fearing that the policemen would interrupt and gesturing to fend them off; but now the young man said, "I don't think I ought to make them wait any longer. My name's David."

"Czepe—I'm afraid the name will stick with me."

David Herron handed the white bag to the priest. "Tell her..." But he did not finish the sentence. He turned and walked over to the policeman who stood nearest to him.

"I won't give you any trouble," he said. "I'll come right along. No fuss. Only tell me this: How did you find me?"

The policeman's face was still stiff with fatigue, even now

as he looked at the young man with some surprise. "You are Dudic, aren't you?"

"Who?"

"Petar Dudic. At any rate, that's what the passport said."

"What's the trouble?" The young man was already beginning to understand.

"Somebody tried to sell the passport. It's a Yugoslavian passport, and the name on it is Petar Dudic. It's forged. You were using a forged passport!" He tried to inject some authority into his voice, but it was too weary. He was brooding over his own problems: how was he going to explain the fuss he had caused, back at headquarters. It would be a good while, what with all the formalities, before he'd be able to get out of his wet uniform.

"Who was it?" Herron had a hard time sounding serious. "A young girl with white boots, a miniskirt, only one earring?"

One of the other policemen, who had come closer, said, "She's a hard-boiled baby, one of those types."

"Never mind that!" the policeman with the tired face said. He turned to the young man again. "Well, what's the story? Are you or aren't you using the name Dudic? Did you take a room in the Hotel Austria under that name, and sign that name? Don't you know it's a criminal offense to use a forged passport?"

The little prostitute—so that was what it was all about! That was why they'd found him so fast. The passport had been in the windbreaker she took with her. She had tried to sell it, make a little extra money on it. They traced him through her to the hotel, from there to the Professor. That was all. He need only laugh, he felt, and everything would turn out to be a bad dream. Perhaps he would have been able to laugh if Milli had not been there, if he had not seen her.

Her brother, Czepe, had again joined her under the umbrella. He was holding one arm around her slender body, which showed under the wet white dress. In the light of the flashes that still split the sky her face was white. Her lipstick had smeared and her eye shadow was running down her cheeks in streaky lines. She was holding her shoe—and now her small white handbag as well—pressed close against her body. She was looking over in his direction, but he was not sure she really saw him.

For a moment it occurred to David Herron that he could still make a break. It had been so foolish to have doubted her, to have imagined she could have betrayed him! Yes, he could still escape them in the rain and darkness. These officers did not look as though they would shoot at someone merely because he had used a forged passport.

He could hide out for three days and leave the city with the Professor. Perhaps there was even a way to get his new passport from Sally and recover the money from the hotel. He wondered how long it would otherwise remain undiscovered in its hiding place. Presumably a very long time, unless the wires needed repair at some point. He could come back years from now and recover that money—but he knew he would hardly be likely to return to this city. Too many things had gone wrong here; he had made too many mistakes, minor, seemingly unimportant ones, and today undoubtedly a major, crucial one. No, he thought, this is no city for me. But there would be others. And he would manage things better, more carefully, next time.

Why didn't he seize his opportunity? After all, he had made himself a promise back then, a year ago when he deserted his unit, that they never could get him. Why give up? Why now, of all times, just when his old self-confidence was coming back?

But then, when he looked over at Milli for the last time— she had not stirred, and Czepe, her brother, still had his arm around her—he knew that he could not possibly take flight while she was watching.

"All right, come along," the policeman said. "Dudic— that's not your right name, is it?"

"You'll find out," the young man said. This would be another way to leave the city, he thought. At the moment it seemed to him the simplest way. Let matters take their course.

He followed the men to the vehicles. With their wide-open doors they still appeared to him like oversized, four-winged insects. He entered the first car, sat down, and waited tensely for the next step, as though it were still possible that the car would soar into the air.

And Milli? If she looks over here, he thought, if she looks over here at all, she'll also think it possible.

Part Three

29

The two furniture vans almost completely blocked the traffic along the narrow one-way street. The first van had already been closed. The second was also packed full. The movers were bringing from the house the sort of things that are always found at the last moment—one of the movers emerged from the driveway with a whole collection of dog leashes in all colors.

He was a big, heavily built man, and he was carrying nothing but the leashes. Several were in his hand, the rest he had looped around his neck. He moved slowly with them, as though their weight were enormous, but at the same time he smiled at the joke.

"That's it." He tossed the leashes into the van. "Lock up and follow me. We're going to have a bite first."

A scrawny man in a long gray smock came toward the mover. He had clambered down from an old, battered pickup truck painted in iridescent reds which was waiting right behind the vans to slip into the freed parking space once they were gone.

No one could have said just how he happened to be there. In the morning someone had noticed the signs blocking off the street, and the furniture vans. The word had been passed on. There was no saying how many intermediaries had made up the grapevine, but the upshot was that the junk dealer was on the spot in his old established territory.

He spoke to the mover, who answered with some impatience.

"No, no, you won't find anything in there. The apartment's been cleaned out, not a piece left."

"What about the attic?"

"Nothing but dusty old stuff lying around—old junk, that's all."

The secondhand dealer went back to his truck. His wife leaned out the window.

"What ever gives you the idea there's anything doing here?"

"Just as I thought," the dealer said calmly. "The attic's full of old junk." He laughed. "Well, doesn't that sound like something?"

"All we'll get here is a parking ticket," his wife said.

He did not answer, but sat down beside her to wait for the furniture vans to leave. Old junk...He loved old attics, the smell, the dust, the dim light, the bouncy floor, the surprises. And he could clearly imagine what the attic in that house must be like. He could not say how many years he had had an eye on it—in any case, it was a long time. There were always a few such places in every district, and if you kept an eye on them, sooner or later you inherited the stuff.

Inside in the large foyer, which looked even bigger and higher now that it had been cleared of furniture, the family had assembled: the mother, the priest, Milli, and a solitary visitor. Their personal baggage stood on the floor around them: suitcases, bags, coats, a basket with food and beverages for the long drive.

Czepe Zuckermann was wearing his cassock and white collar; this was the first time since his trip to Rome that he had donned it again. That had been his mother's idea—"I think they'd be pleased to see their new priest wearing the cassock"—and he had followed her suggestion. He was standing behind the wheelchair in which Milli sat, stiff and straight because of the steel brace she was wearing. On her lap lay a canvas grip which she never let out of her hands.

They were ready to leave, were waiting only for Kropik to

appear and say, with an expression betraying no emotion, "Madame, the car is ready," just as if they were not leaving the house forever, but only for one of their regular Sunday-afternoon outings.

The vicar-general kept the conversation going almost unaided. He talked and laughed, as if the empty rooms provided him with a unique opportunity. Either he felt he must alleviate the emptiness and silence all by himself, or else he simply liked hearing his voice resound twice as loud as usual in the empty foyer. He had appeared unannounced—"I do want to see you off"—and had delivered himself of long and elaborate eulogies of the lady of the house and how well she had organized everything.

"No, nothing has been decided yet," he answered a question from his mother. "Reverend Koenig will take over the parish, but whether he will live here is uncertain." He laughed. "Lived in two rooms; can't imagine what he would do with all this space."

"Yes," the mother replied, "it's incredible how much stuff accumulates in time. We don't really see it until we move, and from that point of view one ought to move more often." In keeping with the solemnity of the day, she had chosen a black dress, though the effect was not somber but rather elegant. In addition to her rings, she wore a double-strand pearl necklace and somewhat heavier makeup than usual: more powder and rouge, more lipstick and eye shadow.

"I understand you had an auction," the vicar-general said. "And very successfully. The prices..."

She parried, smiling. "There's not much point in selling things at poor prices, is there? But I did not forget you." She indicated a large object, well packed.

"For me?"

"You remember, you always said this was your favorite of the paintings. Your patron saint." It was one of those lugubrious paintings of St. Sebastian leaning against a pillar and skewered by arrows. The painting had hung in one corner of the living room, where it was not too obtrusive.

"It's signed," she said, observing his disappointment. "Believe me, there's a good market for such paintings. Plenty of buyers who like that kind of torture scene, at least here in this city. If you want to sell it..."

"I would never sell a gift of yours."

"Do so with a clear conscience. And let me know what price you get. I hope you'll be visiting us soon."

"Certainly. I hear you've had some additional renovation done."

"Who says so?"

"I've heard. And you've also had the ivy removed?"

"Common sense always carries the day for me. But it was a pity. The ivy did add a certain note of..." She turned to her son with a searching look.

"A *feudal* look..." her son said.

"That's just the word, Czepe. It looked more feudal with the ivy. But a rectory doesn't have to look feudal, don't you agree?" She turned to the vicar-general, smiling. "After all, we already have that feudal pilgrimage church, Maria am Wege."

The vicar-general looked at her with admiration. "Shifting the whole cost of renovation to the National Trust — I regard that as a minor miracle, considering how tight those gentlemen usually are."

"Of course otherwise I would have kept my word and financed it myself. But why make things easy for these government bureaus? After all, it's a historically precious building. I do hope you'll be visiting us soon. I'll be glad to send the car for you any time."

"Thanks. It is rather roundabout by train. I only hope you won't miss the city in the long run—and your bridge games." He felt he had at last hit on something incontrovertible. "You certainly will miss the bridge evenings."

"Would you believe it, I've already found three good partners in the vicinity. And if one should be missing, Czepe can take a hand any time. Can't you, Czepe?"

"Of course." At any other time such a question would have embarrassed him, but now he readily picked up her cue. He understood what was at stake right now: a demonstration that the family was united and that she was the one who led it. If anyone could lead, it was she. In the past three months she had proved this on every occasion that was offered. But when he thought back over the time that had passed since that strange night, he felt something he had never felt before with such clarity: gratitude, and even submission. It was she—the metaphor occurred to him at this moment—who was leading her people safely out of Egypt, before whom the waters of the Red Sea parted...He himself thought that rather exaggerated, but still he liked the notion.

"I don't see the Pekineses."

"Oh, they wouldn't have been appropriate in the new house. They were perfect here, in the city. But lapdogs in the country, you know..."

Czepe Zuckermann was not really listening; he was only watching out for his cues. He was still standing behind the wheelchair, hands on the back of it. Milli seemed to be abstracted. The movers had perched themselves on window-sills in the empty living room, since there were no chairs or boxes left, and were eating their sandwiches.

"...Two Alsatians, yes; Kropik will bring them in a few days. Magnificent animals...I can't imagine why Kropik is taking so long."

The vicar-general seemed to understand this as a hint. "I'll be taking my leave now. The painting..."

"I've arranged for it to be delivered to you."

He took her hand, bent over it, and breathed a kiss. Perhaps all the rings confused him, Czepe Zuckermann thought, especially the one on her index finger. Perhaps he thought he was holding a bishop's hand.

The vicar-general went over to Milli's wheelchair.

She did not look up and ignored his outstretched hand.

"The vicar-general would like to say goodbye to you," Czepe said.

Her face had changed. Not that it had aged or showed the effects of pain, or the severe operation, the months in plaster casts, the sleeplessness, the enforced immobility. There was some trace of all that in her face, of course, but it would have been hard to determine where. Rather, her face seemed to be going through a metamorphosis that was not yet completed. Only the process itself was visible; it was impossible to say yet what the result of this metamorphosis would ultimately be.

"That must have been a nasty fall!" The vicar-general scrutinized the staircase that let upstairs from the foyer. "These steep staircases are simply murderous." When no one commented, he went on calmly, "I know you'll be especially glad to move into the new house. The garden is so big and beautiful. You're a talented gardener, so I hear?"

Milli seemed to have no intention of replying. Her mother looked at her: a brief raising of her eyebrows, a quick glance from her dark eyes that included Czepe, too. It was a request, an appeal to the two of them. Once again Czepe Zuckermann felt the absolute, powerful sense of belonging to a clan. He leaned forward and touched Milli's shoulder. The feeling seemed to communicate itself to her. Silent and abstracted as she had been up to now, she found her voice. Quite as though she had taken part in the conversation all the while, she spoke up.

"I do hope you'll be visiting us. I'd love to show you the garden. The flowering quinces and the jonquils..."

"Jonquils?" The vicar-general looked around at the others. "I don't know much about flowers—but aren't they the same as narcissus? Would they be blooming now, in October?"

Everyone seemed taken aback except Milli. "Didn't Mother tell you? If I promise to do my exercises every day, and walk a lot, I'm going to have a greenhouse. I'll have the most beautiful jonquils that ever bloomed in October..." She did not look at the vicar-general but at her mother, who nodded appreciatively, a nod barely perceptible to anyone else.

Kropik had entered the foyer without anyone's noticing. Suddenly he was standing there in his brown livery with the double row of buttons.

"Sorry to have taken so long; I had to round up the sexton to give him the keys." Then came the formula they had all been waiting for.

"The car is ready, Madame."

He had a plaid throw over his arm. It was one of those lovely mild autumn days that sometimes come surprisingly in October, but Kropik was a man given to foresight.

His mother led the way, as Czepe Zuckermann had expected. Kropik took charge of the wheelchair and propelled it toward the big door, which had been taken off its hinges. Milli did not really need the wheelchair any more—the doctor had actually advised against it, but their mother had decided that Milli would keep it until the move. At this moment Zuckermann thought this decision also had been correct. After all, he thought as he watched Milli descending the stairs on Kropik's arm, after all, this is all she expects: long walks, working in the garden, decorating the church with flowers. That would be her life. And his would not be much different: devotions, masses, visits to the sick, conferences, teaching, the budget—in short, the whole routine. And perhaps a choir in addition...

He picked up his suitcase and followed the others. The movers in their sweaty undershirts and green aprons emerged from the living room. Two of them took off their leather caps as they passed the priests.

"Simply habit," the vicar-general remarked, "pure habit. But what does that matter? The Church, too, lives from habit. Wouldn't you agree?"

Six months ago he would have disputed that, and for a moment, but really only for a moment, he felt, *There!* There is the answer to all your questions. But the thought slipped away from him.

The vicar-general went on talking as they descended the broad stairs.

"Have you heard anything from your young friend?"

"No."

"You visited him while they held him, didn't you? Or so I heard. What sort of person was he?"

He had in fact seen and talked with David Herron in jail. The conversation with him had taken a very peculiar course, or rather, when he thought about it, the same sort of peculiar course as the first conversation. They never referred to the events of that night, never spoke of Milli, and in general never got around to talking about personal matters. Not that he hadn't tried to bring up such matters; on his first visit, at least, he had made an effort to find out something about him, to persuade him to talk. After all, he was a priest and people confided in him. But he soon gave up—or rather, he did not really give up so much as simply overlook those personal things, as though they were of no consequence.

During his next visits they had talked about the sea, ships, harbors, routes, shipping lines, types of freighters and cargoes, stories and experiences—the sort of yarns sailors swapped when they ran into one another in a port. Only later, when David Herron asked to be turned over to the American authorities, did Czepe Zuckermann consider that he may have missed the strategic moment. Sometimes a single moment is enough, he now thought, if only you know that this is *the* moment. Possibly that first night had been the high point for them both.

"You don't want to discuss him?" the vicar-general went on.

"I really wouldn't know where to begin."

"I take it you liked him?"

Czepe Zuckermann smiled involuntarily, recalling how jealous he had been of Herron. Some of that jealousy had actually recurred on the occasions of his few visits, although in rather different form. He had been jealous of the decisiveness he sensed in the young man, the conviction he brought to everything he had to do. But over and beyond that, there was the sense he radiated of all kinds of possibilities still lying before him.

"So you've never heard from him again? But I assume you learned in the meantime who he really was?"

"Yes, or at any rate I know what he told the authorities."

"Very curious, that. You know, they would never have turned him over if he had not insisted on being sent back. We do not extradite deserters who ask for asylum. The only thing he could have been convicted for here was using the forged passport."

"He seemed to know what he wanted."

"I suppose one could say that, at least in hindsight... He's escaped from them again."

Czepe Zuckermann stopped in his tracks. "Escaped?"

"I've been trying to tell you, my son, but you keep throwing me off. Yes, he's escaped from them. Well—is that good news or not?"

"You're quite certain he's at liberty again?" Zuckermann asked.

"'At liberty'—interesting you prefer that expression, Zuckermann. Yes, he is definitely at liberty. Last night I talked to the man from the American Embassy who was in charge of the case. This Herron, he was sentenced to four months at hard labor in an American military stockade in Germany for desertion. Seems he had hoped for a bad-conduct discharge too, but he was denied this. He was to return to active duty... That's when he deserted again... The Embassy had just received the news."

"Then there is no doubt?"

"No doubt at all. Your young man is at liberty. You always were partial to such strange birds..."

The car stood in the middle of the courtyard, gray and gleaming, polished so that it reflected everything around it, diminished and distorted: his mother; Milli, in her white dress and pink scarf leaning on the cane; Kropik, folding the wheelchair and stowing it in the trunk.

There was silence in the yard, except for the beating of wings of the pigeons that swooped over the roofs, settled down on the cornices, and then flew up again. Soon they would have the yard to themselves, and they seemed to know that.

Kropik helped Milli into the back seat. He returned to the house once more to bring the remaining hand baggage. The vicar-general had departed; he could be seen at the far end of the driveway, standing in the street outside the building. With the gate open, the driveway looked like a long tunnel, dark at the courtyard end, bright at the other end.

Czepe Zuckermann deposited his suitcase in the back. He went over to his mother to help her into the car. She always took the seat beside Kropik when the four of them rode together.

"Is something wrong, Czepe?"

He looked at her and saw how tired she looked beneath the heavy makeup. He could not recall ever seeing her this tired.

"I'm all right, Mother," he assured her.

His mother gazed through the open window of the car at the gray façade, at the windows, now without curtains, which gave the impression that the apartment had been empty for a long time. Only Milli's balcony seemed unchanged, wreathed in luxuriant vines which still showed blossoms here and there.

"It's not the house, Czepe—or is it? It's not because we're leaving it, is it, Czepe?"

"No, Mother." He too looked up. He saw the tall antenna that towered above the roof. It would have been foolish to dismantle it and take it along—would have cost more than a new one. And he was not certain that he wanted a new one anyhow.

"No, not the house. I liked it; in a way I even think I'll miss it; but it isn't that. It's simply—" He turned toward her. "Sometimes it seems simply absurd that life..."

This time it was she who picked up his cue, helped him continue. "That life goes on, you mean?"

"Yes."

She smiled. "That's just how it is, Czepe. Things don't happen the way they're supposed to. They don't lead up to a grand, crowning final tableau. They just go on. But for that very reason life is naturally full of surprises and hope." Her smile grew brighter. "I hope that doesn't sound too much like the vicar-general. Come, get in so we'll be all ready when Kropik comes. Don't we have a lovely day for the ride? And for moving! Moving in the rain, Czepe—I tell you, *that* can drive a person to despair."

He got into the back beside Milli. A glass pane separated them from the front seats.

"Everything all right?" he asked. "Are you sitting comfortably?"

She nodded. She was holding the grip in her lap; again her hands were resting firmly on it. He asked himself whether he should tell her the news; after all, it ought to be good news for Milli, or so he felt, but he hesitated.

During the period after David's arrest, when he'd gone around trying to find out details, fitting in an item here, a trifle there, he had wondered if Milli would not be able to supply the missing pieces to fill out his incomplete picture. He had waited for her to volunteer something. But not a word about David crossed her lips. It was as if she had forgotten that the young man ever existed, or as if she believed him dead. Perhaps she would have liked to believe that. But even there he was not so certain. While she had been packing the last of her clothes a while ago, he had seen her holding a transparent blue nightgown. She had immediately concealed it from him, stuffing it into the grip she now had on her lap. Although he had suspected some connection, he had avoided any comment—just as nothing had ever been said among the three of them about how Milli's fall down the stairs had taken place...

It had happened that same night. Not even the nurse who slept in Milli's room had heard Milli leave her bed. Had she walked in her sleep? Had she slipped on the stairs? Had she thrown herself down?

Questions that remained unasked, and presumably would remain forever unanswered. After she screamed, they had found her at the foot of the staircase with a broken hip and severe fractures of the vertebrae.

Behind them, the trunk was snapped shut. Kropik had stowed away the last of the suitcases.

"Are you quite comfortable?"

"Oh yes."

"Wouldn't you like the throw? That dress is so summery."

"Thank you, Czepe, I'm perfectly all right. I only wonder..."

"Yes?"

"Do you recall the last time we drove out to the new house? The crickets..."

He could not recall. Had there been crickets there?

"What about them?"

"Oh, nothing special. I was just wondering whether they'll still be there."

"In October?"

She laughed. "I know it's October. The vicar-general thought I'd lost track of time, didn't he? Is that what you think too?"

He felt helpless to deal with her.

"Are you sure that you don't want the throw?"

"Czepe, don't digress! Don't you know that there are crickets inside houses, especially old ones? And once they're there, there's no getting rid of them. They simply belong to the house like...Well, they simply belong to it."

"Yes, I've heard about that."

"In the summertime they're lovely to listen to," she went on. "Those millions of crickets out in the fields, in the grass, at night—you hear them through the open window. It's hot, you can't sleep, and there's the noise of the crickets...It's like a heavy curtain dropping down over the house..."

Kropik had started the motor. It was almost inaudible, simply a vibration passing through the car before the chauffeur shifted into gear. Milli had fallen silent, but she seemed to be still listening intently.

Inside the car it became dark for a moment as they drove under the archway of the driveway. Then the sun struck Milli squarely, blindingly, so that she closed her eyes in pain. She closed them—and then she heard the sound distinctly.

The crickets. Yes—not just a noise. The sound dropped down around her like a soft, protective curtain. She smiled, eyes closed. She was feeling very well, very secure behind the curtain woven round her by the chirping of the crickets.

30

It was still totally dark and there were few other vehicles on the highway. The lights of the instrument panel spread a green fluorescent glow in the cab. There were a large number of dials, not only for the truck itself but also for the refrigeration system of the twenty-five-ton trailer with its load of frozen lamb. The powerful motor produced a low, steady, lulling tone, and at times during the night, especially during the past hour—with nothing but the deep darkness around them and the hum of the motor, very much like the hum of a ship's engines—the young man had had the feeling that he was not in the cab of a truck but in a heavily laden boat sitting low in the water and gliding along over a smooth, nocturnal sea.

The man at the wheel was a good driver. He kept a steady speed, never braked too hard or accelerated unnecessarily. He was around forty, rather short, so that he needed two cushions on his seat. The odd thing about him was his smell. Sometimes while driving along, he would take out a small flask, shake it into the palm of his hand, and rub his neck with what was apparently some kind of eau de cologne. For a few moments it would smell very sweetish and obtrusive, but with the window open the scent was quickly dissipated by the wind.

The driver took one hand from the wheel and pointed mutely at the glove compartment on the passenger's side. The young man took out the blue pack, shook a cigarette into his hand, and held it out to the driver. He replaced the pack.

Finally he broke the silence.

"Why do you keep them there?" He spoke slowly, with an accent, and he divided the simple sentence into three parts, like a tourist who has learned his question out of a phrase book: "Why do you/keep them/there?"

"I'm not supposed to smoke."

"It doesn't make you smoke any less. The pack was full six hours ago and now there are only two left—so what's the difference?"

"No difference." The driver inhaled the first puff and let the smoke escape slowly out of his nose and mouth. "But it helps me feel I'm fighting it." He opened the vent window. The night was cool, not frosty, but cold enough to indicate that summer was over and autumn well along.

"You don't smoke at all?"

"No."

"Then don't ever start!"

The young man leaned back. The smell of the cigarette, the scent of the eau de cologne, and the odor of the truck itself mingled and suddenly seemed to fit very well together. But perhaps he had that impression only because he was feeling good for the first time in three months. He resumed the conversation.

"There were two Greeks who fled into the mountains— this was years ago. They moved only in the dark of night, living on what they had in their packs. They had hiding places in the mountains and they set improvised traps to catch game, since a shot might have given them away. They never entered even the tiniest mountain village—they were two very wary men."

The driver gazed straight ahead at the road, but it was apparent that he was listening with close attention.

"Go on."

"They planted tobacco; well, it helped, but still their homegrown tobacco wasn't the same. It got to be more and more of an obsession with one of the two men: Sometime, somehow, somewhere, he swore, he was going to smoke a real cigarette again"

"Oh yes, I can understand that."

"After I don't know how long a time, anyhow it was years, he decided to take the risk, creep into a remote mountain village at night."

"And was caught?"

"Yes."

The driver looked at the cigarette between his fingers, with the smoke rising from its tip. He took a deep puff, and as he slowly exhaled the smoke he said, "I don't know—for a woman, maybe. Did they have women during those years?"

"No."

"That never would have happened to me," the driver said decisively. "A woman, now, that's something else again..."

"It really was a woman."

"That makes me feel better about it. At least that's a good reason."

They were quiet again for a while and gazed ahead into the darkness, which even the powerful beams of the headlights seemed unable to pierce; where the cone of their light ended, the endless broad sea of night began.

"You really know a lot of stories for a fellow your age." This time it was the driver who broke the silence, his eyes fixed straight ahead.

"You hear all sorts of things knocking around," the young man said.

"All I ever see is National Seven: Perpignan to Paris, Paris to Perpignan. Frozen lamb half the year, pottery the rest of the year. National Seven for more than twenty years. Can you imagine that? Seven used to be a terrible road. Then it was improved, and now it's going bad again. Now and then a detour, then back on Seven. That's all I ever see." He took a last puff and crushed out the cigarette. "Of course, up to three years ago, when I was still driving into the city, to Les Halles— that was a lot better. Do you know that quarter?"

"No."

"Oh, I forgot; you said you'd never been in Paris...Now that they're tearing everything down and moved the market out of town, all that's over. Now all I ever see is this dreary Rungis. But Les Halles—let me tell you! Girls by the dozens, any kind you wanted. Those were the days back then!"

He threw a glance at the illuminated dial of the big watch on his wrist.

"Around this time I would always be getting real jittery—excited, I mean. Once I got off Seven at the Porte d'Italie, I couldn't move fast enough. Avenue d'Italie, Avenue des Gobelins, Rue Monge, Rue Lagrange, Quai St. Michel, then the Boulevard du Palais through the Cité and across the Seine—man alive, was I worked up by then..."

He dropped into silence. The young man leaned forward slightly in his seat. He stared into the big windshield that reflected his face, or else into the darkness—in any case, it was as if he were reading something there, and he said, "Wouldn't it have been better to take the Pont d'Austerlitz?"

The driver looked away from the road, though only briefly; he had not done that all through the night.

"I thought you'd never been there."

"That's right," the young man said.

"You know, it's odd—all the other drivers on Seven took that route. Pont d'Austerlitz—sure, the other drivers were always for that!"

The young man looked contentedly into space. So he'd been right; you couldn't fool a veteran truck driver. He sensed the city, its fabric, its skeleton, its organs, its blood circulation. As yet he was still at the stage of listening, sounding out, collecting, checking, evaluating data. In the course of this one night he had asked many questions and received answers; by now he felt that in selecting Paris he had made a good choice.

Easy to enter and equally easy to leave. Route 7 was far from the only main artery. There were many others, all leading into the city and coming out of it again, like the blood vessels that supplied the heart: Twenty, the route for airplane repair parts from Toulouse and china and shoes from Limoges; Ten, bringing wine from Bordeaux, along with grapes and poultry. Thirteen brought nautical goods and fish from Cherbourg. Tea and gin from England came on One from Calais. Two brought beer from Brussels. And still there were more. Five from Lyons and Marseilles was a good road, as was Fourteen to Le Havre. And there was always the river, the Seine, used for transporting cement, gravel, pipe, and coal.

Lots of highways, lots of trucks and drivers like this man from Perpignan. From him he'd learned a good deal more than routes. He already knew the names of other drivers, the numbers of their vehicles, the days on which they came to Paris. The truckers all knew one another, met in Rungis early in the mornings, unloaded their vehicles, washed, changed their shirts, and shaved, before hitting their return routes. He even imagined he knew some of them as well as he did the man from Perpignan. He knew what they looked like, knew some of the idiosyncrasies—things that were important if you were depending on their giving you a ride.

He was not actually counting on having to leave the city soon. All this was merely a matter of weaving a safety net, taking advantage of a favorable opportunity, so that once the city was before him and he set out to enter it, he would no longer have to think about escape routes...

The darkness around them seemed undiminished, but there were more vehicles on the highway now, and to the right, very far away, a delicate strip of gray was beginning to appear. The man from Perpignan was still thinking about the girls around Les Halles.

"You know, Paris—how should I put it...? I mean, these Paris girls, they don't make a big to-do about love. That's got its points for a man who's just driven Seven all night long. It's got its points, get me? What I'm trying to say is, I might not recommend them on a long-term basis. I wouldn't know; I've never stayed longer than a few hours."

"Maybe you ought to try Paris for a longer time."

"Me? Oh no. Therese..." He spoke the name as though it had become familiar to the other man in the course of the night. "You see, many girls dream of going to Paris, but Therese says the only thing waiting they'll find there is heartbreak. *Paris va te crever le coeur, vous comprenez?* Thinks a girl should stay in Perpignan. Perpignan's the sort of place where a girl keeps a sound heart. That's Therese all over."

"Has she ever been outside of Perpignan?"

"Therese? If she's ever dreamed of other places, she sure hasn't told me." He laughed. It was a very lively laugh for a man who had driven some five hundred miles in the night, almost in one bout, with only brief stops—fewer stops, at any rate, than regulations called for.

"Maybe you'll ride down there with me someday. Life is pretty good there."

"It sounds good, what you've told me about it."

"Ah, but wait until you see it! One hour's drive away, you're in the highest mountains. Fifteen minutes and you're at the sea. And nice girls—girls like Therese, of course. They think of nothing else but marrying and having kids. Sometimes I think they're born that way in Perpignan, already mothers. But still they're wonderful girls. Think it over; there's no hurry."

"I will."

"You won't forget my name?"

"Absolutely not — same as the great bicyclist."

"Yes, only Alphonse, not Louison, unfortunately. And when you ask for me in Rungis, it's not *tête de verre* but *tête de fer*, Old Ironhead, Louison Bober—there's a man for you. He could enter the Tour de France at the age of forty-two and still win. Or what about that fellow Robic? And the kind of bicycles they raced, not these lightweight super-machines. Endurance is what makes a good rider, I always say. Whether it's two wheels or four. Endurance makes the man, don't forget that."

"Right, I'll keep it in mind."

"Your name is—David?"

"Yes, David."

"Not a bad name...I really was in luck meeting you." He took another cigarette. "You know," he remarked, "I wasn't so sure when I picked you up. See, if I do pick up a hitchhiker, I want someone who keeps me entertained"

"Haven't I?"

"You have, but at first..." He cast another brief, analytic glance at the young man. "Hey, it just struck me. Your French sure improved in the night. At first I thought I wouldn't understand a word of your stories."

"But you did understand them."

"Yes...Now we're almost there." He shifted to a lower gear, very gently.

The young man noticed the shifting only by the changed sound of the motor. A few drops fell on the windshield. The man from Perpignan made no motion to switch on the windshield wipers, and the drops vanished. It had stopped raining. The two men lapsed into their silence again, a sign of harmony, but also a harbinger of their impending separation.

While those few big raindrops fell on the windshield, the young man recalled the night of the thunderstorm, the lightning, the masses of water pouring from the sky, the girl in the soaked dress under the big black umbrella, her hair too heavy for her, hanging down on both sides of her face, her white face under the flashes of lightning, and the priest with the strange name—both together on that weirdly illuminated meadow that looked like a turbulent blue sea.

He knew he would never again see Milli—how well the name suited her. But he would always remember her, as he would always remember that other girl: the deserted village, the empty road in the noonday sun, the stillness, twelve men moving forward through the burned grass with bated breath and dazzled eyes, and then something suddenly moving... What had come first, what had he shot at, at a sudden movement or a living being, a child? At whom were those shots directed? At the silence, the fear, the shimmering heat waves in the sun, or was it a human being after all? This question would remain forever with him; and one other: What made me do it?

He had tried to forget, to wipe out that noon. He had not succeeded. Only since he'd been living with it, since he'd accepted it as something that would be part of him for always, had he found a new freedom.

He still did not know what to do with this. Perhaps it would turn out in the future that he had not really gained very much. Perhaps in the future he would no longer have the stamina for the life he was leading, and would have to put something else in its place. But now, at this moment, there was time neither for the past nor for the future, but only for what lay immediately before him.

The sound of the motor changed again.

"That's Rungis over there," the driver said. "I can take

you in there. Or should I stop at the exit? There's plenty of traffic by now. You'll find a car into the city easy."

"The exit," the young man said.

They drove on a short distance, again in silence. The orange directional sign set its glow into the cab as the truck swung to the right, then stood still. The motor under the hood continued to idle, sounding more than ever like a ship's engines. The young man lifted the green duffel bag from the floor, laid it across his knees, and picked up his green plastic rain cape. He was wearing brown slacks, a checked shirt with open collar, and no kerchief.

"Well then." He extended his hand.

The driver took it, held it for a moment, and said, "You know where to find me. Old Ironhead, don't forget. Every Monday and Friday." He released the young man's hand and looked at his watch. "Half past five. You can set your watch by it—whether or not I have a flat or something else delays me, somehow or other I always manage to be here on the dot."

"Well then," the young man said. "Good luck on Seven today." He opened the door.

"Good luck in the city." And then, after the young man had walked around through the dimmed headlight beam to the other side of the truck, he leaned out the window once more, and as his truck slowly rolled ahead, he said, "There, day is breaking already!"

The young man waited until the red taillights had merged with the lights of the Rungis market. The darkness seemed to him quite unchanged. A cold wind was blowing into his face, and it grew stronger as he started to walk. The wind came from directly ahead. He walked on the side of the highway, along the narrow strip of dusty green. Several times he changed his speed and the length of his steps, as though he were trying to find the proper pace.

He had not walked for long when he heard a car behind him. The car passed him, braked, and stopped a few yards in front of him, on the right shoulder of the road. By the time the young man reached it, the driver had cranked down his window. He leaned across the passenger seat, looked up, and asked, *"Americain? Voulez-vous un lift?"*

The young man shook his head. The driver hesitated, as though expecting his offer to be taken after all. Finally he started ahead again.

A lift might have been a good idea at that. He could still see nothing of the city and it seemed far away. But it was better to enter a city on foot, he reflected, especially one you were seeing for the first time. You acquired a better feel for it walking, you paid it more honor. After all, his baggage weighed little. He peered straight ahead, but the darkness was illuminated only by headlights and by the taillights of the cars that passed him.

He tramped on, looking straight ahead, waiting. He did not know what for. He walked, inhaling the air deeply, paying attention to sounds. His footsteps were even and steady now, as if he had found the proper rhythm.